THE MAMACITA MURDERS

A NOVEL

by

DEBRA MARES

A JUSTICIA HOUSE BOOK

This is a work of fiction. All the characters, organizations, and events portrayed in this novel are either products of the author's imagination or are used fictionally.

The Mamacita Murders

A JUSTICIA HOUSE BOOK
303 Broadway, Suite 104-103
Laguna Beach, California 92651

Book cover design by Perlman Creative Group

Printed in the United States of America

for
all victims
those who have survived
those who have passed
&
their loved ones

If anything good can come out of The Mamacita Murders, perhaps they will show someone how our criminal justice system works when an individual commits what the law calls murder; but my greatest hope is they serve those who search for closure.

—DEBRA MARES, AUTHOR
THE MAMACITA MURDERS

The single, most effective way to reduce the crime rate and build public confidence in the criminal justice system is to serve your community. Outside the courtroom, I serve as a pin-up girl at The Mamacita Club. My younger clients request me as Katy Perry and my older ones as a mob wife; but my Latin clients prefer me as Jennifer Lopez.

> — Gabriela Ruiz, Assistant Prosecutor
> Tuckford County

THE MAMACITA MURDERS

VOLUME ONE

SCRATCHING THE SURFACE

The rush of cool air entering the courthouse resets my makeup after a short walk from my office in Old Town Tuckford. Wheeling my briefcase down this grand hall feels like I'm walking through the Vatican. This courthouse would make any beach city housewife sitting sixty miles away rethink calling Tuckford County the armpit of this state. The high ceilings create spectacular, long-lasting echoes of my red stilettos. Some say we all look the same, but my curves and dance moves may remind some jurors of Carmen Miranda, while others of Jennifer Lopez.

I pass all my jurors and smile calmly at each one, pretending to have everything under control. My given name might be Gabriela Ruiz, most call me Gaby, but today my nickname is Grace Under Pressure. Don't flinch. Walk steady. Breathe deep.

As I enter the double doors of Department Thirteen, the defendant, courtroom clerk, and deputy sheriff are all on time. But still, there's no sign of Laura.

Laura promised me to be here this morning at 8:30. I read the courtroom clock. 8:55 a.m. With my ten unanswered calls to her in the last half hour, I've transitioned from the assistant prosecutor in her case to her official stalker. I wheel my briefcase up to the counsel table, sit down, and lean my head back into the chair.

The witness stand surrounded in dark oak is empty. Yesterday, I told the jury that seventeen-year-old Laura would be here this morning to testify. She's supposed to tell the jury that her stepfather Javier sexually abused her. My eyes scale up the rich brown walls of the courtroom. The hand-carved block letters painted in gold at the top of the wall distract me from the knot twisting in my stomach. It reads, "He has a right to criticize who has a heart to help — President Abraham Lincoln." I don't feel so bad saying Laura is probably wrapping her legs around some gang-banger while snoozing her alarm clock instead of being here.

I met Laura when was I was assigned to this case a year ago. She was sexually abused by Javier, her mom's twenty-seven-year-old husband, more than just the one time I charged him with. It left her family divided with Bess, Laura's mom, taking Javier's side. Seeing glimpses of myself in Laura, including her pin-up girl style, gave me a huge heart to help, but plenty of confidence to criticize her. Laura is smart and pretty, but looks for love in all the wrong places; something easy to do in the gang-infested RV park she lives in. Or just something easy to do if you're a divorced professional female like me. But I have hope I'll find the right kind of love this year. I'm not so sure about Laura, though.

Since I met Laura last year, I had been pushing Bess to sign her up for The Mamacita Club, which I run out of my Vintage Airstream motorhome. I noticed her and her mom's relationship became strained after an anonymous caller reported the abuse. Laura blamed Bess for her stepfather abusing her. Bess blamed Laura's provocative ways. I couldn't entirely disagree with Bess after reviewing Laura's sexting history with her twenty-six-year-old pimp, Clown. She met him on GangScene, an Internet chat room for gang members.

Along with a text message saying, "Bang this," Laura sent him a self-portrait sitting up straight on her bed, with her legs crossed. She had white socks pulled up to her knees with black heels on. Her hair was up in a vintage-looking bun and she was wearing one of Bess's red lace teddies exposing her breasts.

I told Bess in Spanish "I'll work a miracle," using my Latina background to build a rapport. I promised to work on Laura's self-esteem, figuring it was worth summoning my magical powers at some point to help her. After all, not all of this was her fault. But Bess wasn't interested in my help.

First, she told me she couldn't find a ride for Laura to get to the club. So a couple months ago, Angela, Riley, Kiki, and I, a.k.a. The Mamacita Club Directors, drove the Airstream to Leafwood RV Park, the same trailer park Laura lives in. We started hosting meetings there, but that didn't work, either. Bess told me these types of clubs went against her culture's grain. Plus, my office thought it would be a conflict of interest for Laura to join since she was a victim in an active case.

The courtroom door flings open and Investigator Dylan Mack walks in. I tell him to follow me outside.

The attorney room outside Department Thirteen gives Dylan and me the privacy we need. I stand up straightening my backbone just enough to perk out my breasts, hoping to compete with any twenty-something-year-old Dylan had in his bed last night.

"What's going on?" asks Dylan curiously.

"Laura's mom called me this morning saying Laura went AWOL last night and she hasn't seen her since. Laura told her she's not coming back to testify. I saw her last night and she promised me she'd be here by 8:30. We met at the Airstream. She seemed a little nervous about testifying, but that was it," I say.

Dylan has always reminded me of Matthew McConaughey, mixed with the style and class of John F. Kennedy, Jr. I don't know if you call it a Bostonian or San Franciscan look. Whatever it is, it's yummy and way too refined for the country bumpkins in the backwoods of Tuckford County.

"Shit, Gabriela. Why didn't you call me?"

"For what? Laura said she'd be here. I had no idea she told Bess she wasn't going to testify until this morning. What would've you done last night?"

"I would've at least made sure she showed up this morning."

"I told her I wasn't going to mess with her business as long as she came to court. It was an understanding we had," I say.

"Understanding for what?" Dylan asks. "Obviously, she didn't care about that understanding because now we don't have her. We can read her statement to the jury that's in the police report, right?" Dylan asks.

"No, we can't use her statement. That's all hearsay."

"What about her interview? We have that videotaped."

"We can't play that either. We need her on the stand or this case is done."

"Where do you think she went?"

"I don't know but she got into a fight over Bess seeing a couple of text messages to Clown. She just took off and never went back home."

"Was that before or after you saw her at the Airstream?"

"I don't know. I saw her around eight."

"Dammit, I told her to stay away from him."

The door to the side room opens and two men walk in continuing a conversation about some million dollar settlement. They might have expensive suits on, but I'll take my job over their boring civil cases any day. Dylan lowers his voice.

"What's going to happen with the trial? Can you use your powers to work some magic?" Dylan asks hopefully.

"No way. Laura needs to show up and help herself. I'm not getting her out of this one."

"Can you ask the judge to postpone it?"

"I can but I need Javier to agree. This can get really ugly for me."

"How is this your fault?"

"Are you kidding me? It makes me look bad that Laura's not here. I run The Mamacita Club for at-risk girls that I had to convince my office to support. I should at least be able to get her to show up to court."

I look back at the civil attorneys, who are both on their cell phones. At least they don't have to deal with stuff like this.

"Let's get back in there," I say, turning to walk towards the door.

As I reach for the door handle, I stop and turn back to Dylan.

"By the way, you look nice today. I like your suit," I say flirtingly.

Dylan's blue eyes gaze into mine before I open the door to walk out.

Tuckford County was rated a top place for having the rudest people in the country. But I haven't found this to be true, except when it comes to defendants. I stand on one of the steps leading up to the jury box where the defendant, Javier Sanchez, sits feet away from me. The clanking sounds from his foot and wrist chains fill the courtroom. The voices on the deputy's walkie-talkie and the clerk's whispers add to the noise. Dylan keeps a close watch on me from the counsel table.

"Hi, Mr. Sanchez. How are you this morning?" I ask.

Javier stares at me and sits in silence. He is facing one felony count for having nonforceable sex with his stepdaughter Laura a little over a year ago. He's also facing at least twenty years in prison because of his prior criminal history. Javier hasn't given me any clue either way if he did what he's accused of. Some defendants admit to having sex with the victim but say it was consensual. It helps explain away any semen, DNA, or physical injuries that might show up. But Javier invoked his Miranda rights asking for an attorney from the moment police arrested him. He never gave a statement. By the time Laura reported the sexual abuse, any injuries or DNA was gone.

As a prosecutor, I've always been as mindful of my role to protect defendants, especially ones like Javier. He went pro per right before trial. I try not to beat up too much on defendants who decide to represent themselves. I don't want the case reversed on appeal. But I always wonder if the judge and jury take them seriously. They can come across as crazy and too emotionally involved, like a wife who represents herself in her own divorce.

"Mr. Sanchez, you don't need to speak with me, but you chose to represent yourself, so it's helpful to everyone if we communicate. Laura won't be here this morning. I'm going to ask the judge to postpone the case so we can make sure she gets here. Do you have a problem with that?" I ask.

"Yeah, I have a problem. I want my speedy trial. You can't delay it. You have no case if she ain't here," Javier says defiantly.

"Mr. Sanchez, if you don't agree to postpone the trial, I'm going to ask the judge to," I say. "It's as simple as that. You can agree with me or you can object. But I'm only asking for some time so we can find Laura and bring her to court. Don't you want to ask her some questions?"

"I ain't postponing this," Javier says.

"Do you even care what happened to her?" I ask.

"What happened?"

"She went AWOL last night. She's probably afraid of testifying or something. You don't have anything to do with her not showing up, do you?" I ask suspiciously.

"What do you mean? I'm locked up in county. What would I have to do with it?" Javier asks.

"You're lucky to be in custody right now," I say. "You should think twice about pushing this trial forward. Even if you were released, you're already labeled as a sex offender. Worse, you had sex with Clown's girlfriend. The Lincoln gang is going to be after you the moment you hit the streets. You've already been beaten up once in jail over this case.

"If someone confronts you on the street and you try to defend yourself, the police might arrest you. Where are you gonna go if this case is over? You can't go back to Leafwood. Lincoln is waiting to get at you, Javier. I know what's going on in the streets. You don't. You've been locked up for a year," I say.

Javier looks straight ahead. He's looking at my legs, which aside from my nude nylons, are bare.

"Why don't you think about this, Javier," I say.

"Let's see what the judge says," he replies.

I take a deep breath and look around the courtroom. The deputy and clerk are talking to each other. Dylan is looking down at his cell phone.

"Javier," I say, bending bend my torso down towards my knee, which is elevated on the stair leading up to where he's sitting.

Javier's eyes make their way down to my chest as I rest my elbow on my thigh.

I soften my voice.

"I would really appreciate if you agreed to a brief continuance," I say in a sweet and slow cadence.

After giving Javier a smile like I mean it, I walk back to the counsel table.

Some criminals can be swayed with tough girl tactics. But more hardened ones like Javier are harder to get to. He's distrusting of law enforcement, he's been through the criminal system, and he knows how the streets work. But he's a man and he has blood pumping through his veins. I'd be naive to think he's not influenced by perky breasts or toned legs from time to time.

I sit down next to Dylan at the counsel table, then move my chair to face the jury box. I slowly cross my legs, and look up towards Javier.

"Fine. We can postpone it. But only til tomorrow," says Javier.

"Madam Clerk, we're ready to speak with Judge Hoffman," I say.

Watching Judge Hoffman climb his way up to the bench gives me a moment to compose myself. I'm always nervous he's going to trip on his way up because he wears a permanent eye patch over his left eye. Rumor is that he used his Brazilian Jiu-Jitsu to fight off five men who tried to rob him. One of the fighters used a shuriken to stab him in the eye and slash his throat. That's why he always wears a red checkered bandana around his neck above his black robe. He was attacked on his first date with his now wife. Three months later, he proposed to her. I too would marry a man thirty years older than me if he could protect me like a young stallion. That's sexy.

"Remain seated, come to order, court is now in session," the deputy says.

The courtroom clerk and reporter stare at me, wondering what's about to happen. Other than several low level assistant prosecutors, the audience section where the victim's family normally sits is empty. On Javier's side, his court-appointed investigator sits.

Just as I'm about to turn back towards the judge, Angela walks in. Angela is my good friend and Angel Therapy Practitioner who works at The Mamacita Club. Like the other club directors, when she's counseling women, Angela dresses up in different outfits. Her Angel Gabriel alter ego helps her bond with the women in the club the most.

"Good morning, Ms. Ruiz, Mr. Sanchez, Investigator Mack. It is 9:15 a.m. and the jury has been waiting now for fifteen minutes. Are we ready to begin?" says Judge Hoffman.

"Good morning, Your Honor. No. The People are not ready to proceed. Laura was told to be here this morning at 8:30 and she hasn't shown up. Her mother informed me that she ran away last night. Since Laura's testimony is the bulk of the People's case, I'm inviting the court to delay the trial just until tomorrow. I'd like to make efforts to bring her to court. I've discussed it with the defendant and he is agreeable to this," I say calmly.

The tough part about being a prosecutor is keeping my composure, thinking on my feet, and figuring out the best way to advocate. One thing about judges like Judge Hoffman is that they are quick to make hasty rulings. They don't want jurors waiting around and they want cases moved out of the system, not delayed. The judges have to answer to the PJ, the presiding judge, who makes the administrative and calendar decisions for the bench. The PJ expects the cases to move and courtrooms to stay buzzing with trials, hearings, and motions. "Inviting" Judge Hoffman to delay the trial is code word for listen up and please do what I'm asking you to do.

"You're asking me to keep my jury waiting for a day while you look for a witness who probably doesn't want to be found? Do you even know where to start? She's a runaway and troubled girl. That much is obvious from your trial brief. I'll bet this isn't the fist time she's gone AWOL. I need some assurance you have a good likelihood of finding her. If I postpone this, I'd expect a manhunt. And in this economic time, I wouldn't expect the Old Town Police

Department to have the resources for something like that. Isn't that correct, Investigator Mack?" says Judge Hoffman.

Dylan laughs.

"Your Honor, may I approach sidebar?" I ask.

"Yes," Judge Hoffman replies.

Sometimes, it seems that when a judge first puts on a black robe, it comes with an attitude, similar to a new car coming with a warranty. It usually wears off after a few years, but there's an occasional one that comes with the extended warranty. Judge Samuel Hoffman is somewhere in the middle. He makes rulings based on law and experience. The thing I like most about Judge Hoffman is that he cares about the integrity of his judicial appointment.

At sidebar, I stand eight inches away from full body contact with Judge Hoffman. A real sidebar allows unobstructed contact with a judge, without the big desk between the attorneys like you see on television. I explain to him in a very calm tone that it really is in the best interest of justice to grant a brief continuance. I also remind him politely that I tried to get Laura housed at juvenile hall during the trial because I was afraid she'd run away, but she couldn't be held because she promised everyone she'd show up. I reminded him that we all agreed she appeared cooperative. After giving Judge Hoffman a smile that says "pretty please," I walk back to the counsel table.

"Very well, Ms. Ruiz. Under the circumstances and because you are only asking for a short continuance, I'll grant your request. But I'll expect an extensive update about Laura's whereabouts. And I'll want to hear about efforts you personally have made to secure her testimony. I'll have my clerk inform the jury we won't be in session today. Everyone is ordered back tomorrow at ten o'clock a.m."

2

ANONYMOUS ANGEL

No longer than fifteen minutes after Javier was looking down my blouse in court, Dylan looks around my office. He picks up and studies a photo of the group of girls in The Mamacita Club sitting framed on my credenza. My office is one of the nicest ones in my building. It's big, tucked away, has a separate sitting area and floor-to-ceiling windows. I have a view of the Old Town Castle where many famous people have stayed. During the Christmas holidays, the Castle turns into the North Pole decorated with lights and life-size dolls. Horse-drawn carriages whisk visitors around the Castle to experience the festive display.

Last year, I requested to move into this office. It had been used by the "Producer," a sophisticated defendant in one of our fraud cases. He stole a building access card one of our prosecutors left behind in court. And he began using the office to host weekend auditions for aspiring actresses in his pilot show called "Crime, Justice and Panties." After that, no one wanted this office. But I didn't shy away from it.

After I moved in, coworkers joked with me asking if I found any underwear in my desk drawers. Whatever circumstances got me into this office, it earns me instant esteem. Law enforcement officers and professionals who visit me to discuss cases are always impressed.

"So what did you do to get Javier to go along with you?" says Dylan.

"Invited him back to the Airstream," I reply.

Dylan and I start laughing.

"Seriously," says Dylan.

"I just sprinkled a little of my Latin spice on him," I reply.

"I figured. If I remember correctly, you tend to do that very well," says Dylan playfully.

"Let's talk about Laura," I say, changing the subject. "I want her cell phone pinged so we can trail her. We need to get her to court."

"There's no way that's gonna happen."

"Why?"

"Because, this isn't the type of case we can do that on."

"I have a witness who took off last night refusing to come back to testify. She was ordered back for this morning. What do you mean this isn't the type of case?" I ask.

"Even if we do track her down, we can't even arrest her. You didn't issue a warrant for her," Dylan says.

"I couldn't. She's a juvenile. Her mom's the one who's supposed to make sure she shows up to court. And Bess doesn't even know where she is. The last thing I'm going to do is hold her responsible."

"If Laura just wants to take off and act like an adult, we should treat her like one. If she were eighteen, we could've issued a warrant."

"She's still a victim. Seventeen or eighteen, I can't say I would've issued a warrant. So she can be picked up and arrested and spend the night in juvenile hall? That's victimizing her even more," I say.

"You tried to keep her in juvenile hall before," Dylan says.

"That was just a tactic. I knew they'd never hold her and I needed to save my reputation in case she didn't show. I reminded Judge Hoffman at sidebar about that this morning."

"I'm not asking for the search warrant. There's no way my Sergeant will authorize that."

"I just need to find her," I say. "I'm pretty sure I can convince her to come to court if I just get a chance to talk to her face to face. How do you expect that to happen if we don't trace her phone?"

"I have no legal authority to do that," Dylan replies.

I return my focus out the window to a tall white cross that sits on top of the local Catholic church.

"Hey, I just thought of something. Bess is the only person who can complain about a warrant. She pays Laura's cell phone bill. And she's not going to care. She wants us to find Laura," I say, spinning my chair back towards Dylan.

"Look. If you want me to write the search warrant, I will. But getting a judge to sign off on it is a whole other deal," says Dylan.

"Javier is twenty-four hours away from being released on a case he deserves to do life on. Let's write the warrant. While we're at it, let's get all phone records. Laura's,

Clown's, and Bess's. It will help us establish a time line," I say.

Twenty minutes after we get a hit on Laura's cell phone, Dylan and I sit at the intersection of Main Street and Amazon Avenue in Leafwood. Low income housing, black iron gates, and graffiti decorates the neighborhood. It makes sense why they call Leafwood the concrete jungle.

"This intersection is the best we're gonna get off tracking her. There's twenty-five apartment complexes down that alley, two motels down this way, and some residential houses on both of those streets. Where do you want to start?" says Dylan.

"Pull into the motel right here," I say, feeling pressure to the back of my head every time I look at Motel Leafwood. "If anyone asks how we knew Laura would be here, let's just say she told me she prostituted here."

"Am I still the only one at work who knows about your powers?"

"Yeah. Well, sort of. Angela obviously knows."

Dylan drives his truck slowly through the parking lot of Motel Leafwood, which has three floors of motel rooms. Cars with missing windows and films of dust fill the parking lot. Between the motorhome taking up a couple of parking stalls and the tent pitched next to it, there's no doubt we're in Tuckford County.

"Can you ask your angels what room she'll be in? There's thirty rooms here and I'm not about to knock on each door. Half of them are probably occupied by dope dealers and the other half by prostitutes," says Dylan, turning his truck ignition off. "Are you sure she's going to be here?"

"That's what my angels are telling me. And they've never been wrong."

Dylan's laugh fills his county truck with sarcasm.

"What should I put in my police report for the angels' address? Heaven? Hell? Somewhere in between?"

"Mine live in heaven. Yours, on the other hand, would definitely live down south."

"Seriously though. Are you just taking a stab in the dark with this place?" Dylan asks.

"You still don't believe in my magic," I say.

"I live in a world based on facts. You know I solve my cases with real evidence, not magic," he says.

"I'll win cases my way and you solve cases your way," I snap back.

"I'm afraid to ask you how many leads you've given me from your angels," he says.

"Just assume that every time I told you a tip came from an anonymous caller, it was probably my angels."

"How far back?"

"To that first call-out I met you at."

"How'd you hide it so well?"

"I had to, at least until I trusted you. What was I supposed to say on that first call-out? 'Hi, I'm Gaby Ruiz. I'm on the homicide pager. Nice to meet you. By the way, my angels told me Chris Jones killed Allen Edwards.' You would've thought I was crazy."

"I wasn't even convinced that Jones was our guy until his DNA came back on the knife. Did your magic put his DNA there, too?"

"My magic doesn't plant evidence like some agencies are accused of. Mine gets the bad guys and frees the innocent."

Before Dylan has a chance to respond, a door on the third floor of the motel landing opens. My heart starts beating fast as a young girl with dark hair the same length as Laura's walks out.

"Is that her?" I ask excitedly.

"Shh. She's saying something to someone inside," says Dylan quietly.

The young woman, wearing cut-off jean shorts and a plaid shirt tied up in a knot sitting on her exposed and tattooed belly is too far up on the third floor for me to tell whether it's Laura. She closes the door and starts walking down the landing.

"She's walking like Laura. That's something she'd wear. I think she has those same color Converse shoes," I say.

She makes her way down the side staircase and comes walking straight towards Dylan's truck. I start crouching down in my seat while taking a good look at her as she walks past my window.

"I thought for sure that was her," I say disappointedly.

"So why didn't your angels tell you it wasn't?"

"I freaked out and didn't listen to my gut," I counter.

Dylan rolls his eyes.

I close my eyes, breathe deeply, and calm my fluttering eyelids. I focus on the darkness and one question while trying to ignore my disappointment. *Where is Laura?* I ask the Universe. I feel the warmth of my mom and her soothing voice. I feel calm. Once I hear her words and see the numbers, I open my eyes and unbuckle my seatbelt.

"She's in room 333. Let's head up there."

Dylan and I walk towards the motel. The pool surrounded by a black iron gate is floating a murky scum. A female Hispanic housekeeper in her early forties pushes her cleaning cart filled with towels, cleaning supplies, and toiletries up on the third floor.

"Quite a chateau, huh," says Dylan.

"The health department should be called out here."

"This is nothing. I've seen far worse."

"It reminds me of some of the places we used to pull into for an afternoon quickie," I say.

"Yeah, you knew how to pick them. Remember that one with the mirrors on the ceilings?"

"You picked that one, silly."

The quiet of the motel would have you thinking it's close to dawn, but it's already a little past ten in the morning.

Our knocks at room 333 go unanswered. I look at the cleaning lady a few yards away sweeping the third floor landing. "Señora, can you please unlock room 333?" I ask.

"I'm sorry but I'm not allowed to do that," the cleaning lady says, holding a broom in one hand and dustpan in the other.

"Look, we need to get into this room. There is a young woman in here who was supposed to show up to court this morning and she wasn't there. It's a long story, but we need your help," I say.

"You will need to speak with the manager. His office is down there on the first floor on the other side of the pool," she says, pointing down to a shack close to where Dylan parked his truck.

"Are you about to clean room 333?" I say.

"No, there's a 'Do not disturb' sign."

I take out my prosecutor golden shiny badge and flash it at her. I remove one of my business cards and hand it to her.

"Look, I am from the Prosecutor's Office. I don't want to startle or alert the manager, because I'm afraid the girl we're looking for inside might run. Do you have any children?"

"Yes, I have two teenagers."

"Can you imagine if one ran away and you had information she was in this room. You'd want someone to help you find her, wouldn't you?"

"My daughter has run away before. In fact, she just came back last night from the streets."

"Keep my card. If there is anything I can help with or if you want me to speak with her, I work with teenage girls with problems. I can help her. But I'm asking for your help right now."

The cleaning lady looks down at my card and takes a deep breath.

"Let me put some fresh towels in the room back there. I'll be right back to open it up."

Less than ten seconds after repeated unanswered knocks, unlocking, and going inside Room 333, the housekeeper runs back onto the landing looking like she had just seen a ghost. Shivering and through chattering teeth, she repeats the words, "My God," five times before I reach into my blouse and free my Lady Smith .38 Special and slowly walk into the room. Dylan follows behind with his gun drawn, too.

Room 333 is ransacked. A body lies face up on the queen-size bed. She has milky white skin and her black lace panties are pulled down to her ankles. Her long brown hair covers her face, which is rested to the side of the bed. Her arms are resting down by her pelvis and her wrists are restrained with a white belt with shiny black rhinestones. Her breasts are exposed and her dark brown nipples are hard. Each side of her pelvis is tattooed with a dolphin jumping up and as though they're arcing out of the water facing each other. She is blindfolded with two long white cotton socks tied together, covering her eyes and tied to the back of her head. I run up to her.

Dylan screams, "Police, police!" as he searches through the closet and the bathroom.

I move the girl's brown hair to look at her, then grasp for one of her wrists. I feel a faint pulse.

"She's alive," I shout.

Her body feels cold. I loosen the socks tied together around the back of her head and feel the pressure around my own head release. I loosen the belt that's tied around her wrists. I barely recognize her swollen and bruised face, but I know it's Laura. She has the pink band around her wrist imprinted with The Mamacita Club I gave her when I met her for the first time and was trying to recruit her. This is the first time I've seen Laura wearing it.

Dylan begins frantically making calls. First it's to 911 dispatch, then the paramedics, and next the Special Homicide Team Sergeant. I grab the bed sheet and wrap it tightly around Laura and tell her help is on its way. I crawl into the bed with her and hold her, rocking her back and forth, telling her everything is going to be okay and to hang in there. She grunts several times when I squeeze her. Her eyes stare right through mine and the white parts around her pupils fill with thin blood vessels.

Laura's blank stare reminds me of my mom in a picture I had seen of her when I was thirteen years old. I was sitting in the witness stand of my stepfather's trial, and the prosecutor, Mike Tanner, asked me to look at a big projection screen.

My mom was projected life-size lying in her bed in our mobile home. She was pale and her eyes were wide open just like Laura's. Her silk Kimono night robe, untied and draping to her sides, exposed her breasts and stomach. A long red scratch ran down her arm and a deep gash cut down her temple.

I cried for five minutes straight on the witness stand until the judge ordered me to answer Tanner's questions.

I hug Laura and promise her I won't leave her side. Footsteps sounding like a stampede become louder and louder until they come through Room 333.

Within thirty minutes of paramedics arriving to Room 333, Laura is wheeled out the front door on a gurney. Her mouth is filled with a tube and a plastic mask covers her face. Blood droplets fall from her head off the side of the gurney onto the motel landing, marking her path down to the ambulance as I watch her being whisked away. I return back inside the empty room as Dylan barks orders over the phone for crime scene forensics to meet us at the motel.

A ceramic vase with the body of a bird rests in a puddle of blood near the bed. The bird's head is broken off and missing. Fake plastic flowers spread around the bed. The blue, mauve, and white bedspread sits swirled up in a cocoon on the floor near the night stand. A matching vase with what I can now see is an intact pink and cream colored flamingo rests on a night stand with a black zip-up hoodie and a white sock draping over it. A pink cell phone sits on the night stand near the vase.

Looking ahead up to the bed, where I was just curled up with Laura, I see the socks lying on the floor that were once blindfolding her. The belt from Laura's wrists lay next to the socks and a pair of pants. A black cell phone lies on the floor nearby. The motel room reeks of blood, alcohol, and the smell of sex.

It reminds me the first time I lost my virginity to my boyfriend Marco after his high school prom. I was fifteen. It happened at a motel one star higher than this one, which his older brother rented for us. After five minutes of something that felt like sex, I said to him, "Is that it?" I thought my first time was supposed to be something special. I couldn't believe I had lost my virginity to fast rabbit humping.

Dylan's phone ringing takes me out of my virginity paradise lost. He silences his phone.

"Did your angels forget to tell you what we were going to walk into? At least if I knew, I could have called in the forensic team beforehand," says Dylan.

"That's not how it works. I asked my angels where we could find Laura and they told me. I never asked what condition she'd be in. But I'll for sure do that next time."

"Okay, so when my boss asks me what supposedly led us to this room, what should I tell him? I'm going to need something to put in a homicide report."

"Homicide?" I say dramatically.

"Laura is practically dead. It's just a matter of time before the coroner is performing the autopsy on her."

"Don't rule this a homicide so quickly. Laura's a strong girl; she'll pull through this."

"Who are you trying to kid?   Did you see what I just saw?"

"Yes, Dylan," I reply.   "I was here holding her while you were on your phone.   I saw everything."

"I'm taking it that this will be your case now.   You're the on-call homicide prosecutor, right?" Dylan asks.

"It's not a homicide yet.   Stop saying she's dead."

"She couldn't even talk.   I've seen these cases before.   She had a huge gash to her head.   That's where all the blood was coming from.   It's just a matter of time.   She was comatose.   It was like she was barely even responding to us."

"You weren't doing anything to talk to her," I counter.

"You looked like you had everything under control.   I was making all the calls to get help out here," Dylan replies.

"Like I said earlier.   You work your cases the way you want.   I'll work them my way.   Let's go get the canvass interviews done so we can get outta here."

3

MY WAY

The motel check-in desk is no longer than five feet wide. Dylan stands on one end while I stand on the opposite end. A sign saying "Be back at" with a clock fixed at 11:40 will give Dylan eight minutes to take notes on the canvass interviews we just did. The window air cooler hums into the small space.

Dylan starts scribbling in a small notepad. An hour of interviews with the esteemed Motel Leafwood residents, mostly who were missing teeth or fingers, produced the typical "I don't know," "I didn't hear anything," or "I was sleeping" responses.

But Mr. Barry in room 331, right next door to Laura's room, heard about five thumps against the wall at five o'clock in the morning. He didn't think much of it because earlier in the night, he heard what he thought was rough sex a couple different times and saw men coming and going. He suspected room 333 was being used as a flop house for prostitution.

Around midnight, Mr. Thomas in room 221 saw Laura with a young man, with light skin, spiky hair, and tattoos including a letter L on his right bicep. I'm almost certain that had to be Clown. His tattoo is a dead giveaway. Plus, one of the cell phones left in the room belonged to him.

Around six o'clock in the morning, the housekeeper heard a car leaving at a high rate of speed. She remembered a strange rattling sound coming from the engine. I don't think the housekeeper Blanca would have given us this information if it wasn't for Laura's blood on my clothes. I told her we all had a role in helping to solve this crime. I love the instruction judges read to juries, how flight is evidence of guilt. We should have this case wrapped up once we get DNA results back from the hotel room.

I turn to Dylan. "I think we're wasting our time waiting around here. The person we're waiting for is the motel owner. He's not going to give us any information about who checked into Room 333. He's gonna want a search warrant. People in this motel know that room was being used as a flop house. The last thing he'll want to do is help us figure out how he could be responsible for what happened to Laura," I say.

"You're probably right, but we need to find out exactly what I need to write a search warrant for. I need to know how they keep information on check-ins, if there's surveillance cameras, do they take credit cards, stuff like that," says Dylan.

Sometimes policemen get into a routine and investigate their cases strictly based on habit. Some seem to have a set pattern of how they solve a case and rarely will they change it up. Most of the time they get it right. But sometimes, there's a better way like my way.

"Do you see that notepad on the other side of the desk up there?" I ask.

"Yeah, this one with a bunch of writing on it next to the bell?" Dylan asks.

"Is that what you're talking about? The check-in roster?"

"Looks like it," says Dylan, looking up from the notepad he's been scribbling in.

"Why can't we just look at it?" I ask.

"I don't want it to become a problem for us later. I already crossed the line in getting Laura's phone traced. Plus, there may be surveillance watching us in here right now."

"Do you really think there's surveillance cameras in this motel? They can't even update their bedspreads," I say.

"Who knows?"

"Why do you think the owner's gone right now? He saw us walking down here and I don't think he wants anything to do with us. He didn't come up one time to 333 to see what was going on," I say.

I move closer to the notepad sitting on the other side of the desk. A large log with a leather cover sits on the desk with a pen resting on an open page covered with lines and writing.

"Don't do that. Let's just wait. It says he'll be back at 11:40. That's just a couple minutes away," says Dylan.

I reach over the desk and turn the book around so I can read it. There's room numbers, dates, times, and names. Room 333. 9:40 p.m., check in. +1 guest. $45.00. July 6. Paid.

That was easy.

"What does it say?" says Dylan.

"Remember, you do things your way. I'll do them my way," I say.

The door opens as a jingle bell hanging from the knob rings the sound of Christmas. A man's voice yells out. "Can I help you with something?"

"Hi. I'm Gaby Ruiz. I'm from the Prosecutor's Office and this is Investigator Mack with the Special Homicide Team."

"Hello there. I'm Bob, the motel manager. Sounds like you had quite an army out there this morning."

"We did. You run quite a motel here. How long have you owned this place?" I say.

"Oh, I just run the place. I'm not the owner."

The first sign of someone lying to me is always a bad sign. It makes me wonder what else they are hiding. Our canvass interviews already informed me that Bob is the owner of this motel.

"How long have you run this place?" I ask.

"Oh, twenty years now," Bob replies.

"Wow, you could have paid off the mortgage on a place like this if you bought it way back then. That's too bad. It would have been a nice chunk of retirement you could've been sitting on," I say.

Bob is probably sitting on this motel as a piece of retirement. He pays no maintenance, which is obvious from the pool scum and unattended flowerbeds and lawn areas around the parking lot. The rooms are outdated and he hasn't put any work into it other than patching things up to make it habitable. The spackle on some of the walls is not even painted over. The rent he charges is so low and every room is occupied. And he's willing to rent to pimps and drug addicts.

"Yeah, too bad I don't own the place. What can I do for you guys?" Bob asks.

"Well, do you want the good news or the bad news first?" I ask.

"I don't want any news from the police," says Bob.

"That's fair. Most people don't. Let me help you then. I'll start with the bad. The bad news is that we found a corpse, almost dead, in one of your rooms. It was a girl, seventeen years old. She was supposed to be testifying in one of my cases this morning and she didn't show up. That's why I'm here. Can you tell me who was occupying Room 333 this morning?" I ask.

"Well, I'd have to search the registration logs. We keep all the information on the motel guests in that log."

"No problem. I can wait right here while you check."

"It would take some time to research. I'll have to call my corporate headquarters and get permission to release the information."

"We can wait."

"It's not that easy. Maybe you don't understand."

"Maybe *you* don't understand, Bob. I'm asking a simple question. And my common sense tells me you probably have some sort of registration log you keep right here, like a notebook, with the names of people who checked in. What do you do when people want to check out of your motel or you need to contact them in their rooms for something? Do you have to call corporate headquarters?"

"Well, that depends."

"Depends on what?" I ask. "How high on drugs they are? What room they're in? Whether they're a regular guest?

Whether they're using your facility to pimp out and turn tricks?"

"I don't know what you're talking about," Bob says.

"Where are your headquarters, anyway?"

"They're in Old Town."

"Is that your house in Old Town you're talking about? Is your wife at home who you call your headquarter?" I ask.

"Look, you're going to need a warrant to get any records from this motel," Bob replies. "It's just standard procedure."

"We will be getting a warrant," I assure him. "And let me tell you what my standard procedure is. Once I review those records, if there are any convicted pimps on that register that you've been warned not to rent rooms to, I will take the personal pleasure in filing charges against you for aiding and abetting prostitution.

"You and I both know that you're the owner of this motel. And I bet if I look into it, you've been told not to rent your rooms to certain people including the one you rented 333 to last night. Do you know what a blacklist is, Bob?" I ask aggressively.

"Yes, it's people we're not supposed to be renting to," he replies.

"Exactly," I say. "I'll put twenty dollars on whoever you rented Room 333 to last night is on that blacklist."

Bob is silent, staring at me wondering what's going to come out of my mouth next.

"Ma'am, like I said, you'll need a search warrant for the motel records," he says.

"Very well," I reply. "Now that was the bad news. Let's talk about the good news. The good news is that we are done processing Room 333 and it's all yours. Our forensic team is finishing up, as we speak. You may have a bit of a clean-up to do in there. And I don't think you'll want to send in your housekeeper. She's rather distraught. She found the girl's body.

"You should think about hiring a crime scene clean-up crew. They have these great steam cleaners and heavy duty equipment and cleaners. They'll be able to get out the blood that soaked into your bed and carpet with just one steam clean. My grandmother had to hire one," I say, walking myself out with Dylan.

"Did your grandmother really hire one of those companies?" asks Dylan.

"No, we cleaned it ourselves. I don't think those companies existed back then," I reply, holding back my tears and regretting that I mentioned this.

"What did that roster say?" Dylan asks.

"Clown checked them in last night. Let's head to the hospital. I'll need an update on Laura to give Judge Hoffman."

There's nothing glamorous about the hills of Mason Valley on our ride to the hospital. If it had its own TV show, it would star some trailer trash hillbilly actress. Dylan turns down the country music playing in his truck so I can answer my ringing cell phone.

"Gaby Ruiz," I say. It's Maribel, the front lobby receptionist at my office.

"Hi, Ms. Ruiz. A man by the name of Rodrigo Garcia just walked into our office. He's asking to speak to you on a case you're investigating," says Maribel.

"Thank you, can you transfer me to the O.D.?" I ask hurriedly.

The O.D. is the officer of the day. Every day there's an investigator assigned to the front desk. He watches the front lobby, monitors surveillance throughout the building, and is in charge of helping prosecutors with last minute favors.

"O.D.," says a man on the phone after a minute of symphony music.

"Who is this?" I ask quickly.

"Investigator Chuck Van Dyke. Who's this?"

"Hey, Chuck. This is Gaby Ruiz. I need your help," I say. "There's a man that's waiting in the lobby. He looks like a hardcore gang-banger. His name is Rodrigo Garcia and he goes by the nickname Clown. You can't miss him. He has this big joker smile with big jowls. He just walked into the office asking to speak to me."

"Hold him there. Well, don't hold him, but keep an eye on him and make sure he doesn't leave. If he starts to leave, assure him I'm on my way. If you need to, put him in an interview room and offer him some coffee. He's a suspect in a serious assault that I'm investigating right now."

"Can I hook him up?" asks Chuck.

"No, don't hook him up. I don't think we have enough on him yet. Plus, I want him at ease as much as possible when we talk to him. He won't talk if he's in custody. He came to the office for a reason. I don't know what that is. But I don't wanna spook him. I should be there in about half hour if there's no traffic," I say.

"All right, see you in a bit," says Chuck as I hang up the phone.

"Are you kidding me? You don't want him arrested? You don't think we have enough!" says Dylan sarcastically as he redirects our route to head towards my office.

"I just want something more. We don't even have the DNA," I say.

"What more do you want? A confession? A videotape?"

"The moment we make an arrest, the clock starts ticking. I don't want the forty-eight hour pressure with a case like this. The DNA will take at least a week to get back," I say.

"A week? That will give him just enough time to leave the country," Dylan replies.

"Assuming he could afford that. The only things we have right now is that he checked into the motel, his phone is in the room, and he's seen with Laura hours before she's found. We have no cause of injury, no time of assault, no DNA," I say.

"He's a pimp. He could afford to leave the country. And DNA will take weeks to get done. We can't wait for that," says Dylan.

"Let's just see what he has to say, then we can hook him up. What if he's a witness? Why would he be coming to speak with us?"

"Oh, come on, that's ridiculous."

"Call me ridiculous. I call it proving a case beyond a reasonable doubt. You can hook him up. I'm not filing it based on what we have now. And if you hook him up and he gets released because we haven't filed charges, you can definitely guarantee he'll run. Let me do all the talking when we see him. I know how to deal with him. I've spoken to him before on Javier's case."

Being minutes away from interviewing a possible attempted homicide suspect is as adrenaline-laced as riding a roller coaster or drag racing. You never know what story he'll give or whether he's dumb enough to even talk. It's never a good idea for a criminal defendant to give a statement to police, much less testify.

Clown has prior violent felony convictions for carjacking and burglary, which subject him to double digits of punishment just like Javier, if he commits any felony in the future. He's served a total of six years in state prison and has miscellaneous drug, child endangerment, and hit and run misdemeanor offenses.

"Pull over right here. I don't want him seeing us just yet," I say.

Clown is pacing back and forth in the lobby of my office. Dylan turns the ignition of his truck off.

"On the count of three, let's get out and start walking towards the front door," I say. "One. Two. Three."

I jump out of Dylan's truck, glancing at my hair in the reflection of the tinted passenger window. I run my fingers through my hair from my forehead back. I catch Dylan watching me primp myself. Women magazines firmly believe that when a man watches a woman primp, it causes him to be sexually aroused. Dylan and I walk towards the front double glass doors of my office.

Before I could even see it coming, Clown rushes at us. He slaps his palms against the exit bar of the door, pushes it open, and runs full speed down the stairs and across the street. I lose sight of him as he's running past the Men's Old Town Jail. Chuck, the Officer of the Day, runs out of the office, then stops dead in his tracks.

"Don't bother. I'm not filing even if you detain him," I say.

"He's a fugitive and dispatch just said he has a warrant for his arrest. He didn't show up to court in the past," yells Chuck.

"What? Did you know that, Dylan?" I ask.

"You want me to go after him?" Chuck asks.

I think for a second. If we arrest him now, it will force everyone to wrap this case up and make a filing decision within forty-eight hours. I'm supposed to be on a plane in two weeks to start my international vacation, which I've been saving for the past three years. I've scouted out the best and cheapest motels. How can I miss three days on the beach, two nights at a quaint bed and breakfast I booked, and the wine region?

Chuck snaps me out of my travel dream. "We're gonna lose him. We need to start now if we're going to do this. And I need Dylan to back me up," says Chuck.

"His fleeing at least gives me more to work with. Go ahead and hook him up," I say, reluctantly.

Dylan and Chuck take off running.

4

POINT OF NO RETURN

Thirty minutes after the chase, I sit in the office of Karen Alvarez, the head of the Investigator's Bureau. Dylan and Chuck sit at opposite ends of the rectangular table I'm at. Karen's office on the thirteenth floor is spacious and lined from ceiling to floor with windows. Karen and my supervisor Joanna Medina sit closest to me in the middle. Special Assistant Prosecutor Stevie Sapp sits directly across from me. We sit in silence, waiting for Mike Tanner, my boss's boss. I haven't spoken to Tanner aside from meetings like this since he prosecuted my stepfather in my mom's murder trial. A freight train makes its way down the train tracks parallel to the freeway. I start counting the train cars hoping it will calm my nervousness. It was something my mom and I used to do when I was young.

Stevie Sapp interrupts my counting.

"How's your girls' club coming along, Gaby?" she asks.

I give Stevie a big fake smile.

"Thank you for asking. The Mamacita Club has been wonderful. I've bonded with some of the toughest girls. A lot of them come from the mobile home parks we're hosting in. I hope to continue doing it and growing the club. I've been recruiting all kinds of women to mentor; in fact, many are from your unit," I say, hoping to upset her.

When I started The Mamacita Club, Stevie Sapp was anything but supportive. She didn't like the idea that a high ranking prosecutor would want to drive around in an RV helping the community instead of earning a trial stat she could add to her monthly report.

"How's the mobile home holding up?" asks Stevie.

I look at her, disgusted.

"It's a *motor*home, not a mobile home," I say.

"Is there a difference?" says Stevie rudely.

"Yeah. A big one. A mobile home stays in one spot. Most of them aren't drivable unless you hook them up to a truck. Mine's a Vintage Airstream, custom-made classic. I can drive it to different RV parks," I say.

"And you *live* in that thing?" says Stevie.

"Just occasionally. It's really not that bad. I grew up in a trailer park," I say.

"I guess you can take the girl out of the trailer park, but you can't take the trailer park out of the girl," says Stevie.

I give her another big fake smile. "That's right. You should try camping in one. You'd probably like it," I say.

"No, thank you," says Stevie dismissively.

I roll my eyes at Dylan.

"We've received several complaints about that thing being parked in the trailer park. People are concerned your group is a law enforcement club. And that their park might be targeted by gangs, etcetera, if they are associating with *you*," says Stevie, emphasizing the word "you" like she's the real one targeting me.

"That makes absolutely no sense. There's no evidence of that even being remotely true," I snap back.

"Well, this case we're about to discuss involves one of the girls from your club. Doesn't it?"

"No. I wanted her to join, but the office said it was a conflict. I have to wait until her case is over. Plus, her mom never gave her permission," I say disappointedly.

"I don't know if you're aware, but Ed Vanderbilt is already in talks with the trailer park about the liability of you being there. It may be too much of a problem to have your club meetings on their premises," Stevie says.

"That's okay. We'll just drive the Airstream to another trailer park."

"You might want to hold your horses and check with Ed before you set up camp anywhere else."

Mike Tanner walks in, interrupting my frustration and concern about Stevie's comments. He wastes no time before laying in on us.

"What the hell is going on, Karen?" Tanner asks. "There was a homicide suspect in the lobby of our office thirty minutes ago. He had a warrant for his arrest. Why the hell would he not be detained? Explain that to me, because the prosecutor and the press are going to want an explanation for this."

I look at Chuck before I look down and stare at the maroon swirl pattern of the table.

"We were told to hold off and not make an arrest. The only information we had was to keep an eye on him. And we were told there was no probable cause. Chuck was the one who discovered this man had a warrant," says Karen.

"I'm going to ask you again. Tell me why, after Chuck realized there was a warrant in the system, you did not hook him up right there?" asks Tanner.

I can feel Chuck looking at me as I'm staring down at the table. I can't stand confrontation. There is silence in the room.

"It's my understanding that Chuck was told not to make an arrest," says Karen.

"I hope that was the prosecutor who made that decision. And I'm not talking about an assistant prosecutor, I'm talking about the appointed prosecutor. If that suspect hurts anyone, goes out and continues his killing spree, or turns up missing, do you know who's going to have to answer questions about this decision?" asks Tanner dramatically.

"Sir, we still know nothing about this case," Karen says. "The only information we had was that this was a possible homicide suspect, his physical description, and that there was not enough PC to arrest him. He had walked into the office asking to speak with Ms. Ruiz and we were to keep an eye on him. We were never informed about any warrant. Chuck found the old warrant when he ran this fellow through the criminal database. We would have only been making an arrest on an old warrant issued when he failed to appear on a drug case. You know we would have booked him across the street and the jail would have released him. There's no room for him over there."

"I was under the impression he had a warrant for a murder. Was I misinformed?" asks Tanner.

I stay quiet. And I try to tune out the screaming. Everything will eventually stop. At least that's the way I survived my stepfather's alcoholic rages late at night when I was young. I would listen to him scream at my mom in the next room. I would stay quiet, paralyzed under my covers, squeezing Zip my stuffed monkey and crying until things calmed down.

"Yes, you were misinformed. And Chuck was misinformed," Karen replies. "I don't think Ms. Ruiz or Investigator Mack knew that he had an outstanding warrant. Chuck was specifically instructed not to arrest him."

"It sounds like this was a colossal crater of misinformation," says Tanner.

I stay silent.

"Investigator Mack, it is my understanding you are assigned to this homicide case and were assisting Ms. Ruiz in her trial. Is that correct?" Tanner asks.

"It is, sir," says Dylan.

"Is it fair to say you never informed her of any warrants this suspect had?" asks Tanner.

"That's correct. I wasn't aware of any warrants," Dylan replies.

"Did you check a database or run his criminal history?" Tanner asks. "I'm sure the warrant would have been in the database."

"Sir, the Leafwood Police Department is the investigating agency on this case. It is an attempted homicide, not a homicide, so SHT hasn't officially taken it over. The Leafwood Police Department never mentioned the warrant," says Dylan.

Dylan should know better than to try to blame another agency. Mike Tanner is a skilled prosecutor. Tanner knows the pass-the-buck blame game and Dylan just got caught doing it.

"You certainly know what a criminal database system is and what a dispatcher does, don't you?" asks Tanner condescendingly.

"I do," says Dylan.

"It would be within the color of your authority to use those things to check for warrants, wouldn't it?" Tanner asks rhetorically.

Dylan stays quiet.

"Never mind, don't answer that," says Tanner laughing.

"This isn't as bad as I thought it was walking into this room. Investigator Mack, I'm going to ask you to step out of the room for just a moment. I need to speak to Ms. Ruiz briefly," Tanner says.

Dylan grabs his portfolio and gives me a nervous smile before walking out and closing the door behind him.

Mike Tanner is an overall distinguished looking man in his late fifties. He has a full set of brown hair that looks fluffed and hair-sprayed neatly. He has on gold rings, a gold watch, and gold cufflinks. His starched white shirt sits flat inside his tan and dark brown suit. Sitting ten feet away from him after he sent Dylan out, I'm able to study his appearance for the first time. It cries out top prosecutor of the county. It's no wonder he was able to convict my stepfather based on his appearance alone.

I know my mom's case struck a chord with him. Twelve years later, he helped to get me hired behind the scenes. At least that's what the rumors were. I haven't spoken with him aside from staffings or mandatory meetings like this one.

This reminds me of when he examined me during my stepfather's trial. At thirteen years old and crying on the witness stand, Tanner asked the judge to order me to answer questions about hearing my mom scream for me to call police the day she died. Tanner and I haven't spoken since. It was mainly because of that picture he showed me of my mom when I was testifying.

A couple years after the trial, he visited me. He tried to apologize to me and explain that he needed the jury to feel my pain. My stepfather was a sympathetic defendant and Tanner was worried the jurors wouldn't convict him.

What was most insulting about his visit was that he left some brochures on the Alateen program for me. He told my grandma it had to do with a group that helps family members of alcoholics. Nana told him she didn't believe in that type of stuff.

From time to time I wonder if the past twenty years would have been different for me had I started going to Alateen. I never forgave Tanner for showing me that picture.

"Ms. Ruiz, I know you and I have not spoken in a very long time. Almost twenty years, I think. Any of the people in this room will tell you that I have nothing but respect for you, your trial work, and your contribution to this office. However, I am less than thrilled with your involvement in the fiasco that just happened," says Tanner.

I look directly at Tanner in the eyes for the first time in a long time. "What fiasco? If we would have arrested him, a) he wouldn't have spoken to us, and b) the jail would have cite released him," I say.

"We could've asked the jail to hold him. And besides that, what's even more concerning to me is that you had no idea he had an outstanding warrant. What exactly have you and Investigator Mack been doing?" Tanner asks.

"Do you know how hard I've been working on this case? This victim was supposed to start testifying this morning in my trial and she went missing. I've been running the past six hours through Leafwood and Mason Valley trying to gather as much information as I can. Judge Hoffman wants a full report when we return to court. That's what Dylan Mack and I have been doing. And why would you think we've been doing anything other than investigating this case?" I ask.

"Well, for starters, you two were involved in other things in the past," says Tanner.

"You have no right to pry into my private life. You know what your problem is? You don't know when to stop. If you want to talk about work, that's one thing. But you've crossed the line. And this is not the first time you've gone way too far. Mr. Tanner, you and I will never see eye to eye," I say bitterly.

I look back down at the mahogany table patterns. A warm tear drizzles down my cheek before it drops down onto my black suit blazer.

"Dylan is the investigator on your case assigned to *my unit*. Your relationship with him is my concern. When this case is filed, I want you off. Your lack of diligence in having this suspect arrested is reason enough to have you removed from the case," says Tanner.

"Good. You go find someone who will care half as much as I do about Laura or this case. No one will fight like I will to get her justice. I know her and this case better than you ever will or anyone you reassign it to. Are we done here? Because I'm through speaking with you," I say standing up.

"I have nothing else. Karen?" asks Tanner.

Everyone looks at each other and stays quiet. I walk out and slam the door.

5

EMERGENCY SEARCH

Within thirty minutes of leaving Tanner's meeting, I pull up to Laura's mobile home at the Leafwood RV Park with Dylan. It sends chills down my back. I come here all the time to the Airstream, but the last time I came here with Dylan was a year ago. Not much has changed, even my feelings towards him, which date back to the first time I laid eyes on him two years ago.

I've always thought he was the one. The smell of Dylan's cologne and his big blue eyes were my biggest weaknesses. His eyes standing out against his tan skin and thick light brown hair catches the eyes of women in all demographics. Two years ago, I became another woman who threw herself at him.

"You think he's here?" Dylan asks.

"Just put it this way. I know he's here," I reply.

Dylan rolls his eyes, half-believing me. We jump out of his truck and make our way slowly up to Laura's mobile home. The front door is open with the screen blocking our way inside the house. A Mexican soap opera is on the television in the front room.

Several call-outs for Bess don't receive any response, and my heart starts beating fast thinking Clown made it to her before we could. My worst nightmare is that some violent perpetrator got loose onto the streets to hurt someone else because of a bad call I made.

"Señora Sanchez," I yell several times before telling Dylan we need to go inside.

"On what basis are we entering this house?" Dylan asks. "There needs to be an emergency or we need a reason to do a welfare check to break through this screen door."

"Why can't we just say he came in here?" I ask. "He's a wanted fugitive. And responsible for Laura's assault."

"Because you know that won't fly," Dylan says. "We have no credible information that he is even here. And no, your angels do not count as a credible or reliable source of information. I need a solid tip that he's here."

I see a man in jeans and a white tank top and suspenders crossing the dirt road in the trailer park towards us. I've seen him before, but have never spoken to him.

"How about we talk with this guy right behind you and see if he saw anything. Hey, Sir! You live here, right?" I ask.

"Well, I sure do and that's why I came to speak with you. I recognize you from the Airstream. That's a fine trailer you got there. And a nice thing you're doin' for them girls," he says in his hillbilly accent.

Within seconds, Mr. Smith is rattling off the names of his six kids and wife Georgia, who live in the trailer across the way. His style reminds me of my fourth grade, redneck cowgirl costume my mom and I created for my Halloween contest at Tuckford Elementary School. My mom wasn't feeling well enough to take me shopping the night before Halloween. When she wasn't icing her black eye, we dug through our closets to see what we could come up with. We found a pair of my stepfather's suspenders.

"I saw something suspicious. Someone pulled up, ran through that front door. It happened about ten minutes ago. Next thing I knew, about ten minutes later when I was watching TV, I heard the car start up and take off real fast," says Mr. Smith.

"What did he look like?" I ask.

"Dark hair, spiky, a letter L on his arm, light skin. He looked young, in his 30s. I think I've seen his Lincoln in this neighborhood before. Engine has a strange rattling sound," says Mr. Smith.

"Thank you for the information. Go ahead and go back to your home," I say.

"That should be enough for us to enter. And if anything has happened to Bess inside, that should be enough for us to get fired from our jobs. I can see the headlines now. Possible armed suspect breaks into the victim's home to kill her mother after the Prosecutor's Office drops the ball. I'm going in," I say.

Dylan follows me down the hallway of Bess's small mobile home. Watching Dylan's gun drawn up in front of him just like I have mine causes my chest to tighten and my heartbeat to pulse throughout my body. It's times like this that my CCW permit comes in handy. After receiving threats while I was working gangs, I decided I needed a Concealed Carry Weapon; so my boobs and thighs got strapped, literally.

My .38 Special Lady Smith either hides beneath my boobs in a space below my bra or the inside of my thigh when I'm wearing skirts or dresses. Both locations give me easy access to guarantee any surprises go my way.

The books that line a bookshelf in the hallway of Bess's home catch my attention. *The Secret. The Alchemist. The Five People You Meet in Heaven. Go Ask Alice. The Freedom Writer's Diary. Scars. The Diary of Anne Frank. Muchacho. Tuesdays with Morrie. Love in the Time of Cholera. The Long Walk. Fruitflesh. The House on Mango Street. One Hundred Years of Solitude.* These weren't here the first time I came to this house. I can't believe Laura bought all the books I've recommended to the ladies at The Mamacita Club.

There is no sign of Bess or Clown. Dylan and I creep our way down the hallway and I watch Dylan clear every room, looking under beds and through closets to make sure no one is there.

An open window off the kitchen at the end of the hallway catches my attention. A white cotton curtain with a yellow lace fringe is blowing in the wind. I look closer to make sure the screen is not off the window, thinking for a second that Clown skipped out of the window leading off the kitchen. The screen is missing.

"So how did you figure he would be here?" asks Dylan.

Just as I want to remind Dylan about my powers, I stop.

"Why do *you* think he was here?" I ask.

"I asked you first," says Dylan.

I shrug my shoulders and smile. Dylan smiles back at me and holds my gaze.

"Well?" Dylan asks.

"I figured this place was worth a shot. Tanner's pissed at me. And you seemed really upset trying to get the fugitive team after him. I figured, why not try Laura's house," I say.

"Why do you think he would have picked this place?" asks Dylan.

"I don't know," I say.

I start looking around the home. Dylan starts to remind me I wasn't supposed to be snooping. We were only supposed to enter the house for an emergency reason, like to save a life. I wonder where Bess had gone in such a hurry leaving her front door unlocked and open. I walk into a small room off the hallway. It's Laura's room.

Laura has a long dresser with a mirror on top. A white lace doily drapes across it, with a jewelry box sitting on top. I open the box and the piano music fills the air. A ballerina pops up and begins spinning with her arms in the air. When I first came to this house to talk to her about Javier's case, I admired this same jewelry box. It was the same kind I had always wished for when I was younger.

My mom promised me one for my birthday, but then she died before it came around. So I never got one. When my grandmother offered to buy me one later, I told her that I wanted to wait and buy one if I ever had a daughter. I didn't want Nana buying me what I wanted my mom to. These days, I wonder if I'll ever have that chance.

"We probably shouldn't be touching anything," says Dylan.

I stay silent as the room becomes blurry from the tears in my eyes.

"I know this is hard and you really liked Laura. You were trying to get her to join your club. I remember when we came here and she invited you in here, while I was talking to Bess. I still remember the beige suit you had on. There was something about you that was glowing that day," says Dylan.

"It's funny you say that. I was thinking the same thing coming over here. I never could have predicted anything like this would have happened to her," I say.

"What's with the jewelry box? You want one?"

"The timing's never been right," I say before picking up my vibrating cell phone.

"Hi, Gaby. It's Maribel from the front desk. I have Detective Shawn Ford on the other line. Is it okay if I transfer him to you? He says it's urgent."

"Go ahead," I say.

After a couple loud clicks, I hear static.

"This is Gaby Ruiz," I say.

"Hi, Ms. Ruiz, this is Detective Shawn Ford. We have Rodrigo Garcia in custody at the Leafwood Police Department. Get on over here. We're getting ready to interview him."

6

MEN IN UNIFORM

Detective Shawn Ford, the lead detective handling Laura's case for the Leafwood Police Department, meets Dylan and I at the back door of the police station.

"I have Rodrigo here, ready to interview. He was located twenty minutes ago two blocks from Motel Leafwood," says Ford.

Often, suspects will return back to the crime scene to watch their mess unfold or to try and get information about the investigation so they know how much of a viable suspect they are to police.

"I wanted to let you know that it's a bit questionable how he was pulled over and stopped by our patrol deputy."

"What do you mean?" I ask.

"Officer Cruz radioed that the suspect had a chain hanging from his rearview mirror. That was the reason he gave dispatch for pulling him over, but there was no chain.

Cruz is familiar with him and his Lincoln Continental from the neighborhood," says Ford.

"He has that warrant out for his arrest. Why do we care about the reason for the stop? Cruz could have pulled him over just because he has that warrant," I say.

"I know, but Cruz didn't know about the warrant when he pulled him over. Cruz hadn't run the plates through dispatch. The all-points bulletin hadn't been broadcasted yet. Cruz just knew we were looking for him to talk to. He's young, eager, and just put the cart before the horse, that's all," Ford says.

"Is Cruz's reason for stopping him recorded on the dispatch radio traffic?" I ask.

"Yes, and it appears in the dispatch log as well. There was a woman in the car with him too. He took her at knifepoint, but she's okay," Ford replies.

"Oh my God," I say. "It wasn't Bess was it?" I ask, seeing my entire career flash before me.

"How'd you know?" asks Ford.

I change the subject, not wanting to explain that my angels led me to Bess' house.

"Do you know if we get a confession from him right now, his attorney would have a good shot at getting it thrown out? Why are we even bothering to question him?" I ask.

"I know," Ford says. "That's why I'm telling you this."

"Look, it's gonna be Cruz's word against a convicted felon's. Who do you think a judge will believe?" asks Dylan.

"What if they ask where this supposed chain is that he had hanging from his rearview mirror and Cruz can't produce it because it doesn't exist? Or what if Bess says something. She'd be the most believable in this whole thing. Anyway, now that you gave me this information, I'm obligated to tell the defense about Cruz's mistake."

As a prosecutor, I am bound by an ethical duty to tell the defense anything that may exculpate or set his client free. It's my duty to inform the defendant of any evidence that might point to his innocence or help his case. This responsibility is non-negotiable in my eyes. And violating this requirement can cost me my Bar card, something that is not worth putting the most heinous defendant away for.

I'll use my other weapons — my magic, my Latin spice, my assets, my sweet talk, my attitude, and sometimes my mean girl tactics to make sure justice is done. But I won't rob a defendant of his right to know everything that might help his case. That would jeopardize my powers.

"I know Cruz screwed up, but we can't undo the past," Ford says. "I already advised his Sergeant and he's going to speak with him later today. He'll probably invoke his Miranda rights and not speak with us, anyway. He's been around the block before. He's a Lincoln gang member, he has a serious criminal history, and is looking at a case being filed in the next forty-eight hours.

"I've already spoken to Bess, so I know the history between Laura and him. But let's hear what he has to say, then we'll go from there," Ford says, waving his key card in front of a black square on the side of the wall and opening the door for us.

The booking area of the police department where young, fit police officers, handsome and fresh in well-ironed beige uniform shirts with army green pants, greet us with big smiles. I forget about Cruz until I see him in the booking area. He's not as clean-cut as the other officers and his wrinkled shirt looks like he grabbed it from the dryer this morning, but it's hard to pick on him. He just detained our attempted homicide suspect, which may have saved me my job and my office some embarrassment.

"Hi, Detective Ford. We have the suspect here waiting. He's been searched and patted down; he's all ready to go," says Officer Cruz.

"Great, thank you, go ahead and put him in the interview room. I'm going to take Investigator Mack and Ms. Ruiz to the monitoring room. See that the recorder is up and running," says Ford.

"Done. We already set it up for you. Just hit play on the black box and you're good to go. Anything else you need, let me know. There's coffee and water in the Detective Bureau. Help yourself," says Cruz.

It hurts the case and justice all around when evidence gets thrown out because a police officer doesn't play by the rules. I have no problem letting a police officer get yelled at in open court by a judge because they did a bad search or traffic stop. I'll even yell at them myself. It teaches them a serious lesson, to not abuse their power, or in Cruz's case, to just be patient.

For whatever reason, I take the opportunity to keep my mouth shut and, instead, just smile at Cruz as I pass him. I learned from Dylan that emasculating a police officer, especially in front of their superiors, is never a good idea.

Walking through the Leafwood Police Department following Dylan and Detective Ford reminds me how hard these guys work. They are tapping away on their computers, cranking out police reports, writing search warrants, and running criminal rap sheets. They sit in crammed cubicles in their bulletproof vests, with photos of their wives and kids thumb-tacked up on the walls lining their cubicles. It's easy to forget how hardworking and simpleminded men like these are.

They risk their lives every day. It's easy to take that for granted and just remember any unlawful search they've done because sometimes it seems that's all the media portrays. But this job has showed me another side — the reality.

This agency is a demonstration of the best and ripest apples. They put their lives on the line for ours. In some respects they are like military men. No one wants to do their job, but we're the first to criticize them when they make a wrong move, whether it's arresting an innocent person or killing an innocent civilian during war. Sure, there are bad apples in every line of work including police work, but they are the exception, not the rule.

Passing the smell of fresh brewed coffee in the Detective Bureau tempts me. Three weeks ago I gave up caffeine after my friend Riley, The Mamacita Club holistic doctor, said it adds stress to my body and can prevent me from having kids. That was all I needed to hear to get on the no-caffeine wagon. At thirty-one years old, I might be still learning about love, but I'm hoping someday I'll meet the right person to use my magical powers to summon a second marriage and two-point-five kids. Plus, my same aged girlfriends have been having a hard time getting pregnant. I've started to question how much all the birth control pills taken over the years have to do with this.

"Is there any decaf around here?" I ask.

"Are you kidding me? These men drink coffee for the caffeine," says Dylan.

"I figured," I reply.

"Did I hear someone asking for decaf?" a voice says. Out from behind a cubicle wall, Officer Miguel Perez comes out.

"Perez!" I yell.

Dylan does a double-take, watching every move of Perez as we hug each other. Perez was the first officer I ever examined on the witness stand. It was during my first preliminary hearing of a domestic violence case. Thank goodness he had his belt recorder on and tape-recorded his conversation with the victim because she later went sideways, recanting everything she told Perez. At one point, her lies got so bad that I had to have the judge order her to answer the questions truthfully. I was only twenty-six years old, didn't really know what I was doing, but Perez led me through the whole thing. I always thought he was extra nice to me because he had a crush on me.

After I divorced, Perez tried to pursue me, but I wasn't interested. One night when Dylan and I were dating, Perez and I were discussing an upcoming case late at night after he ended his shift. Dylan confronted me about why Perez and I were on the phone so late. I told Dylan he was accusing the wrong person of cheating, especially after what I had been through with Neil.

"I actually do have decaf, and I will brew you a pot right now. You don't drink caffeine?" Perez asks.

"Nope, not as of three weeks ago," I say.

Dylan stares at both of us as if he's trying to look for any remnants of chemistry. It's nice to see him still care enough to be jealous, because I haven't stopped thinking about Dylan every night since we broke up.

"You gonna be in the monitoring room? I'll bring it to you there."

"Yep."

"It's good to see you, girl, don't be a stranger."

"Thanks, Perez! I miss you."

The small ten-by-ten foot room with a television monitor broadcasts live feed from a nearby interview room where Clown is sitting. The coziness of the room gives me a chance to sit close to Dylan. We sit in silence for a few minutes together watching Clown. There are no cameras visible to him in his room. With television these days, you'd think that all suspects knew they were being video-recorded. But it always amazes me how some suspects will pick their noses when the interrogator steps out of the room, get on their knees and pray, secretly try to erase data from their cell phone, or just put their heads down and cry. Some creep up close to the walls examining them for cameras. There are really some dumb criminals out there. Let's see what this one does or if he's savvy enough to know he's being videotaped.

I watch the television and begin watching the interrogation. Voices come through the sound system of our room.

"Sir, how old are you?" asks Ford.

"Twenty-six," says Clown.

"Where are you originally from?" Ford asks.

"I grew up here in Leafwood," Clown replies.

"When did you join Lincoln?"

"When I was fifteen years old. I got in because of my older brother Sniper," says Clown.

There's several ways to get into a gang. You can be jumped in, which means the gang beats you, literally. Your job is to fight back. You can be crimed in, where you need to commit a robbery, burglary, or assault. Girls can be sexed in, where they have sex with multiple gang members. Or, like Clown, you can be grandfathered in. A family member sponsors you and you're walked into the gang. It's like getting a full ride scholarship without doing a darn thing.

"How do you know Laura Paula?" asks Ford.

"She's a hood rat. Everyone knows her," says Clown.

"This guy totally did this to Laura," says Dylan in our monitoring room.

"You think we have the right person?" I ask.

"Yeah. Look at how hardcore he is. He won't even admit to dating Laura. He's calling her a hood rat. If he didn't have anything to hide, he wouldn't be so concerned about admitting he dates her. He'd be concerned about her and want to help," says Dylan.

"Even though he's a gangster?" I ask.

"Yeah. He should at least be asking what this is about," says Dylan.

We focus back on the television monitor showing the interview room.

"Clown, do you know why you're here?" Ford asks.

"Did they Mirandize this guy?" I ask Dylan.

"I can't remember. Did they do it at the beginning?" asks Dylan.

"I don't think so," I say.

Every suspect who is under arrest, in the custody of police and being interrogated about a crime must be read their Miranda rights. If the police don't Mirandize the suspect and get him to waive his rights, the confession can be kept out of court. Clown is certainly being held in police custody, in a police station, and is about to be asked questions about his girlfriend's attempted murder.

I stand up, walk out of the room, and head to the interrogation room. I open up the door and motion for Ford to walk outside the room.

Ford closes the door to the interview room and stands close to me near the officer cubicles in the general area of the police station.

"I know you're about to read him his rights at any point. I'm just concerned about you softening him up before reading him his Miranda rights, especially because of the questionable stop. I know he'll be more likely to spill his guts without the warning but I personally don't like it done this way," I say.

"I was about to read him his rights. Is this what you came to interrupt me for?" asks Ford.

"I just wanted to make sure you didn't forget. Case law looks unfavorably on not advising him of his rights sooner than later. So I just wanted to make sure we were on the same page," I say.

"I don't need you watching over my shoulder. I know how to do my job," says Ford, walking back into the interrogation room.

Experienced homicide detectives like Ford know how to tread close to the line and get the confession they want without violating rights. But I worry in this type of case. With Cruz's questionable stop, a judge will not want to see Ford softening Clown up before reading his rights to him. It just looks bad.

I walk back to rejoin Dylan in the monitoring room. "I think he may have actually forgotten to Mirandize him. That's the only reason I went in there," I say.

"You don't have to explain to me," says Dylan.

We focus back on the monitor.

"You have the right to remain silent, anything you say can and will be used against you, you have the right to an attorney, and if you cannot afford one, one will be appointed for you. Do you understand these rights?" asks Ford.

"I would like to speak to an attorney and see what they have to say," says Clown.

"Do you understand these rights?" Ford, ignoring his response, asks again.

"Yes," says Clown.

"Having these rights in mind, do you wish to speak to us?" asks Ford.

"Well, like I said, Laura is just some hood rat. I don't know how she wound up at that motel," says Clown.

I bury my head in my hands.

"This man just invoked his Miranda rights and is asking for an attorney. He should stop questioning him. I hate when they do this," I say to Dylan. We focus back on the monitor.

"Sir, are you telling me that you knew Laura was found in a motel?" says Ford to Clown.

"The police told me that," says Clown.

"No, they didn't. I know for a fact that the police did not give you that information. How did you know that?" says Ford.

"I want an attorney," says Clown.

"Is there any reason your name appeared on the check-in log for the motel room Laura was found in?" Ford asks.

"No, sir, I have no idea how that happened," says Clown.

"Sir, what is the truth about your relationship with Laura?" Ford asks.

"Like I said, she's a hood rat, puta sucia (dirty whore). We call her Bang Bang, because that's all she does and everyone knows it," says Clown.

"I know she gets around. And you seem upset about that. How is your relationship with her? Do you get along with her?" Ford asks.

"I don't know her like that," Clown replies.

"Then why was she taking naked pictures of herself and sending them to you? I know you met her on GangScene," Ford says.

"Sir, I don't mean any disrespect, but I need to talk to my lawyer," says Clown.

"Laura was found almost dead. She is in the hospital right now and just had brain surgery. We are trying to find out who did this to Laura and we need your cooperation. You were seen renting the room she was found in and I need you to answer questions because your story is not making sense. Did things just get out of hand with her? Did the sex go a little too far with you guys?" Ford asks.

"Sir, I don't know," says Clown. Burying his face into his hands resting his elbows on his knees, Clown stays in that position for at least five minutes of silence.

I look at Dylan. "I don't know why suspects start out by lying. What does he think, we're not going to check the motel roster?" I say to Dylan.

Usually I can explain away why someone would lie. They don't want to get involved in a lengthy criminal investigation, they don't want to get dragged to court to testify, they don't want to miss work. Sometimes they don't want to get in trouble for something they did that has nothing to do with the crime. But I can't think of one reason Clown would rent a room in this ghetto motel for Laura unless he was somehow involved in hurting her.

"Do you think we need to look at anyone else for this? Could he have had help?" I ask.

"Anything is possible, but I doubt it. He was seen leaving alone from the motel," says Dylan.

It's important to keep an open mind when investigating a crime. It's too easy to dismiss people or overlook possible suspects. You never want to leave any stones unturned, but you also don't want to spin your wheels for a dead-end lead.

"In this case, it's pretty clear we got our guy. I know he's not confessing, but in my book, lying about his relationship with Laura and about renting the room are two huge things pointing to his guilt," Dylan says.

Ford comes walking into the room taking deep sighs. "What's your thought, you want me to keep at it with this fellow? I think he has a lot more to say, but I don't want to step on any toes. He's asked for an attorney twice now," says Ford.

"Yeah, I know. I think we need to stop questioning," I say.

"I know. Plus, he seems really irritated at Laura's hood rat ways and I'm wondering if he may have taken her to the motel to confront her. I'm going to ask him one follow-up question, if he did this to Laura. I just want to see his reaction, then I'll leave it at that. I really don't want to go any further," says Ford.

"I'm ready to make an arrest. It's clear this is our guy. Just the fact he's lying about the extent of his relationship with Laura and renting the room is big. We have Laura leaving to go with him last night, he rents the motel room, he leaves his phone in the room, then he's seen taking off in his Lincoln Continental right after the crime.

"The DNA will take some time to get back unless you can put some pressure on the Crime Lab; but even without that, I think we have enough. I'm ready to do this. What's your thought?" Ford asks.

"This is our guy," says Dylan.

Ford makes it back into the interview room and Clown looks up from his hands with a shocked look on his face. "Sir, are you placing me under arrest?" says Clown.

"Well, is there something you think you should be arrested for?" asks Ford.

"It's just that...never mind," says Clown.

"Sir, I have one last question for you. Did you do this to Laura?" says Ford.

"I need an attorney, sir," says Clown.

"Sir, place your hands behind your back. You are being placed under arrest for the attempted murder of Laura Paula," says Ford.

7

THE MAMACITA CLUB

An hour after leaving the Leafwood Police Department, I pull my car into the parking lot of the Leafwood RV Park, which is in the hairy part of Tuckford County's armpit. "Think empower, empower, empower," I say.

"Think Dylan, Dylan, Dylan!" says Riley.

"Why did you have to bring him up?" I ask. "I wasn't even thinking of him."

"I know you still have feelings for him," Riley says.

"I do. But he's just not that into me."

"You're crazy, Gaby," Riley says. "You're beautiful, successful, and a lawyer. If he's not smart enough to realize that, good riddance!"

Riley is a holistic doctor who volunteers to help me run The Mamacita Club. She helps victims and their families with medical diseases, ranging from cancer to alcoholism. She teaches women about health and wellness at the Airstream. She believes most problems, including depression and other mental illnesses, can be cured with positive thinking. If not, she turns to her Native American medicines and herbs.

In exchange for volunteering, I let her use the Airstream to meet with patients and conduct drug and alcohol interventions and meetings.

When Riley was twelve, the same age I was when my mom died, her sister overdosed on drugs. Because of this, I've always been able to open up to her about things. Riley knows almost everything about me and I trust her.

"The Universe has a plan for you. This investigation is bringing you and Dylan together for a reason," says Angela.

Angela is an angel reader, spiritual coach, and grief counselor at The Mamacita Club. There's nothing that can prepare someone to be the victim of a crime, especially a violent or sexual one. But Angela tries to make the aftermath less traumatic. She finds them a place to sleep, helps them with restraining orders, or relocates them to another county or state if their situation is really bad.

In exchange for Angela's helping out at the Airstream, she gets to use it for angel readings, therapy sessions, life coach workshops, and to house any of her abused clients that need temporary shelter. People like Riley and Angela seem to have the biggest hearts to help and for the right reasons.

"Girl, maybe if we create a little costume to send you over to Dylan's in late at night, like a trench coat and garters, that just might do the trick for you both," says Kiera.

The four of us all start laughing. This is what I love the most about Kiera. She makes me laugh and makes me feel alive. Kiera, a.k.a. Kiki, is our wardrobe stylist at The Mamacita Club. She creates all of our costumes and pin-up outfits.

Kiki also scouts out different mobile home and RV parks around Tuckford County. Then she negotiates rent for parking my shiny chrome Vintage Airstream motorhome for eight weeks, the block of time we need to build a rapport with our clients at The Mamacita Club.

In exchange, I let Kiki keep her costumes inside the Airstream and drive it to film sets where it duos as a dressing room and wardrobe closet. Kiki might be one of the most fun people I know. She comes from a well-to-do family, but never once has she flaunted it. She helps me let loose, reminding me how to start playing like a kid again.

Playing dress-up with her rehearsing our chosen alter egos is a blast. She helps us come to life and dress and act like women in recovery. Once, she even helped me put together an evening of red wine, chocolate, and strawberries for a few women marking their one year anniversary in walking away from their spousal abusers.

At the Airstream, I teach the women about abusive relationships including domestic violence and sexual abuse. Riley, Kiki, and Angela laugh when I yell out, "Ladies! Just like the world, the Airstream's a stage, so let's get in our costumes and I'm Bettie Page."

I also help the women with any legal issues and teach them how to gain independence, especially the financial kind. Speaking Spanish really gives me an advantage in helping the women.

My RV with its pink neon *The Mamacita Club* sign gets us instant credibility and into some of the worst areas in the county where the women need our support. Kiki, with her bubbly personality, has recruited some of the best women from these low income mobile home parks.

Angela, Riley, and Kiki know I'm fine with using the Airstream for anything that helps us empower women, including field trips that give our clients the opportunity to visit places they would never see. Sometimes I even use it as a place to sleep when I don't feel like driving back to Blackbird Beach. Most importantly, the Airstream gives us a comfortable place to meet weekly with the girls recruited for The Mamacita Club. It's all decked out fifties' vintage style to match the pin-up girl, Hollywood starlet, criminal, country western, musical, cultural, pop icon, spiritual, musical, political, and other alter egos we adopt to mentor the women.

The Airstream was handed down to Neil and I as a wedding gift from his family who owns most of the RV Superstores in Tuckford County. It was the only thing I got in the divorce. So I turned it into the best thing I knew how to — The Mamacita Club.

At The Mamacita Club, we help young women grapple real life issues and set goals beyond getting pregnant, addicted to drugs, or dancing on poles.   And we help the older women learn how to live again. Every woman who has come through The Mamacita Club has empowered another woman, whether it's a client or a staff member. We just all help each other. It's my family.

We get out of my car and rush into the Airstream to get dressed in our costumes.

Within thirty minutes of Riley, Angela, Kiki, and I arriving at the Leafwood RV Park, seven young women sit at the table inside the motorhome, writing down their stinky thinking thoughts and sealing them up in a jar we call the

Mamacita Mason Jar. I love this exercise and pull the sheet of paper sitting in front of me closer, pick up my pen, and start scribbling:

Dylan is not that into me. I'm nervous about giving the class today. I hope I can make a difference for these girls.

Crumpling up my paper into a small ball and tossing it into the jar gives the most invigorating feeling of letting go. I make sure to screw on the lid extra tight this time. The idea is to get all the chatter out of our minds and focus on the here and now. The girls love the exercise.

After sealing the jar, I stare into it. I see a Christopher Columbus-looking ship sailing on water inside the jar. I squeeze my eyes shut for a second and open them again. My crumpled piece of paper sits at the bottom of the jar and the ship is gone.

"Well, hello there, lots of chatter upstairs? We have a pretty good turnout today, but we have some bad news, which will be the focus of our class tonight," says Angela.

Angela and I decided before class started that we were going to tell the girls what happened to Laura and see if any of them could give us information about the assault. We're especially hoping to talk to Christina, Laura's best friend, who's here tonight. And we're hoping to do it inside the Airstream, where her bottom bitch is not allowed.

I've suspected for a while that Christina is being groomed to be a sex worker. Sometimes she goes missing from school and the RV Park here where she normally lives with her grandma. When she's reported missing, she still comes to The Mamacita Club, but I've noticed the woman who drops her off hangs outside the Airstream while Christina is inside. The woman is about forty years old and watches her like a hawk. Despite Christina's denials, I alerted the human trafficking division at the Leafwood Police Department.

On the streets, someone like her is called a "bottom bitch," because she recruits young women into her ring to start a cycle of prostitution. The young women are bought nice material things and are encouraged to pay for them by dancing, stripping, and eventually selling their bodies. It's an endless cycle.

"Laura won't be coming back to the trailer park for a while. Something terrible happened to her," Angela tells the girls inside the Airstream.

I'm glad Angela is able to speak about this, because I couldn't deliver the news without getting choked up. Angela is used to grief and talking about these things with her victims. She has cried countless hours and wiped tears for everyone she helps. She's used to this. I'm not. I still can't go a second talking about my mom without getting choked up over that one night I couldn't save her. So I just don't talk about it.

I learned from Angela through angel readings that there's a difference between dealing with losing someone close to you and just coping with the pain. I've done the latter through my whole life. But I'm determined to start coping. It's hard for me to get close to anyone and trust them. I don't want to lose anyone again.

Some of the girls begin to cry as Angela tells them about Laura. All of a sudden, I hear what sounds like the backfire of a tailpipe. Then I hear tires spinning through what sounds like water. It startles all of us.

A couple of the girls and I run to the side exit door of the motorhome that leads to the RV park. I grab two of the girls by the shirt and tell them to stay inside. Then I reach into my thigh holster through the side slit on my long red mob wife dress, free my Lady Smith .38 Special, and open the door to rush outside.

Outside the Airstream, I crouch behind a car, looking up to a cat splattered against the dirt path of the RV park. Its gray fur is almost flush with the dirt as its backbone convulses in slow motion curling up, then falling flat. Another convulsion makes the cat look like a worm. Its lower back convulses up, then the middle of its spine bubbles up and its neck snaps forward. It falls flat again. I watch the convulsions, one-after-another, slow and reflexive from the energy in its body leaving its skin. On the fifth convulsion, my vision begins to blur.

Instead of brown dirt, I see the brown and beige linoleum floor in the kitchen of the mobile home I grew up in. When I was ten, I watched my cat Penny have convulsions. My stepfather, upset over my mom pouring out his beer, ripped Penny out of her hands, then kicked Penny in the stomach.

I ran into the kitchen and kneeled over Penny. "Please don't die, Penny, please don't die." Penny started convulsing, one after another with her fur puffed out like she had just been electrocuted. To peel me from the floor and get Penny to the hospital, my mom kneeled behind me and held onto me tight. She told me told me that it was okay, all cats had nine lives, and Penny would make it. I couldn't stop crying. My mom held me tight until Penny's last convulsion.

I look beyond the gray cat further up the dirt path of the RV Park to the exit leading to the city road. The driver in a black car points a gun into the air and begins shooting. "Pow, pow, pow." I see Christina outside with Riley.

Dust from the ground fills the air like an explosion.

"Get down!" I yell.

We all drop to the ground. Someone is slouched down in the driver seat. The roaring of a car engine echoes through the RV Park.

Riley yells, "Where's Christina?"

Christina stands up and starts running in the same direction towards the car. One last shot from the driver side of the car rings out, deafening me. I see a black pistol and sparkles of dust.

I scream, "Get down!"

The car screeches off and I see Christina's bright yellow shirt down on the ground in between two cars parked in the RV park. My heart pounds against my breastbone. Don't be dead, please don't be dead. This can't be happening, this can't be happening.

"Christina, Christina, are you okay? Please tell me you're okay," I yell, running as fast as I can.

The distance to get to Christina feels like an eternity. The idea of having to tell Christina's grandmother, bottom bitch or drug addicted mom something happened to her, frightens me. If The Mamacita Club is not a safe place, where will incorrigible girls like Christina go? She calls this place home, showing up every week, even when she runs away from the RV Park to probably prostitute. I can't lose another girl. I'm supposed to protect her. And now I've failed. Again. Christina is my only link to Laura. I need to ask her if she knew anything about what happened. Please don't be gone. Please. My heart beats fast and my legs aren't moving fast enough to get to Christina.

Riley pops up from behind a truck parked close to the cars Christina is in between.

"She's fine, she's fine," says Riley.

I stare out into the distance watching the car fly down the street as the taillights get smaller and smaller. A distinct rattle and ticking of an engine fades in the distance. Riley and Christina grab onto me, crying.

"Get back inside and get everyone to the back of the Airstream until police get here. They might come back," I say.

Christina and Riley run back inside the Airstream.

Several different people stand in front of their mobile homes.

"Did anyone get a license plate?" I yell to them. No one answers.

"Did anyone see what kind of car that was?" I yell to them again.

A woman stands in the middle of the RV park.

"They're not gonna help you," she says, turning to walk away. Everyone standing outside walks inside their motorhomes and mobile homes without saying anything. I stop counting after I hear five doors slam shut.

Falling asleep has always been hard for me to do. From the moment I crawl into bed, I've always been that kind of sleeper that stays in one place the whole night long. To make my bed in the morning, I just have to pull the covers back into place. It's from lying in bed, stiff-as-a-board, in sheer terror, every night growing up and listening to my stepfather and mom fight. They say that people go to sleep based on how they were put to sleep as a child. So I usually go to sleep terrified. It's a little better if I have a TV on, someone holding me, or a locked and loaded gun within arm's reach, especially after tonight's shooting.

I lie in my bed naked under a sheet at home in Blackbird Beach a few hours after the drive-by. I pull myself up and lean over to my night stand. I open the cabinet that sits next to my bed to take out my Smith and Wesson Lady Smith .38 special. The revolver's weight and the cool temperature of its steel barrel make me feel safe.

I place it on top of my night stand furthest from my door and position the muzzle facing away from me. I look over at the corner of my room and smile at my twelve-gauge shotgun leaning up against the wall. I let out a deep sigh. That shotgun is the only good thing I inherited from my stepfather.

Just as I start to doze, my outside light turns on. It's on an automatic sensor. I open my eyes and tuck the covers under my chin, trying to listen. All I hear is the waves crashing from a distance. Then I hear rustling against the bushes outside my bedroom window. I strain to listen harder. I hear my side gate creaking. I stay quiet and listen. My outside light turns off.

I pull my body up, bracing myself to reach for my revolver. I feel the resistance as I pull the hammer of my gun back, trying to stay as quiet as possible. I swing my legs around to the edge of my bed and stand up. I walk over to my dresser and rest my revolver on top of it, before heading to my closet.

I make it to my gun safe and rest my fingers in the hand impression on top of it, sticking my index finger into a drop down compartment. The safe door flips open towards me and I reach inside for my Glock. The light outside my window turns back on. I curse myself for buying the discount window shades. Whoever's outside can see in more than I can see out.

I grab my nine millimeter magazine that is fully loaded with bullets and push it into the chamber of my Glock. I hold the top of the gun and rack the slide. The clicking sound makes me feel ready. For what? I have no idea.

Another sound from the bushes outside my window gets my heart pumping fast again. I take two deep breaths in and out. I walk to my bedroom door, close it, and crawl back into bed. I sit up, spread my legs, and balance my body. Then, I hold my Glock. Steady. Good job, Grace Under Pressure. I aim it at my bedroom door.

I've been a prosecutor long enough to know that no 9-1-1 call will ever protect you like you can protect yourself. I've always learned it's best to stay in one place, armed and ready, waiting for someone to come find you. It's better than walking around my place. I know the layout of my place much better than any intruder would know. I'll wait for him to come to me.

I listen to the waves crashing and sit in darkness. I look at my dresser, wondering if I should put some clothes on. My mom used to tell me to always wear clean underwear when I leave the house in case I was ever taken to the hospital. But I'm too nervous to get up. And the only person who's going to the hospital tonight is going to be the intruder who's about to get a nine millimeter bullet right through his chest.

The only sound I can hear is the rush of blood through my body, which sounds like I'm under water. And then, my beating heart, a sound I'm starting to hear a lot more lately.

I hear the screen on my front door open. I look at my alarm clock on my night stand. 10:05 p.m. I grab my cell phone and dial a nine, deciding whether to call 9-1-1. Who would be coming to my door at this hour, on a weeknight? If I call 9-1-1, they'll think I'm crazy.

I close my eyes and grip onto the handle of my Glock. *Please tell me what to do.* Nothing. Why do I do what I do? Is this really worth being a prosecutor? I hate living in fear. I don't get paid enough for this. I think of my mom. And I remember that if my life ended right now, it would be the beginning of a new one with her. My eyes flutter as I grip tighter, careful not to touch anywhere near the trigger.

I look at my other night stand and see my homicide pager lying there. I'm not going to be the next homicide victim. Just as I dial the next number, I hear the screen to my front door close. I stay quiet, then hear a car door open and close, before an engine starts. The sound of a car driving away makes me hang up the 9-1-1 call. I listen. The sound is so familiar. The ticking rattle of an engine, the same one after the drive-by, fades in the distance.

I get up and walk down my hallway, holding my Glock in one hand and my cell phone in the other. I get to my front door and look through the peephole. I can't see through it because something is blocking it. I dial Dylan's number and listen to his voicemail pick up, then hang up and open the door.

A note lies in the iron trap design around the peephole of my door. I grab the note as my sensor light turns on. The sound of my beating heart gets louder as I stare beyond the light. A coyote stares eagerly at me. I slam the door shut, flip my inside light on, and let out a deep breath. I put my phone and gun down and open the note. In purple ink, it reads:

You'Re next. You'Re choice. Bullet, blade, oR flamingo vase!

8

ANGEL'S DEN

The morning after receiving the note, I sit at a small round table inside my Airstream with Angela. She flips over the "Kiki's Closet" chalkboard sign hanging from a pink satin ribbon on the door to read "Angel's Den." I love how she sets the mood, turning our wardrobe closet into our private angel reading room, even during broad daylight.

She pulls the black fabric curtain with bright pink symbols and designs to shut it closed and make the Airstream as dark as possible. Then she lights a candle on the table next to the threatening note I received last night. We study the note.

"This means one thing for sure. There's more to this. Whoever left this note last night was driving the car with that same rattling sound I heard during the drive-by shooting. That's the same noise the housekeeper described at the motel Laura was assaulted at," I say.

"Do you notice all the capital R's?" says Angela.

I look closer at the note. "Yeah. What do they mean?" I ask eagerly.

"I don't know. Nothing specific. Your angels are just alerting me to them," says Angela.

I let out a big frustrated sigh.

"Not everything has significance. Don't get frustrated. Just take mental note of it," says Angela, picking up on my irritation.

"Look, Gaby," Angela continues. "I think you really need to tell someone about this. Someone is threatening you. And it's a direct threat towards The Mamacita Club. I don't think we should be hiding this, especially after the drive-by."

"Give me one good reason. What is the police department going to do with this note? Nothing. They're not going to find fingerprints, DNA, or anything on it. The only thing turning it over is gonna accomplish is shutting us down. My office is already talking about the liability of us being here. You know what people like Stevie Sapp and Ed Vanderbilt think of us," I say angrily.

"I'm just concerned about you and for us. They're targeting the club. You guys have Clown in custody for what happened to Laura, but obviously there's more than just him involved. Maybe they can relocate you or our club for a bit," says Angela.

"Angela, they're going to shut us down. And they're not going to relocate me or even give me any kind of protection. I'm leaving soon on vacation anyway," I plead. "Is this what my angels are saying or is this coming from you?" I say suspiciously.

"It's coming from me, as a concerned friend. For you *and* the club," says Angela.

I look away from Angela, upset.

"Tell me more about the animal you saw last night. Are you sure it was a coyote and not a wolf?" Angela asks changing the subject.

"It was definitely a coyote. It was limber and slender. It was staring at me; really curious," I say.

"Hmmm. Well, coyotes are known as tricksters. They give you the impression that things are not as they seem, until the lesson is learned and the wisdom is gained," says Angela.

"So what am I supposed to be learning?" I ask skeptically.

After pausing and closing her eyes tightly, Angela looks up at me. "I don't know. I'm not getting a read," she replies. "Maybe just the obvious, that this case is not as clearcut as it seems. That there's more to it," says Angela.

"Well, that's obvious from the note," I say sarcastically. "No one would know about the flamingo vase except law enforcement or Clown."

"Are you gonna tell Dylan about it?"

"He already suspects someone's targeting us. I'm not gonna confirm his suspicion. It will get back to my office. I don't want our club to be blamed for Laura's assault," I say.

"Gaby, just hear me out," Angela says. "What if something happens to you or to the girls again? Do you realize the liability for us? Knowing that you've received this threat, then to stay up and running here at the park."

"Do you know how hard we've worked to build The Mamacita Club up? I can't believe you would even think of jeopardizing it by telling police. It's only going to mean one thing. That my office will shut us down. That doesn't mean the same thing for *you* as it does for *me*. You have a family. You don't need The Mamacita Club. I don't have anyone. This is all I have. Plus threats are just that, threats. Terrorism is in the eye of the beholder. I don't want my office to shut us down over terrorist threats. If someone wants to take me out, fine; let them. At least I'd be back with my mom," I say, starting to shake.

"You're right, you're right. We at least owe it to the members to let them know about the threat. And then let them make a decision about whether they want to come back," says Angela persistingly.

"Fine, you can tell them. But tell them they're not welcome back if they quit," I say dramatically.

"Gaby, you're being paranoid. The club will always be their home. They're not going to leave us forever. They love it here too much. It will just be a temporary thing. And I'll tell them to keep this confidential," says Angela.

"Fine," I say reluctantly. "Do my angels have any ideas to get the police department to look deeper into this case without alerting them to the note?" I ask.

"I wouldn't worry about that. Just force them to do their job and comb through all the evidence. Stay persistent. Be the coyote until the wisdom is learned and the truth comes out," says Angela.

9

POINTS OF COMPARISON

Minutes after leaving the Airstream, I pull up to the Fingerprint Office. The thirty-second walk from my car to the building feels like a mile in the humidity. The smell of the cow manure and thick air makes me want to gag. We are minutes from an area that used to house chicken farms. The years of chicken poop must have seeped well into the ground to suffocate the next seven generations.

I open the door to the Fingerprint Office and I walk straight through and up to the front desk.

"Hi there, I'm Gaby Ruiz with the Tuckford County Prosecutor's Office," I say. "I'd like to talk to someone about a fingerprint comparison in a case I'm investigating."

After a few minutes of speaking with a white-haired receptionist, I follow Fingerprint Examiner Linda Dean down a hallway. We pass cubicles and other examiners looking into round handheld magnifying glasses examining fingerprint cards.

"Go ahead and have a seat right here," says Ms. Dean, pointing at two chairs in her cubicle area. "What can I do for you?"

"A forensic technician found a fingerprint in the case I'm investigating. We think the victim was hit in the head with the vase. The technician photographed the print and sent it to you for examination. This is the case number. I just came to see if there were any results."

"Yes, actually," Ms. Dean begins. "I just spoke with Investigator Mack on this from the Special Homicide Team. It is actually a very clear print of a thumb. Typically, I look for ten points of comparison on the actual print in order to be confident that I can read it. It appeared there are sufficient points of comparison. I spoke with Investigator Mack and he actually submitted the suspect's recent booking print to me. I have it right here and I should have the comparison done by Monday."

"Is there any possible way you can do it right now?" I ask.

"I have higher priority cases right now," Ms. Dean replies. "I have prints waiting to be examined from a murder and a child kidnapping case. Those get priority. Our office has strict rules on our caseloads. This case is not a high priority. Plus, I understand you already have a suspect in custody, so it doesn't have the urgency of other investigations where the suspect is on the loose."

"Look, Ms. Dean," I say. "We have similar rules at my job. My trials get priority over recently filed cases. My child molestations get priority over adult sexual assaults. I get what you're saying. But I have a staffing Monday morning and I'm trying to get all my ducks in a row. This is the key piece of evidence. If it doesn't belong to our suspect, that will be a major issue. Either he had help or the real suspect might be on the loose."

"I understand what your goal is, but I can't just drop everything to work on your case," says Ms. Dean.

I breathe in and out deeply and try to formulate my frustrated thoughts before I open my mouth.

"Ms. Dean, sometimes there is no good reason for doing something, other than just to help a girl out. I'm going to get grilled on Monday for why I couldn't get you to give me this information. And there will be no good reason why this couldn't be done sooner than later. You not helping me is going to delay things. It's just one thumbprint and like you said, it's a good one. If anyone gives you a hard time about it, you can just refer them to me," I say.

"Look, I'd really like to help you but..." says Ms. Dean.

"I'm trying to do my job and it's my job to have every question answered," I say, interrupting her. "It shouldn't take you that long to look at it. And then I'll get out of your hair."

"I'm not doing it, Ms. Ruiz. This is how my casework gets behind and I get into trouble," says Ms. Dean.

"I guess this case is not as important to you as it is to me," I say. "It seems like you have dozens of prints you are waiting to compare and it's just another fingerprint that comes across your desk. I wish I had your job sometimes, where I didn't have to look into the eyes of the victims or their family and tell them we are going to have to wait for justice.

"My life would be much easier if I didn't have to fight to figure out who hurt seventeen-year-old Laura. She's sitting on her deathbed in a coma at the hospital. I would love to trade jobs with you so I wouldn't have to look into her mom's eyes and tell her we still don't have an answer. But at least I can tell them I tried," I say, grabbing my purse from the floor and starting to stand up.

"Well. All right. This shouldn't take long. Let me take a quick look and see if it matches," says Ms. Dean.

I sit back down as Ms. Dean puts on her black-rimmed reading glasses and takes out a fingerprint magnifier. She positions it over the thumbprint on Clown's fingerprint card. She looks from his thumbprint to the blown-up photograph of the bloody print, then looks at her points of comparison chart that sits bulletin-pinned on her corkboard inside her cubicle. She takes her glasses off, starts writing some notes down inside her file, and finally puts her pencil down and looks up at me.

"Do you want the good news or the bad news first?" she asks.

"The good," I say.

"We actually have a couple good things here. That print landed in her blood after she was probably hit in the head. It's called a patent print. Additionally, the thumbprint is facing downwards on the vase as if the suspect held it in a way he could strike her with the most force. See how the ridges curve up and around in the core?" says Ms. Dean, pointing to the center of the bloody thumbprint in the photo.

"Wow. You would testify to that?" I ask.

"That's my interpretation. So yes," she says.

"And the bad?" I ask.

"It's not your suspect's print."

10

ORDER OF THE COURT

Within thirty minutes of leaving the Fingerprint Office, I sit in Department Thirteen. The morning sun's rays peek their way through the windows as Javier Sanchez shoots his eyes from Dylan, to me, and then the double door entrance of the courtroom. He's looking for any indication of what's about to happen. The courtroom clerk, reporter, and deputy do the same before looking at one another as though they are placing bets on what's about to happen.

I figure I might as well wait to tell everyone at once what's going on. I don't feel like dealing with the questions they will have about Laura and the case. Plus, Carol Hernandez, a well-respected local news reporter, is sitting in the back of the courtroom. The media PR person at my office alerted me yesterday that she was getting calls on the case when they discovered Laura was found in the motel.

"When are we going to get the DNA results back?" I ask Dylan.

"They are telling me it will take five months," says Dylan.

"Geez, will they speed it up if Laura dies and this case becomes a homicide?" I ask.

"Calm down. I know what you're thinking. But that print can belong to a number of people," says Dylan.

"'Like who?" I ask.

"Laura for one," says Dylan.

I think for a second about whether to tell Dylan about the note.

"Let's get over to the hospital then the Crime Lab as soon as we're done here. I want to see Laura's injuries. And I want to see if the lab will rush the DNA. I'd like everything done before I head out on my vacation. I don't want to worry about things falling through the cracks after I hand it off," I say.

"Sure, but we won't need that stuff for the preliminary hearing. We have more than enough to get a holding order. I think we're solid," says Dylan.

Before I can respond, I'm interrupted.

"Come to order, remain seated, court is now in session. The Honorable Samuel Hoffman presiding," yells the deputy.

"Are we ready to proceed, Ms. Ruiz?" asks Judge Hoffman.

"No, Your Honor, we are not," I say.

"Have you located Laura?" Judge Hoffman asks.

"Yes, Your Honor. I'm not sure if you've had a chance to read the newspaper, but Laura was found unconscious in a motel room in Leafwood. But for the grace of God, she is not dead. She is currently at Tuckford County Memorial Hospital," I say.

"Is Laura's condition the same?" I whisper to Dylan.

"Yep," says Dylan.

"My goodness. I'm so sorry. I realize you may have been close to her," says Judge Hoffman.

I wonder if Judge Hoffman is speaking in a friendlier tone because someone from the media is in the courtroom actually listening to what he's saying and will quote him in the paper. I wish I had a media representative following me around court every day.

"What is her expected recovery time?" asks Judge Hoffman.

"We don't know at this point," I say.

"I know based on our pretrial motions, she had a difficult life and was making bad choices, and running the streets. I'm assuming that had to do with what happened to her," says Judge Hoffman.

"I don't want to comment on that, only because there is a suspect now in custody for her attempted murder. She was unconscious when we found her, but I'm hoping for a full recovery," I say.

"Well, I admire your optimism, Ms. Ruiz. If anyone knows you well, that would be something we would all agree you have. However, for purposes of this trial, which by the way, we are in the matter of People versus Javier Sanchez, case number TUCK1393, it doesn't appear that you have sufficient evidence to proceed. Unless, well, wait a minute, did you have Laura testify at preliminary hearing? Or did she call 911?" asks Judge Hoffman.

"No, neither of those things exist," I say, regretting how the case was handled before I got it. Laura should have testified.   She's a runaway, dabbles in drugs, and is prostituting herself.   The reality is that some of these girls wind up staying on the streets, getting pimped out, or become reluctant to cooperate with law enforcement.   Some wind up dead. You never know if they are gonna show up or even be around to testify by the time trial rolls around.

Derrick Sandy, an assistant prosecutor who was known for not putting in a whole lot of effort into his cases, had the case before me.

"Do you have any other evidence to present in this case?" Judge Hoffman asks.

"No, Your Honor, I have nothing else," I say.

"For purposes of this trial, if the People are not ready to proceed, I'm prepared to release the jury.   I'd like to bring them in, explain what is going on, and let them go," says Judge Hoffman.

"I'll submit, Your Honor," I say.

"Mr. Sanchez, do you have anything to say about what's going on here?   I would assume you have no objection to what you're hearing," says Judge Hoffman.

"Judge, what happens now?   Will I get released?" asks Javier.

"Mr. Sanchez, double jeopardy has attached.   You can no longer be prosecuted for this crime, you..."

I raise my hand up towards Judge Hoffman to get his attention.

"Your Honor, I'm sorry.   I don't mean to interrupt you. Just so we're clear, the panel was not sworn in yet.   So to answer Mr. Sanchez's question, I do intend on refiling charges this afternoon and he will not be released.   Or, let me clarify, he will be released momentarily and then rearrested before he gets out of jail," I say.

"Okay. I forgot. Yes, you're right, the jury was not sworn. In fact, you asked me not to swear them in. Thank you for reminding me," says Judge Hoffman appreciatively.

Double jeopardy attaches to a criminal case forever barring a defendant from being retried for the same acts once twelve jurors are selected and asked to stand up and take an oath to serve on the jury. After we selected the jury yesterday, I asked Judge Hoffman to hold off on swearing them in. I was concerned about Laura's flakiness and didn't want jeopardy to attach. So, technically, I have a second bite at the apple to refile on Javier, start the clock over, and just hope and pray that Laura comes out of her coma.

I have nothing to lose by refiling the case. The alternative is letting Javier out of custody to abuse the next victim. Plus, I need to save face at my office. The news reporter has been scribbling down everything that has been said in this courtroom all morning.

"Given all of the circumstances and now hearing from both sides concerning this matter, reluctantly I have no choice other than to dismiss this case for insufficient evidence and allow Ms. Ruiz to refile charges. Bring the jury in," says Judge Hoffman.

One by one, the jurors file into the courtroom past Dylan and me. I never figured out if the reason they call this county Ole Tucky is because the people here look like the kind of hard-working blue collar people you'd expect to find at a truck stop in Kentucky, or because it actually has pockets of green pastures and farms like Kentucky. Maybe it's both.

The jurors take the same seats they were expecting to listen to Laura's testimony from today. The jury learned a little about Laura during my voir dire two days ago. I got to speak with the jury and tell them a little about the case and read the charges to them.

After Judge Hoffman tells the jurors what happened to Laura, a couple of them begin to cry and reach for tissue boxes sitting on the railing of the jury box. Watching people from the community sit through these cases has taught me that we all have sympathy for everyone involved in the case, especially the victims.

Three of the four men on the jury begin staring intently at Javier Sanchez. Javier looks straight forward towards Judge Hoffman's bench as the stares burn a hole through the right side of Javier's head. Even if we had Laura's prior testimony, I'm not sure that twelve people would have agreed to convict Javier. These cases are difficult. Slim evidence is all I get in most of these sexual abuse cases.

Even though the law says one witness's testimony is enough to convict, the jurors always want more, even the conservative ones who make up most of Tuckford County's jury pool. At a minimum, they want a prosecutor who believes the defendant did what he's accused of; and without Laura, I can't say whether I'd vote guilty.

"Ladies and gentleman, you are excused from jury service. We will see some of you I'm sure next year. Thank you for your service," says Judge Hoffman before the jurors start filing past us to leave. I wait for the last one to leave and watch the door close behind her.

"Dylan, are we one hundred percent sure Clown's the only one involved in this?"

"Yes. We're not looking at anyone else. Why do you ask?"

"I could've sworn the car last night had the same rattling noise the motel housekeeper described," I say.

"You said the car was black. Clown's car is Burgundy. Who else are we going to look at anyway? And that print could easily belong to Laura or the technician that collected it," Dylan says.

"I just don't want to make a mistake."

"You're crazy," he says. "Look, I know you like to be really thorough, but there's no doubt in my mind. I know the drive-by shooting may have startled you, too. But we haven't determined if one thing has to do with the other. We have the right person. So don't get any ideas. This is an open and shut case. I haven't seen many stronger cases in my career. We don't even have any other leads. He's our guy. The Leafwood Police Department feels the same way."

"Dylan, I think there's more to this," I say.

"Gaby, I don't want to hear what your angels are telling you. I'm done with this case. I have several reports to finish and you're going on vacation. We are not reopening this. Clown is our suspect and I'm expecting us to staff this case by Monday morning with your office. I want this case filed before you leave on your trip."

Judge Hoffman returns to the bench, interrupting our conversation.

"Come to order. Court is again in session," says the courtroom deputy.

"As for you, Mr. Sanchez, you are discharged from this case. But as you heard, it doesn't look like you'll be going far. They are going to file the same case on you again, which they can do. There's nothing preventing them from filing it twice. Mr. Sanchez, you have received a huge break in this case. The prosecution did not have sufficient evidence to proceed with their case in chief, so I was forced to dismiss it. Now, don't mess up while you're in custody or when you get out," says Judge Hoffman.

"Your Honor...," Javier says with a smirk.

"I don't want you to say anything. I just want you to be careful. You have a lengthy criminal history and you won't see another break like this. I can guarantee that. Do you understand me?"

"Yes, sir," says Javier as Judge Hoffman gets up to leave the bench.

I turn to Dylan. "Let's get to the hospital."

11

IN HIS HANDS

Dylan's county truck bounces into the parking lot of the Tuckford Memorial Hospital, the ghetto part of a town called Mason Valley. Mason Valley houses a lot of the low income families that relocated from bigger cities over a decade ago to take advantage of the low housing market. Since then, many of these families have lost their homes to foreclosure during the recession.

Dylan and I walk from his truck into the hospital.

"We're looking for patient Laura Paula," I say.

The twenty-something-year-old Latina hospital lobby receptionist bats her eyelashes and brown eyes at Dylan, then twirls her long brown curly hair. After searching her outdated boxy computer, she looks up at Dylan. "You look like a celebrity, kind of like Matthew McConaughey. She's in room 511. Take the elevator up to the fifth floor, and to the ICU."

It's still weird to hear women flirt with Dylan, but I've learned to just appreciate it. I was doing the same thing two years ago. I still remember the first homicide call-out I went on with Dylan. Every young prosecutor's goal is to be assigned to the homicide pager and report to crime scenes when a dead body is found and help out in the investigation. Dylan Mack was the lead investigator, my Law & Order backstage pass to run with the best of the best, the Special Homicide Team. This team handles all gang and sexual assault related homicides in Tuckford County.

There's nothing sexier than a man who takes control of his surroundings. That was the first thing that attracted me to Dylan. When he greeted me at the crime scene and walked me into a room full of testosterone-driven police officers to brief me about what happened, my knees were practically buckling at the attention he was able to command. The entire room full of men in uniform wanted nothing more than to become what Dylan was — a Special Homicide Investigator.

I never thought I'd be drawn to a man in uniform. But his confidence got me hooked. His crazy stamina in his king size bed helped, too. My girlfriends forced me to recount stories of our sleepless nights early in our relationship.

As I wait for the elevator with Dylan, I want to tell him I wish room 511 was our motel room number, like back in the day when we would meet up at any cheesy Motel 6 we could find to have a quickie during lunch. But I stop myself. Those days are long gone. This field trip is related to my profession as an assistant prosecutor, not my obsession with Dylan Mack. We make our way into the elevator.

Hospitals are my least favorite place to be. The hustle and bustle of staff in lab coats wheeling tables in and out of our elevator on the way up to Laura's room makes it seem like everyone's working on the assembly line to death.

"I bet this is the last place you thought you'd be visiting one of your girls," says Dylan.

"It really is."

"How are you doing?"

"I'm okay, I just really don't like hospitals. Just last week I was sitting in one for my first mammogram thinking how much I hate them. Everything turned out fine, but it just reminds me how quickly life can turn upside down."

A smile comes to my face as I think of Riley from The Mamacita Club, who got dressed up in the Madonna Evita costume to get me psyched up for my mammogram recently. I love when Riley dresses as Madonna, who played Evita in a musical, to teach women about cancer, disease, and death. The wife of an Argentine president, Eva Peron, who became known as Evita, was a woman who died of cancer at thirty-three and had a huge heart to help women and those in need. What Evita accomplished by the time of her death amazes me. I tend to become obsessed with legends who died around my age. Angela, my angel reader, tells me it's normal. She says it will be really bad when I approach the age my mom died.

"Mammogram at, what are you, twenty-five years old?" says Dylan.

"Twenty-five? I wish. I'll be thirty-two this month."

"I would've never guessed you were in your thirties, but that's still young for a mammogram, isn't it? Are you gonna be okay?"

"Yeah, they just wanted to make sure everything was fine."

The hardest part about going to hospitals is thinking that a time will come when we are all on our deathbeds in a miserable place where medicine can do nothing to save us. For some reason I've always been afraid of illness, disease, and sickness, especially when it's in the final stages of death. It's worse than looking at autopsy or crime scene photos. I've seen so many naked bodies with bullet holes or stab wounds. Their pale skin, dark lips, and eyes staring blankly at me all remind me of that photo of my mom. The moment someone still has blood running through their veins and has an ounce of life in them, it's hard for me to tolerate. I just want to save them.

As I'm contemplating getting out of the elevator at the next stop and leaving the hospital, I remember my promise to Laura. I told her I wouldn't leave her alone. The elevator door opens to the fifth floor and Dylan and I get out.

I take two steps into the room with Dylan close behind me and see Laura lying in a hospital bed. Her once long hair that I was stroking yesterday at the motel is now shaved. She has a big horseshoe stitching on the side of her head from the brain surgery she just had. The white crust on the sides of her mouth and a pale grey ash tone to her once tan and elastic skin makes me nauseous.

Two weeks ago, her big brown eyes and eyelashes were batting and rolling as she joked outside the Airstream with Christina.

Now, Laura lies motionless in a hospital bed with metal rails at her sides and tubes coming out of her nose and mouth. IVs run through her veins. Plastic tape covers her hands and rubber tubing feeds oxygen and pain medicine from a machine beeping every second. Large red numbers flash on a monitor, which is pulsating near a long plastic sack filled with fluids.

Laura's mother, Bess, is sitting by her side, holding her hand.

"Mrs. Sanchez, I'm so sorry," I say, regretting I haven't said this sooner.

"I was hoping to never have to see you after the trial. But now *this*. And the shooting! What are you trying to do to these girls?" Bess Sanchez says in a thick Spanish accent, glaring at Dylan and me with a look of disdain.

Her tight bun with her severe side sweeping hair-sprayed bangs pulled behind her ear reminds me of one of my Ballet Folklorico dance teachers I had growing up who died a while back. Instructor Maria Flores had fierce Spanish eyes and would open her lacy black fan with one swift click into the air. She'd whip that thing towards me when I messed up my dance routines. It got so bad, my mom had to move me into another dance troupe.

"Look at my mija Laura, my sweet baby. How could you let him do this to her? And then he comes to my house and gets me? You people don't know what you're doing," says Bess angrily.

"Mrs. Sanchez, we will do our very best to get justice for Laura," I say. "The Leafwood Police Department is handling the case. The Special Homicide Team is helping, and Investigator Mack and I are working very hard on it. I'm the homicide on-call prosecutor, so I will be handling the case for now. I want to speak with the doctors about Laura's injuries. That's why I'm here."

"Why is the Homicide Team involved? Laura is not dead," says Bess.

"I know, I said the same thing. But this is a serious case and Laura was almost killed. When we're not sure if a victim is going to survive, the Special Homicide Team gets involved to make sure the evidence is collected properly and the interviews are conducted the right way. Just in case this becomes a homicide, we want the investigation done properly. Plus, I'm familiar with Laura and Clown," I say.

Dylan's cell phone starts ringing and he leaves the room to answer it. Bess turns towards Laura and strokes the top of her head as though she still had a head of hair she was brushing from front to back. Glancing at the monitors, feeding tubes, and number displaying on the beeping equipment, Bess stands up, turns on the light for assistance, and sits back down on a metal chair close to Laura.

"It was too much for her. The trial was too much for her. She was acting strange that night. I know she didn't want to return to court to testify. I should not have checked her phone. I should have let her be. She was under so much pressure. But she wasn't listening to me. I wanted her to listen to me but she was on that phone. I knew she was texting with Clown and then I saw it on her phone. She knows in my house that is not allowed," says Bess.

"You can't blame yourself," I say. "You had rules in your house and she knew that she couldn't be in contact with Clown if she was living with you. He's nothing but trouble. He's nine years older than her and in a gang. I've told her to stay away from him, too."

I look back at Laura, who seems completely unaware that we're sitting by her side. Her eyes are swollen and her breathing is labored.

"What's going on with Javier's case?" Bess asks.

"The case was just dismissed, but I plan on refiling it assuming Laura will come out of her coma. I came to see how she's doing," I say.

"You told me you would make her better. She just seemed to get worse, especially with this trial. She would lock herself in her room, ditch school, and not come home at night," Bess says.

"This is why I wanted her to join the club," I say.

"It had to be the trial," Bess says, changing the subject.

"This situation is hard enough already and we don't need to point fingers," I say.

This is so typical for a mother of a victim to take out their anger and guilt on me as a prosecutor. I've sat through mothers yelling at me for no good reason and have learned to accept it as part of the job and part of the grieving process. Plus, having somebody's mother yelling at me is better than not having one at all.

"The nurse and Dr. Lee should be coming any minute. I just rang them. They can tell you more about Laura," says Bess.

Dylan, Dr. Lee, and a petite nurse in a bright pink smock with Yorkshire terriers spread throughout the shirt walk in.

"How can we help you?" asks the nurse.

"This is the prosecutor on my daughter's case, Ms. Ruiz. She was asking how Laura is doing. It's fine with me if you guys speak with her," says Bess. "I was thinking that I would like to speak to someone about filling out DNR forms," continues Bess.

"We are not authorized to discuss the Do Not Resuscitate forms with you. But I can notify Organ Donation that you'd like to speak with them," the nurse says.

"Yes. I'd like that. I've made the decision. And I don't want there to be any confusion if God forbid something happens to Laura. She has been through enough already and I don't want her to continue suffering," says Bess adamantly.

"Laura was so vain, she would not have wanted her head shaved. Now she has a scar with staples that looks like a horseshoe on the side of her head where her hair will never grow back. She would never have wanted that. Isn't that right, baby?" Bess says, rubbing Laura's face.

Laura, completely lifeless, with her cheek nudging into her neck area from the back of Bess's fingers petting her face, doesn't respond.

"My thought is to just end the life support now. I don't know why she is being fed with all these tubes. That was never her wish and not mine," says Bess hopelessly.

"Well, she came in as a Jane Doe and immediately went into brain surgery. The standard procedure is to keep her on support. Come with me and I will put you in touch with Organ Donation," says the nurse before leaving the room with Bess.

It makes sense that hospital staff can't discuss DNR forms with Bess, so they don't become organ hungry to clear out a bed for the next patient. It would be like jail deputies deciding who to charge with a crime based on how many jail beds they have available that day. But the idea of giving up on Laura, who might still have a whole life ahead of her, makes me sick.

Dr. Lee and Dylan's eyes get bigger and bigger as they stare at Laura.

I hear a grunt that sounds like a barking dog.

"Laura, can you hear me? What is it?" I ask. Laura's eyes are wide open like her mouth. Dr. Lee, Dylan, and I move closer to her bed. The stench from her mouth is like a beached otter groaning; remnants of the fish it's been eating all summer sticking between its teeth leaving a terrible smell with each bark. As quickly as Laura's eyes open, she shuts them. A bloody tear falls down her face.

"Laura, could you hear what your mother was talking about?" I ask.

Her eyelids pulsate at a tremor speed like she has an overactive twitch, or she is possessed. After a few seconds of silence, she let out a long sigh before her eyelids begin to rest.

Nothing.

"I think it's a sign. I think she could hear what her mom was saying," I say.

Dylan looks at me like I'm crazy.

"Maybe she doesn't want any part of it," I say.

"Or maybe it was just a reflex, which is common in comatose patients. Look. She has not been responsive since she hit the door here. She's on a ventilator and hasn't been recovering as well as we expected from surgery," says Dr. Lee.

Dr. Lee, who's rubbing Laura's forehead, looks adverse to my theory. It dawns on me why I don't trust MDs like Dr. Lee or my ex-husband Neil; their practice is not based on miracles, prevention, or signs. Insurance companies and pharmaceutical companies would probably never allow that.

"What is the procedure for removing Laura from life support?" I ask.

"Well, if she was removed from it today, I would estimate she would live for no more than forty-eight hours," Dr. Lee replies.

"However, the more time that goes on with her being nourished, hydrated, and nursed back to health, the healthier she will become and the longer she will continue living once removed from life support.   You hear about those cases, where the patient stays alive for days, weeks, or even longer. I just can't give a definite time frame. It just depends on the patient.

"It also looks like she's having the onset of gangrene around her thumb. We noticed a gash on her thumb. But we're going to monitor it. I may have to amputate any areas that turn black," says Dr. Lee.

Dr. Lee pulls up the blanket that is covering Laura's hands.

Laura has a darkened right thumb area with a chipped French manicure and crinkled skin. It resembles the webbed and wrinkled foot of a bird. Her hand is inverted and the skin around the base of her thumb leading up to her pointer finger is purple.   What looks like bruising is actually gangrene. Marks around her right thumb that show a dark red pooling of blood next to the stitches catch my attention.

"That is the gangrene. It's caused from the compression to the nerve," says Dr. Lee.

"Is that because the belt was too tight around her wrists?" I ask.

"It could be from being too tight or if she was holding her head, whatever struck her could have clipped her thumb. And if she was struggling when she was restrained causing the gash, that could damage the nerves, too," Dr. Lee says.

"Thank you, Doctor. Here's my card. My cell phone number is on the back. Please contact me if there is any decision made regarding the life support or if there is any significant change in her status," I say.

"Of course," he replies. "To be honest, I'm not looking forward to calling you. I haven't had the best experience with your office. I don't know how you do your job. I save lives, but you people seem to wreck them. You call people into court to testify, you arrest people, and you call people for jury duty. I can go on and on at how your profession never ceases to amaze me."

I never looked at doctors in the same light after I married one. Neil, my ex-husband, grew into the biggest asshole I knew after graduating medical school. His head grew bigger each year his residency brought him closer to starting his own medical practice. I started noticing why when I went to a hospital holiday party with him. Nurses in stilettos, fishnet stockings, and backless dresses were gushing over all the doctors. Neil was right there eating all of it up.

"Yes, if you are asking, someday you will need to come to testify about Laura's condition and how your trauma unit treated her or, as you say, 'saved her life,'" I reply.

"Okay, whatever you need."

The sarcastic tone of Dr. Lee's voice sent a wave of goose bumps down my arms and thoughts back to Neil's paternalistic down-talk that I put up with for four years.

"Dr. Lee, we need people like you to come to court on these cases and tell the jury what procedures you did," I explain. "What if the defense later came back and said it was by some fault of the hospital or you that caused Laura to die, rather than her hematoma or beating? Not only would that mean a lawsuit for you, but it would be a huge waste of time and resources. It's in your best interest to cross your t's and dot your i's with this case, so you can explain all the necessary medical procedures you did on Laura."

Dr. Lee looks like his head is about to erupt as he tightens his lips together and squints his eyes at me.

"I run one of the top centers in Tuckford County. I know how to cross my t's and dot my i's."

I give Dr. Lee one of my fake smiles.

"Has any of the brain matter, which I'd assume was removed during surgery, been sent to pathology?" I ask.

Sometimes brain guts are removed by a surgeon, like a clot or hematoma caused by some blunt force trauma or beating. They can be sent for testing to see how large the clot is to show how slow the brain bleed was and when the injury occurred. The look on Dr. Lee's face is an obvious sign he didn't dot this i.

"Ma'am, we don't typically do that; but I will check with Dr. Mai to see if she can send that over for you."

"It's all part of crossing those t's," I say as Dr. Lee leaves the room and the VAT nurse walks in.

12

THE EXAM

I used to think one of the most intrusive examinations a woman can undergo is a pap smear. But a sexual assault exam is a hundred times worse. Danielle, dressed in a dark blue uniform with white skulls and crossbones on top and bottoms, shows up to perform this exam on Laura. She is from VAT, the Violent Assault Team. She conducts her exams quickly, but not always the most thoroughly. Dylan and I stand by Laura's bed at a distance, close enough to observe, but far enough to give the nurse space. Bess walks in and sits next to Laura, holding her hand. Two of Laura's hospital nurses walk up and stand near the doorway.

In most exams, the nurse will conduct a full interview with the victim, asking her all kinds of questions to get a complete history about the incident and what her private parts have been exposed to in the past two weeks. But Laura is unconscious.

"Has she had any surgeries you know about?" asks Danielle.

"She had an abortion when she was thirteen," says Bess.

"Was the father known at the time?" Danielle asks.

"Well. She claimed it was her stepfather," Bess says.

"It *was* Javier," I say dramatically.

"That was the allegation. It was never confirmed," Bess retorts.

"Why would she lie about that?" I ask.

I can't stand Bess right now. This is the typical denial that mothers have about their daughters being sexually abused. Her tone that suggests Laura would have made this up irritates me to the point I almost ask that she be removed from the room. But I remember not to miss the opportunity to keep my mouth shut. I know this must be hard for her.

"Do you know the date of her last menstrual period?" asks Danielle.

I laugh. "Yeah, actually, she was laughing with her neighbor Christina, who's in The Mamacita Club, a couple weeks ago saying she had just started her period. I told them that we women are so reactive to our environments, even our menstrual cycles become synchronized to each other," I say.

"You told that to my daughter?" asks Bess disgustedly.

I glare at Bess.

"Do you know whether she's had intercourse in the past five days?" Danielle asks.

"I don't know. Probably. She did leave with a young man the night before this happened," says Bess.

"That probably wasn't the only person she was having sex with," I say.

"Do we know if she had multiple partners?" Danielle inquires.

"We don't know for certain, but word on the street was that she was being used as a sex worker," I say.

"I see," says Danielle. "So we may have the presence of semen from multiple men inside her."

"Please excuse me. This is a little too much for me. I'm going outside to have a smoke," says Bess, while standing up and leaving the room.

"Do we know whether she used condoms?" asks Danielle.

"I doubt it," I reply.

"Well, it sounds like we have quite an upstanding young lady. She's had an abortion, has multiple partners, doesn't use condoms, and may be prostituting herself out. And you were mentoring her?" asks Danielle in a sarcastic tone.

"I was trying to. I don't know if you realize this, but she was sexually abused by her stepfather. In fact, it was the man that Bess, the lady who just walked out, has been trying to protect. I think that was obvious by her comment about Laura's abortion."

"Yes, I gathered that. I'm just trying to collect as much information as I can about this girl. I know nothing about her and am not here to judge her. All I'm thinking is that there may be factors interfering with findings. It's just something I need to document," says Danielle, backtracking.

"Thank you for your insight. I'm well aware of the factors that may affect the findings in these types of cases. Laura may be a troubled girl, but she is still a victim and didn't deserve what happened to her," I assert.

"How was she tied up?" asks Danielle.

"Her wrists were tied together with a belt," I say.

"To what?" says Danielle.

"Nothing. They were tied together. And she was blindfolded," I say.

"So she could have gotten up?" Danielle asks.

"Assuming she wasn't unconscious, yeah. I guess," I say.

Danielle squints her eyes and shakes her head like something is not making sense to her.

"Do you know whether she's lost memory?" asks Danielle.

"She's in a coma, for crying out loud. I'm sure she's not going to remember pretty much anything," I yell.

Why is it that Danielle wants to be thorough in filling out this questionnaire when she's dealing with a comatose patient? She's never this thorough.

"Let me ask you this. Why do you think she was raped? You're the ones that called me down here for this exam. From your answers, it seems like she was a willing party in any sexual activity," says Danielle.

"The man we have in custody is her pimp. There's only one reason he would have done this; to discipline her if she was trying to leave the ring. It's pretty common for them to rape their sex worker," Dylan says.

Danielle shuts her notepad and puts her pen down.

"I'm ready to do this if you are," says Danielle in a sarcastic tone.

I really don't think Danielle likes this part of her job. Who really would? Looking up the vaginas of women for evidence of physical trauma isn't the most glamorous, but someone has to do it. And I'm glad it's not me. Danielle puts on latex gloves then hands Dylan, the nurses, and me our own pairs, which we all put on.

"Can you help me elevate and spread her legs into these holsters?" Danielle asks.

There are two stand-alone holsters for Laura's legs that are wheeled on each side of her bed. The two nurses, Danielle, and I manipulate Laura's legs into the holsters. Her leg is heavy like a concrete block. Laura is completely out of it, lying unconscious, not reacting to us touching her body at all.

Danielle starts examining Laura's head, neck, mouth, and teeth, swabbing two cotton sticks on the insides of and around her lips.

"Do you notice anything significant?" I ask.

"Other than the obvious marks on her wrists and hands, which I'm sure you caught, no," Danielle says in her rude and abrupt way.

I take a closer look at Laura. Small scratches appear in vertical lines down the sides of her neck. There's nothing worse than being in a physical exam with a victim and the medical personnel is not on your side. Between Dr. Lee and Nurse Danielle, I'm beginning to understand why Tuckford County, the "Big T," is considered full of rude people.

Danielle then hands Dylan a plastic bag, asking him to hold it under Laura's nails. She picks up nail clippers and uses them to snip each of Laura's ten nails, letting them fall into the bag. Next, Danielle moves to Laura's genitalia.

Placing forceps into Laura's vagina, Danielle takes a small wand with a camera, which videotapes and takes photos, and inserts it into Laura's vagina. She asks Dylan to hold a light nearby so she can get a better look inside Laura. Danielle writes down a few notes and begins to swab the area inside of Laura. Thirteen swabs were taken from Laura — vaginal, cervical, anal, and vulva. And they were all taken in silence.

Danielle then removes the forceps and begins to draw Laura's blood, which she seals in a glass tube with a lavender top. Then she starts plucking some of Laura's pubic hairs. Ouch. Ouch. Ouch. Ouch. There's just some things that hurt me as much when I watch. I thought getting a Brazilian bikini wax where a lady waxes the hair off my vagina so it's as soft as a baby's butt was bad, but individual plucking seems a hundred times worse. I feel like I'm absorbing all the shock of the plucking for both Laura and myself, because she has no reflex to it.

"Why can't you just trim the hair?" I ask.

"This is just a standard procedure we go through. I've always used my tweezers to pluck some of the hair. Plus, she's not feeling anything we're doing to her right now. Not on that pain drip she's on," says Danielle, pointing to a sack of liquid.

"You never know. What if she can hear and understand everything's that happening to her, but she just can't respond to us? I wonder if she's paralyzed inside watching everyone prod and poke at her. Did you ever consider that?" I ask.

"No, because that's not what happens," says Danielle.

The idea that even the nurse is giving up on her makes me really sad. I promised Laura I wouldn't leave her side and I'm not about to right now.

Last, Danielle takes out her camera and snaps photos of Laura's body and the injuries on her wrists and hands.

Danielle removes her gloves and looks up at us.

"Were there any sort of findings?" I ask.

"Yes, there were," says Danielle.

She stays silent and starts writing some notes in her chart. She stops, stands up, and puts the pen in her pants pocket.

"Well, do you care to share them with us?" I ask.

"Sure, I can do that," she says. Another round of silence confirms she's playing games with me.

"Well, there's a couple things. My findings are consistent with sexual intercourse in the recent past. It appears she has erythema to fossa navicularis," says Danielle.

"What's that?" I ask.

"How long have you been in the Sexual Assault Unit?" Danielle asks sarcastically.

"Longer than you've been a VAT nurse. How many exams have you done?" I ask, snapping back.

"Roughly two hundred," says Danielle.

"Are you always so pleasant when you conduct them?" I ask, smiling.

"I do each one the same way every time," says Danielle.

"Are you always so skeptical about the victim?" I ask.

"I don't judge," says Danielle.

"Right. I'm sure you don't. I just wonder if these cases involving sex workers get you thinking the victim had something to do with their assault," I say.

"Look at a girl like Laura. This girl is sleeping around and selling her body. She's a hooker and not very sympathetic. She certainly won't be liked by your jurors," says Danielle.

"You're supposed to be a neutral party in this," I say.

"I am," says Danielle looking back at her watch.

"Do you want to know what erythema to fossa navicularis is?" she asks.

"I already asked you to explain that," I say.

"It's basically inflammation to the area between the hymen and the frenulum labiorum punendi."

I hate when medical personnel speak in language I can't understand. They always do it when they're testifying, like I'm supposed to know what a frenulum is. At least I can ask them what that is without looking dumb in front of the jury. But here, Danielle knows I'll have to ask what this is and she wants me to look stupid in front of Dylan, someone I've seen her flirt with in the past.

"I know what a hymen is, but what is that other thing you just mentioned?" I ask.

"Sometimes it's referred to as a fourchette. It's the area right by the back area near the anus," says Danielle.

Now she's speaking in a language I can understand. I remember Neil telling me things I never wanted to hear about the fourchette. He used to joke, "Your fourchette is worth a fortune." That's the only reason I remembered the word.

When Neil worked in the delivery room during one of his stints as a resident during medical school, he said the fourchette can be torn during delivery because of all the stretching that goes on down there. To prevent this, the doctors would make a deliberate cut starting from the fourchette towards the anus.

Neil said when the cut went too far, it left the whole area way too loose to ever make sex enjoyable again. So Neil told me if we ever had kids, I would have to get a C-Section. The fourchette can also be torn with forced acts like rape and sometimes needs stitches to get it back intact. But Danielle said Laura didn't need surgery and there was no bleeding, just inflammation.

"So are her injuries consistent with being raped?" I ask.

"No, not at all. They're consistent with sexual intercourse in general. If she was violently raped, I'd expect to see more than this," Danielle replies. "I'll write my findings in the report. Here are all the samples. I hope you find whoever did this to her. But this girl wasn't raped."

Within one minute of Dylan and me leaving Laura's room, sirens and a loud intercom announcement screams out, "Code Blue, fifth floor, room 5-1-1!" Dr. Lee comes running down the hall with Bess, who is being grabbed by one of the nurses.

I start running behind Dr. Lee and into chaos. Laura is being wheeled out on her bed. Nurses are running down the hall and loud sirens are screeching.

"Irregular heart rhythm!" screams one of the nurses to Dr. Lee, who is running down the hall. Sirens are making it hard for me to hear anything else the nurse says. But then I hear Bess screaming.

"Don't save her. She's not to be saved! Those are my orders!" shouts Bess.

"Save her, please save her," I yell back.

Dylan grabs me by the arm, pinching me so hard it makes the nerves in my nose cringe. I unlock my arm out of his, scream at him to leave me alone, and continue rushing towards Laura. Dylan runs after me and pulls me into a waiting room closing the door behind us.

"What are you doing?" I yell.

"That is not your place to be doing this," says Dylan, pushing me up against the wall.

"They're gonna let her die. She can't die. We need to save her. Please let me save her," I say.

"Gaby. Stop. Calm down. Listen to yourself. You can't save her. Let her go. This is not your decision. Stop trying to control this."

I begin to sob uncontrollably in Dylan's arms with him holding me. I can save her. We can save her. She can't die. I need to save her.

"Shhh, Gaby. Calm down. It's okay," Dylan says.

Everything around me starts to look blurry like I'm looking through a hazy white film. My ears start ringing loud, my head feels warm, and I feel like I'm passing out.

I must have only lost consciousness for a couple seconds. I'm lying down on my back on the floor of the waiting room. The fogginess starts to clear up. I start focusing in on a television pinned to the wall showing some soap opera. I study the seats around the room that are attached to the floor and see Bess sitting in one of the seats. The coolness of a wet rag lying across my forehead sends chills through my body.

Bess reaches into her shirt and removes a black beaded rosary from her bra. She closes her eyes, bows her head, and begins to slowly move her fingers across bead after bead while mumbling.

"What happened?" I ask.

"I think you went into a little shock," says a nurse crouched down towards me. She removes the damp rag from my forehead.

"I thought we were going to have to check you in. You turned from a bright pink to a ghost white in a matter of seconds. I was a little worried about you," says Dylan.

"What happened to Laura?" I ask.

"Dr. Lee gave her a cocktail of drugs to calm her down," says the nurse.

"Is she alive?" I ask.

"Yes. But she's still in a coma. She does have a pulse, though," says the nurse, smiling at me.

"She made it," I say.

"Yes, she made it," says Dylan.

"You got your wish," says Bess, glaring at me.

"What are the drugs for?" I ask.

"Just to help out with her anxiety and stabilize her blood pressure. She was having an irregular heart rhythm that set the monitor off and triggered the Code Blue. It may have been triggered by the exam," says the nurse.

"But I thought she couldn't feel anything," I say.

"We don't really know what she's experiencing right now. And it's just in case," says the nurse.

"I thought you guys were going to let her die," I say.

"We resuscitate everyone within 48 hours after they come through our doors, Sweetie. But she pulled through this one, all on her own. She's a little fighter," the nurse says.

"Can I go see her?" I ask.

"Of course. Do you feel okay?" asks the nurse.

"I'm fine. I just want to see her," I say, reaching for Dylan's hand as he helps me up. We walk to Laura's room.

Standing next to Laura, who's resting in her hospital bed, makes me wonder what she can hear or feel. She looks dead to me and her coloring is more pale than it was when I saw her less than an hour ago before her Code Blue. I ask Dylan and the nurse if I could be alone with her for a minute and they leave the room.

"I'm sorry I didn't get to you sooner, Laura. I know if I went to that motel just a little earlier, I could've saved you. I'm sorry. I won't let them kill you. I know you're gonna make it. I will fight for you to the end. I won't let them put you in a casket.   I won't let that happen to you, I promise you."   I stare at Laura and see my mom's face in hers.

I stare at Laura hoping she'll open her eyes and see me. "Laura, please don't leave me.   Hang in there.   I need you to wake up and tell us what happened.   I need your help.   I need you to get better and testify in Javier's trial, too.   Don't leave me and I won't leave you.   I promise to come back every day to check on you until you wake up.

"Let's do this one day at a time, together.   Heal yourself. I need you to promise me you won't give up on life.   I need signs from you that you aren't calling it quits.   I'll be back tomorrow to check up on you and let you know what's happening in the investigation.   Please, please, live through today," I whisper to Laura.

13

THE CRIME LAB

Less than an hour after Laura's Code Blue, Supervising DNA Analyst Miranda Jules greets Dylan and I with a fresh smile and youthful glow at the front lobby of the Crime Lab. Miranda would meet the qualifications to work on the TV show CSI. She doesn't fit the crunchy scientist stereotype. She's trendy and wears glasses like the rest of her colleagues; they're Coach ones, giving her a Pippa Middleton style that comes through even with her white lab coat on.

"Hi, Ms. Ruiz and *Dylan*, it's nice to see you again," says Miranda. With Miranda having Dylan on a first name basis and winking at him, I'm instantly suspicious if he's dated her. But I stop myself and remember to put first things first. I'm here for Laura, not to investigate Dylan's dating history.

I clip my guest badge onto my suit jacket and am now authorized to walk the halls of this sterile laboratory with Miranda and Dylan.

"Thanks for meeting with us on such short notice," I say.

"Of course, anything for Dylan, my favorite investigator. Dylan and I have worked on many cases together. What was our last one? That home invasion over in Mason Valley?" asks Miranda.

"Yes. You did an amazing job on that case," Dylan says, trying to butter her up.

"Miranda located one of the suspect's DNA on a ski mask he left at the crime scene. That was the only piece of evidence we had linking that guy to the scene.

"She built a profile within forty-eight hours on the case. She even stayed the weekend. I remember coming into the lab over the weekend to get the results. If I trust anyone with my cases, it's Miranda. We're in good hands," he says.

"Aw. You're sweet. Thank you, Dylan. Let's go down this hall," says Miranda endearingly.

I grab onto my guest badge like it's my security blanket, making sure it's still in the same place I clipped it thirty seconds ago. I can't stand hearing Dylan and another woman gush over each other's case victories right in front of me. Remember, Laura, Laura, Laura. This is all about Laura.

The Tuckford County Crime Lab, when under time pressure from my office, can analyze DNA found at a crime scene in two to three days if they're pushed. Usually, it's all based on case priority. If you have a good relationship with the crime lab supervisor and get him or her on your side convincing them the case is important, they'll work hard to get the job done. They'll even work over the weekend to help you, like Miranda.

The Crime Lab is over-flooded with work. A piece of crime scene evidence can sit at the laboratory for years before a criminalist takes a look at it, finds a DNA profile on it, then uploads it into a criminal database with offender DNA profiles — and possibly finds a match. The more serious the crime is or high profile the case is, the greater chance you have at the criminalists working up your case.

If you saw their meticulous notes and sterile lab, with all the quality assurance measures they go through to look at one piece of evidence, you'd understand why it takes so damn long. They aren't just running a black light over the piece of evidence like you see on television. There's a whole bunch of procedures they need to follow to make sure they keep up with standards and regulations of the state. I know Miranda can get the DNA done in Laura's case if I can find a way to convince her.

"Why don't we make a right down this hall and use this conference room to discuss the case? I think I read about it this morning in the paper," says Miranda.

The medium-sized conference room gives me room to spread out my file. Dylan places his Special Homicide portfolio on the table and stares at Miranda.

"Is this the one where a young girl was found bound in the motel room, but she's still alive?" asks Miranda.

"Yes," both Dylan and I reply in unison.

"I'll let Gaby tell you about the case. She has a personal relationship with the girl. She has been trying to recruit her into her club, so the news was shocking. They met in another case we were prosecuting. Laura is the victim in a sex case," Dylan explains.

"Did the lab do any DNA work in that case?" Miranda asks.

"No, she didn't report the sexual abuse until months later. There was nothing to test," I say.

"Okay, well, tell me what pieces of evidence we have in the current case," says Miranda.

What I've learned about DNA cases and the Crime Lab is that sometimes it's better to give them less information about the facts of the case or the suspected perpetrators. It helps keep them unbiased if they don't know whose DNA we hope they will find. When they are testifying and the defense is trying to make them look like our puppets, it helps when they know little about the case or the suspect. They can say they just were given items of evidence and looked for semen or fluids and figured out whose DNA it was. When they can testify they had little or no information about a certain case or suspect, it shuts down any potential defense of bias in our favor.

"We have a belt," I tell her.

"Where was that found?"

"Around her wrists. Her hands were tied up and she was lying on the bed."

"Was she tied to the headboard or any part of the bed?"

"No. Her hands were tied together and resting like this," I say, holding my hands down by my lap.

"Were they tied to any other part of her body?" asks Miranda.

I shake my head back and forth. "They weren't tied to anything. She was blindfolded, though," I say.

"With what?"

"A sock."

"Was she found lying face up or down?"

"Up."

"What else do we have to examine?"

"We have a ceramic vase."

"Why is that important?"

"It has blood all over it."

"Where was that found?"

"Next to the victim."

"What condition was it in?"

"Partially broken," I say.

I used to make pottery when I was young. The hum of the wheel and the touch of the cool clay after dipping my hands in the water and kneading my clay always felt so soothing. I made my mom a vase one year. She loved it. My mom would wake me up every Saturday so we could pick roses from our garden and put them in our vase. I would do anything to hear her sing one more time, "Rise and shine and get some glory glory."

One time, my stepfather cut our Saturday ritual short when he saw my mom talking to our neighbor John. I could still smell the alcohol on his breath when he stood over my mom at the kitchen sink as she filled our vase with water. I can still hear the crash of the vase when he shattered it against the wall. The white walls of my hallway spun around me like a moving tunnel as I ran to my room for cover that day.

"Ms. Ruiz, did you hear me?" asks Miranda.

"No, I'm sorry. What did you say?"

"Is there any other evidence you'd like examined?"

"Yes. Let me think," I say. "There are exams from the suspect and the victim, who by the way is named Laura."

"Was there any other evidence collected around the scene that might tell us who was there? It seems quite a task for someone to do this alone. I read in the newspaper that the entire room was ransacked in addition to the girl being tied up and her panties were pulled down to her ankles. Is that accurate?" Miranda asks.

The thing about news reports on crimes is they rarely report the details of crimes under investigation. Sometimes the media gets more information about a case than I may initially have. They are good about going into the community and interviewing people about the suspect or the victim. They will show up at memorial sites and take the time to speak with the people who are affected the most.

"Was that really in the paper? That the room was ransacked and about her panties?" I ask, surprisingly.

"Yes, that's what I read," says Miranda.

"I wonder where they got those details. I'm surprised because they're actually true," I say.

"Those are typically things law enforcement would not release, especially this early in the case," Dylan says. "I know I didn't release that information and I can guarantee Ford wouldn't have released that. The press release from the Leafwood Police Department didn't contain that information, either."

When it comes to details of the crime scene, however, they rarely have any. They are usually not allowed beyond the yellow crime scene tape or given much information by police, so the investigation is not jeopardized. Prosecutors can't even give any more information to the press other than charges a suspect is facing, the maximum sentence a suspect is facing, and any other public information that takes place in open court on the record, like court rulings, testimony, and motions. Law enforcement never releases details other than the location something occurred, the suspect's name and the victim's name, assuming she's not a minor.

"Ms. Jules," I begin. "I know how swamped the Crime Lab is. Every case I send here seems to take three to six months. But this case is very personal to me. I was prosecuting Laura's sex case when she didn't show up to testify, and then we found her in the motel.

"I was trying to recruit her into The Mamacita Club where I mentor at-risk women like Laura. Helping them is my passion. They come from broken homes, low income neighborhoods, and mobile home parks. They've been subjected to violence, gangs, and drugs. Laura is sitting in a coma over at the Memorial Hospital and can't tell us what happened to her. We need science to tell us. This is an important case.

"I brought some pictures taken during one of our field trips. Laura's best friend Christina is in this one," I say, pushing one of the photos I printed on my desk jet printer early this morning towards Miranda.

"Who's this lady?" asks Miranda pointing to the woman we visited.

"The girls met a cancer survivor whom they really bonded with," I reply.

Miranda studies the photo with an expression that seems to recall something inside of her.

"This picture is what Laura looks like now," I say, handing her one of photos taken by a tech yesterday.

Miranda looks at the photo and points to the horseshoe on Laura's shaved head.

"I'm assuming this is from brain surgery?" Miranda asks.

"Yes, but for the grace of God, she didn't die. Whatever you can do to get this DNA processed within the next forty-eight hours, it would mean a lot to me," I say.

"The person you have in custody is her boyfriend, is that correct?" Miranda asks. "I read that in the paper, too."

"Right," I say. "Well, it was more so her pimp. We believe he was pimping her out from that motel room."

"Why would her boyfriend or pimp have ransacked the room?" asks Miranda.

"That's a good question," I say, looking at Dylan.

"It's pretty common for a suspect to make the scene look like a burglary occurred," Dylan replies. "They do it to throw off the police and make it look like a random act. Or, the perpetrator, even when they know the victim, shuffles through the drawers looking for money or other things to take. Criminals are just greedy. They'll grab things near the exit door of a store they just robbed. Some are just freeloaders, especially someone like Clown."

"You're pretty confident you have the right person?" questions Miranda.

"I am," says Dylan firmly.

"And you?" Miranda asks, turning her focus to me.

"That's why I'm here. I want science to answer that question for me. I wasn't there," I say.

I could feel Dylan staring at me. Miranda looks down at the pictures of Laura and my group of girls with the cancer survivor.

"Our crime lab has triple the amount of cases as other crime labs, and we have far less criminalists to handle the caseload. I'm going to make an exception in this case and get this done by tomorrow. That's the best I can do. I can see how important the case is to you. Plus, I want you to be confident you're charging the right person," Miranda says.

"You're an angel. Thank you," I say graciously.

Sitting across the table from Dylan at Farmer Tuck's Burgers, taking bites of our burgers and fries, starts to calm my stomach after visiting the Crime Lab. A fix of greasy food always calms my stomach when it's queasy from photos or evidence we have to look at. But Dylan always has a way of disrupting any of my calm moments, or maybe I just let him.

"What did you do in there? Did you really have to bring those photos?" Dylan asks.

I don't want to have this conversation on a topic that is so sensitive to me, especially with a man I care about. I've learned I get defensive about the girls I mentor.

"I need the Crime Lab to get the DNA done before I leave on vacation. They won't get it done if we don't pressure them a little bit," I say.

"Why did you have to make it sound like you don't know if we have the right suspect?" asks Dylan.

"I need to believe I can prove this case beyond a reasonable doubt before I recommend my office file charges. My burden is different from yours, Dylan, you know that. Plus, I'm concerned now because Laura wasn't raped. Your theory is Clown raped and assaulted her for wanting to leave the ring. And that's not what the exam results are showing. Plus the print on that vase isn't even Clown's, " I say.

"You made it seem in front of Miranda that you don't believe he's the one. That makes me look bad," he says.

Dylan's deep blue eyes and puppy dog face look desperate. I usually find men who are whining about something a complete turn-off. But Dylan, right now, is endearing. I feel closer to him now than I did at the Crime Lab when Miranda Jules was drooling over him. However, that might be because I'm hormonal right now.

"I just want the Crime Lab to work up this case and care about it. If I didn't show those photos and lay it on thick, she might not care about this case. Look, if Clown's our guy like you believe, there should be DNA all over the belt, her nails, the VAT exam. Why are you worried about it if you're so confident he's the one?"

"Why are *you* questioning Clown's involvement?" Dylan asks, shifting the focus on me.

"Mainly because of the fingerprint. I just think there's more to this. And like I said, I just want everything in order. I don't want any stone left unturned in this case. It's for Laura," I say.

"You're up to something. I can tell. You're acting weird. I don't trust you," says Dylan.

"You don't have to trust me," I say. "You work the case your way and I'll work it my way. I set the staffing for Monday morning at nine a.m. Hopefully, we'll get preliminary results from Miranda by then and she'll just confirm what you already suspect, that it's Clown."

A worker cleaning the tables comes and asks me if I'm done with my burger, half of which is still sitting on my plastic tray. I tell him to take it all away since I just lost my appetite.

"Do me a favor?" asks Dylan.

"What?"

"Don't ever disagree with me in front of the Crime Lab again."

"What is that supposed to mean?" I ask.

"You know exactly what I mean," Dylan says angrily. "Do you know how embarrassing that was? My reputation could be on the line with the Lab if we had the wrong suspect. They'd start getting curious on all the cases I've made an arrest on and start testing all pieces of friggin' evidence."

"What would be so bad about that?" I ask. "I'd love to test the entire evidence locker of stuff in most my cases."

"For what? What would that do? Just because there's someone's DNA on a piece of evidence doesn't always mean they're the killer," says Dylan hotly.

"Chill out. Why are you so defensive about testing everything?" I ask.

We focus on eachother in silence. Neither one of us looks away.

"I might as well tell you this now," he says, finally turning away. "I'm a little concerned. Can I trust you with something? I'm still looking into it as we speak."

"Of course."

"There was a business card found inside the pocket of Laura's pants found near the bed. It was the business card of a police officer. It didn't belong to any of the officers that reported out to the scene," he says.

"Then how'd it get there?" I ask.

"I don't know," Dylan says. "My concern is this getting leaked to the press. For all I know, he could've contacted her or stopped her sometime earlier and she had the card. We're looking into it."

"Since when would an officer give their business card to someone they stopped?" I ask.

"I don't know. I'm just guessing."

"Has anyone spoken to the police officer?"

"No," Dylan replies. "The only thing I know is that he was placed on administrative. And rumor is that it's over this case."

"So who's gonna talk to him?"

"I haven't received permission from admin to make contact with him since he's been on leave," Dylan says.

"Since when do we need permission from admin to speak with a potential witness in an attempted homicide investigation or any investigation for that matter?" I ask.

"Well, he might have certain rights and may be disciplined internally, especially if he was at the motel for questionable reasons, having nothing to do with the assault," he says.

"Like for prostitution?"

"For anything. I'm looking into whether he was on duty that night, whether he radioed in to make a stop at the motel. There's a number of things I'm looking into before we go hunt him down to speak with. All this needs to get cleared through the administration at Leafwood PD."

"You might have to go through admin, but I don't. What's his name?" I ask.

"I'm not releasing that to you, just yet," Dylan replies.

"Are you kidding me? Since when do you, a Special Homicide investigator, start withholding information from the assigned prosecutor on the case? Are you trying to cover something up?" I ask.

"No, I just don't want you interfering with my investigation," Dylan says.

"You've completed your investigation. You've arrested your suspect. It's my case now and you need to turn over all the information. There's no hiding the ball. If you were still investigating, you shouldn't have made the arrest," I say.

"We haven't submitted the filing request to your office yet. Plus, you're not staffing it until Monday. Give me until then," he says.

"Fine, Dylan," I say, giving in. "You have until Sunday night to come clean with this information and tell me what's going on. I want to know the exact reason that card is in the pocket of a girl who was nearly dead. Laura never mentioned meeting up with an officer when I saw her the night before we found her. And I highly doubt she had a networking event where she was exchanging cards with police officers. If I don't have an answer by the staffing, I'm going to recommend my office investigate what this officer has to do with Laura."

"Get off my back, Gaby. I didn't even have to tell you about this," Dylan says indignantly.

"Oh, and wait for me to stumble upon this card in evidence when I'm looking through the property room one day preparing Clown's case for trial? Would that be the right time to tell me about it?" I ask sarcastically. "I'm giving you til Sunday night."

14

TO SUMMON OR NOT TO SUMMON

Thirty minutes after leaving Farmer Tuck's, I sit with Angela inside my Airstream focusing on the candlelight inside Angel's Den. After sitting down across from me, Angela holds my hands as I close my eyes to summon my energy. Deep breath in. Deep breath out.

"What's bothering you, sweetie?" asks Angela, staring at me with her big brown eyes sparkling from the light of a candle lit beneath us.

"I need to get to the bottom of something. A police officer's card was found in Laura's pocket at the crime scene. Dylan won't tell me who it belongs to," I say.

"Tell me more," says Angela.

"That's all I know. I think he's starting to realize there might be more to Laura's case. But I'm not even sure where to begin," I say.

"Comb through all the evidence yourself and see if you can find the answer that way. Don't wait for it to come to you," says Angela.

"That will really upset Dylan. But he's already mad at me. I hate when we're fighting, especially when it's over work stuff. It's so hard because I still love him," I say.

"Let me ask you this. If you feel you're in love with Dylan, why don't you summon your powers?" Angela asks.

"I don't know. Can't you give me the answer. I thought you're supposed to help me figure this out. Can't you ask my angels?"

"It's your angels that are asking you this."

"Fair enough," I say. "I think it's because I don't feel like he's the one, so I don't want to summon the powers."

"Let me ask you this. What do you like about Dylan?"

"Hmmm. He's handsome. His wavy hair almost looks like he has these sun-kissed highlights. He's always tan and has this stomach of steel. He works out almost every day and I remember how good it felt against mine. His smile glows and his blue eyes sparkle at me. He has these long eyelashes, too, for a guy.

"And he's one of those guys that anything you do with him, even just hanging out with him during an investigation, is fun. He's sweet to everyone, but the moment he feels threatened, he's fearless and throws these temper tantrums. It's sexy, though. Plus, he's good at his job. It's not anyone that gets assigned to the Special Homicide Team."

"All those things are great, but let me ask you this. Have you spent much time with him outside work lately? You know, to get to know him again?" asks Angela.

"Not really," I answer.

"Why don't you suggest doing something outside of work? He looks really appealing to you because he is at the top of his game. It's sexy to many women. But that's not what it will take for the long haul. You know this. This is what attracted you to Neil."

I stare at Angela worrying she's not reading Dylan correctly.

"There's no way Dylan is like Neil," I say.

"I'm not saying Dylan will mistreat you, but he might not be enough for you. He might not bring out the best in you. That's all I'm saying," Angela says.

I look at her hopelessly.

"Your angels are asking you to return to the ocean. You haven't been down there in a while and I can tell you're off-balance. You're in a slump right now. Go down to the ocean and I promise you will start living well and get the answers you are looking for," Angela says.

Two hours after sitting across from Angela in Angel's Den, I walk around Blackbird Beach. Even though I was born and raised in Old Town, I've always loved the ocean. Since I was old enough to walk and play in the sand, the ocean has given me peace of mind. My mom used to drive me from Old Town all the way here to Blackbird Beach. If it wasn't here, it was having tuna sandwiches with Nana at beaches further up the coast. Being by the ocean was one of my mom's favorite things to do. Plus it's where I had my very first experience with my powers.

After my mom died, I was playing in the sand wishing so much she was there with me. The next thing I knew, she appeared right next to me and we played all afternoon.

Things like that kept happening to me from time to time. I'd hear her voice and see her everywhere like in the clouds, in the ocean, or just walking in the street. If it wasn't her or someone who looked like her, it was a vision shaped like an angel, the wings and all.

The other strange thing that kept happening was that I'd see the number three in odd places. Sometimes it was 33 or 333 on license plates, trucks passing by, billboards, telephone numbers, clouds, gas station prices, digital clocks, case numbers, cash register totals. The number three in different sequences appears everywhere, still today.

For a long time, I wanted to forget about the power of my mom, the universe and their signs. I only used to tap into it when I needed it most. Breathing in and out, remaining calm and allowing my mom into my world was always so easy, when I actually did it. But for a really long time, it was too painful. Because it meant coming to terms with the fact that my mom was gone forever, at least physically. And that's always been so hard for me to accept. Even though I know she's with me spiritually.

It wasn't until things ended with Dylan, that I really started to call on the Universe and my mom for answers. I was at such a low from the pain of losing Dylan. I felt the same abandonment I did as a kid losing my mom. Around the same time, Angela joined The Mamacita Club and started helping me hone my powers.

Like other angel readers I've met, she knew right away I had something special. She explained numerology and how the number three represented the trinity, a higher power and angels making me aware of their presence. She explained I had a mission in life to carry out my passion for helping victims like me and bring them serenity. The Universe and my mom have always sent me gifts in strange ways, especially when it's to help women and those who have died. And that's why my career has always thrived.

I like bringing the girls in The Mamacita Club down here to the ocean because it gives them a sense of hope, wonder, and freedom. People come from around the world to vacation here. If you just walk around here any summer day, you'll hear at least five different languages being spoken around you. My favorite part about Blackbird Beach is at night, looking up into the sky and seeing stars everywhere because the neighborhoods are so dark. I've always thought Blackbird Beach is one of the most amazing and serene places on Earth. And I don't just say that because I live here. I've talked to people who have traveled all around the world. And they say Blackbird Beach is still their favorite. So it was an easy decision to settle here after Neil and I divorced.

Dylan helped talk me into moving here. I still remember his advice: "Decide where you live based on where you want to spend the weekends, not the weekdays. A job is a job. You should live for the weekends," Dylan said.

Of course, at the time he was living two cities away from here. We were chatting over margaritas at a cantina with an amazing view of the Cove. After a night of drinking, dancing, and a last minute check-in to a nearby motel, I was sold on Dylan's idea of moving here and I've never regretted it. I knew I needed to be close to the ocean.

Afterall, I'm a Cancer sign, a crab. And I constantly need to hide away in my shell and live close to the water to live a balanced life. The amazing ocean views, seals and dolphins I see year 'round playing in the water, help recharge me after working the week as a prosecutor and at The Mamacita Club. Plus, the vast ocean, looking at it and asking it for advice and questions, gives me the most clarity, serenity, and balance in my life.

Angela is right — the ocean answers all my questions and I haven't been back to the Cove to summon its powers since last October. It's now July.

When the weather is right, the tide is calm, and no one is around, I walk down to the Cove. It is the rockiest point of Blackbird Beach, just down the hill from the main park. Around seven p.m., when I know the lifeguard is off his tower and all the tourists have packed up to leave the beach, I head down and sit on my favorite rock. It doesn't take much concentration, and Angela has taught me how to meditate and summon powers quickly because at any moment, people could disrupt the channels.

The first thing I see is a school of dolphins. Not one, not two, but about a hundred. Their grey backs breach the water and their fins dive back into the water, one after another. Their playing reminds me to have fun, be playful, and never lose the love for those close to me. When I ask the ocean what this means for Dylan and me, I'm reminded that we are part of a team of people that do good and help others. I'm encouraged to continue playing and working together and let life be. The answer comes quick and it makes sense. When answers come and don't make much sense to me from the ocean or my angels, I keep pressing to figure out if I have channels or answers that are crossing one another.

My next question is about Laura. Tell me how to handle Laura's case. The ocean gets very still. Water is barely crashing onto the shore. It's trickling onto the sand. No wonder there are no lifeguards manning their stations right now along the coast. It's so quiet and silent, there's no need.

The ocean tells me to remain still, quiet, and calm. See what happens. The answer seems logical.

When you serve justice, you can't control the outcome. Things just happen. You can work hard, do your job, and try your best. But that's it. The ocean knows there's no point in fighting the inevitable. Over time, I've learned that, too. It's so hard for me to relinquish control and give it up to a higher power beyond me.

As a kid, I couldn't control what was going on around me. Anytime I feel I don't have a voice, it brings me back to those tough times growing up. I'm learning to relax, because it becomes exhausting when I don't. I'm learning to offer my problems to a higher power for help to figure them out.

I recite the Serenity Prayer.

God, grant me the serenity to accept the things I cannot change, the courage to change the things I can, and the wisdom to know the difference.

I breathe in very deeply and release it with the flow of the water going back out to the vast ocean. All the dots will connect someday soon. It will all make sense.

I have one last question. I've learned to never ask too much and three is enough. Who did this to Laura? It didn't take long before the waters turned rough and the most beautiful ship caught my attention in the distance. Its huge sails reminded me of the Nina, Pinta, or Santa Maria. The huge mast of the ship looks like those ships with sails you see inside a glass jar that you can buy with a cork inside at Knott's Berry Farm or some other amusement park.

I don't understand the meaning of the ship. But what I do know is that the Universe doesn't give me clues when things are the way they're supposed to be. The water turns rough when something's wrong. If Clown were the right or only suspect, the Universe would not be telling me to look for a ship.

Just as I'm thinking I might see a pirate come to the ledge spearing his sword around, I keep staring out into the ocean, but nothing is out there, including the ship I just saw. The waters remain rough and the sound of the waves crashing against the shore get louder and louder until they're almost deafening.   It's not often that my powers scare me. It's starting to get dark and I rush back home.

15

THE PROPERTY ROOM

The morning after my vision of the ship on the water, I decelerate the beast to exit the freeway towards the Leafwood RV Park. When I turn up my air conditioner, I hear a strange noise coming from my engine. Driving this beat-up old Celica, which still has a cassette player, makes me wonder if I'm still a struggling college student trying to get by or a professional with a law degree.

The job of being an assistant prosecutor is not a highly paid one. But it's one that pays a consistent salary. It's barely enough to maintain a comfortable lifestyle, which includes my gym membership, keeping a fully stocked refrigerator, and maintaining a fashionable enough wardrobe. People envious of my lifestyle forget I'll be paying down student loans for the next twenty-five years.

Being a prosecutor, however, has never felt like a day of work for me, except for times like when I'm threatened. I've always told people it's worth the risk and danger that comes along with it. It's important for me to do what I do not only for my mom but because it's something not many people are willing to do. Whenever I've worried about my safety, I just think I'd be that much closer to my mom if my life ended. So it would be worth it if I died today.

But the drive-by shooting and the death threat have made me think for the first time how much I want to keep living. I want to keep working with young women like Laura and help them forgive themselves, believe in themselves, and follow their dreams. Even with all the curveballs the girls throw at me, the acceptance they have given me makes the danger worth it.

Angela once told me that 99.9 percent of people dislike their jobs. Every day I thank God I'm in that percent of people that like theirs. I wouldn't give it up for anything, except to have my mom back.

I pull up to the Airstream. Kiki, who's dressed in a sexy police pin-up costume, jumps in.

"What's this all about?" she asks.

"It's a really long story," I say. "And I haven't really figured out all the details yet. But what I do know is that Dylan is hiding something from me."

"Like what?"

"A police officer may have some information about Laura's assault."

"Wait. Slow down. Start over. Which assault? What police officer?" Kiki asks, confused.

"The one in the motel room. Dylan told me that a business card of a police officer was found in Laura's pocket when the forensic team was collecting evidence. But Dylan won't tell me who the police officer is and why his business card was in Laura's pocket," I explain.

I slow my Celica down at a lighted intersection on a main street and watch a man multitask. He's talking to himself while crossing the street in his tattered dark blue jeans held up with a brass belt buckle. His dirtied, cream-colored cowboy hat contrasts nicely against his red-and-white checkered shirt. Moments like this remind me that I'm sixty miles and a world apart from the coast.

"So what are you thinking the police officer knows about Laura's assault?" Kiki asks, interrupting my thoughts.

"I don't really know," I reply. "What I do know is that Dylan is not giving me the information. And I want to get it myself. I want to see that business card and find out who it belongs to."

"And then what?"

"Go talk to him," I say. "I don't want to go over Dylan's head, but this looks really bad. I just want to make sure that the Leafwood Police Department is looking into all potential suspects in the case, including one of their own."

"Gaby, you're crazy," Kiki says. "Are you out of your mind? If the Leafwood Police Department finds out that you're conducting an investigation into their investigation, do you know how pissed they're going to be?"

"Well, I can't just sit back and wait for Dylan to get me the information," I say. "I point blank asked him who the officer was and what this had to do with Laura's case. And he wouldn't answer me. He said he was still investigating it."

"Well then, let him investigate it and wait to see what he says," Kiki replies.

"Clown is in custody on the assault. We only have 'til Monday to file charges on him. And if we don't, he's gonna be released. My office is gonna want my recommendation. And part of it is based on whether I think there are other suspects. Dylan's dragging his feet. He hasn't given me an answer either way why a police officer is showing up in Laura's motel room," I say.

"This is crazy," says Kiki.

"Do you trust this guy that works in the property room?" I ask.

"Totally."

"Why?"

Kiki stays quiet, then opens the sun visor on her side leaning close to it looking in, before snapping it shut.

"I just do," she says finally. "We've been through a lot together."

"Like what?"

Kiki stays quiet and starts twirling her hair nervously.

"I've never told you this," she says. "But do you remember my ex-boyfriend? The guy I used to live with before I moved out here?"

"Yeah, vaguely," I say.

"I met him when I was doing wardrobe for that show."

"Oh, yeah."

"He used to hit me," says Kiki.

"Aw. Kiki, I'm sorry," I say.

She looks out the passenger window.

"So this guy who works in the property room. He was the only one I told when it was happening. I made him swear he wouldn't report anything and he never did," Kiki says sadly.

"Wow," I say.

"I know. But please don't judge me."

"I'm not. And Kiki, thanks for sharing that with me."

"I was just going through a rough period," she says. "He was showing me a lot of attention. I didn't really like myself back then. We only dated a few months. But I couldn't handle it anymore. The long distance relationship, plus getting hit when we saw each other, was getting really old. He'd tell me he was gonna stop, but he never did. My mom started getting really suspicious. Plus, she felt bad, cuz I watched the same thing happen to her."

"What made things change?" I ask.

"Someone told me to take one hard look at myself in the mirror and ask myself what the hell was I doing," Kiki says. "So I did. I realized I was canceling other dates so I could drive three hundred miles to spend time with him and get hit. I look back and think, 'What the hell was I thinking?'"

"Don't you think it's part of the cycle of violence? You were destined to have the same thing happen to you that happened to your mom," I say.

"Even when you're in the cycle, you can make a choice. You can write your own ending. It doesn't have to be based on what's happened to you in the past. Your destiny can end the way you write it," Kiki says.

"That's an interesting way to look at it."

"I feel like I have even more of a responsibility to stop the cycle, being a part of it and all," she continues. "Plus, I can't blame it on my mom anymore. My problem was that I didn't like myself. I got what I felt I deserved. I didn't realize I deserved much more."

"How did you end things with him?" I ask.

"We got into this huge fight. He threw my high heel at me and it hit me in the lip. I got this huge cut that started bleeding. I had to make up some story to my mom, saying it was from falling," Kiki replies.

Kiki's story reminds me of all the times I had to watch my mom make up excuses for her cuts and bruises. The worst time was when I almost missed my second grade school photo. My mom and stepfather got into it over the muffins she over-baked. He took her bare hand and forced her to take the hot pan out of the oven.

My mom was so busy treating her burns that I had to braid my own hair that morning. By the time we got to my school, the photographer was packing his stuff away. My mom convinced him to set back up. She told him we were having car trouble. I still have that class photo where my braids are lopsided.

I look back at Kiki.

"Was it hard to leave him?" I ask.

"I had to," she says. "I told Vince he hit me with my high heel. Vince told me I had to leave him or he was going to report him."

"So that's why you trust this guy?"

"Yeah."

I look at Kiki and smile at her.

"I'm glad you got out of that relationship," I say.

Kiki smiles back at me.

"I'm sure you know this," she says. "But if Dylan or the Leafwood Police Department doesn't want to tell you what's going on with that officer or how he's connected to Laura, chances are they're not going to let you find out, either."

"I know, but it's worth a shot," I say, punching the code Kiki hands me on a piece of paper into a small box at the back gate of the police department. We pull up to the side of a small building and park my car.

"Let's try and go through that door right there," says Kiki.

Within twenty minutes after arriving at the property room, I look at brown paper bags with yellow evidence labels. Kiki is leaning over the counter and making flirty small talk with Vince. I'm impressed by Kiki, who's batting her eyelashes and grinning at Vince. I begin to understand why she picked her police pin-up outfit to wear today.

I sort through thirty pieces of evidence, including the trash they collected outside the motel room. Crime scene technicians always collect all sorts of things, because no one knows what might be important later. One time, a fedora hat was collected from a crime scene in a case I prosecuted. A shooting had happened at a wedding reception and I was able to get the suspect's DNA off the hat, placing him at the scene.

The technicians in Laura's case even collected a plastic soda bottle and a cigarette found on the landing near room 333. Once I get to the thirtieth piece of evidence, I see an envelope that is entitled "card." It says, "Located in pants pocket southwest of victim location near bed." I turn the item over and notice that the bag is sealed.

"Kiki, this is the card I think I'm looking for," I say.

"Great, whose card is it?" she asks.

"I don't know, we need to open it up," I say.

"You want some scissors?" asks Kiki.

Once I cut open any piece of evidence, I'm forever in what's called the chain of evidence. Any person that cuts open an evidence bag must cut in a certain place on the bag, and not into someone else's cutting. Then, the bag must be sealed back up and initialed on the cutting. This guarantees that anyone who had access inside the bag is accounted for. It's a quality control measure that every police department in Tuckford County uses.

As a prosecutor, I never want to be in the chain of evidence, because then, I can become a witness. If there is some allegation the evidence is tainted, I could be called as a witness. For this reason, and the fact I don't want Dylan to know I was here, I'm not going to open it.

"Hey Vince, I've looked through pretty much everything. And it doesn't seem like there's anything I need to be concerned about. Most of it is just stuff from the crime scene, like fabric swatches, broken glass, and stuff like that. But there's a card in this envelope and I'm not quite sure who it belongs to. Do you think there's any way you could open it, so I can just take a peek? I want to make sure I'm not missing anything important," I say.

"Sure, where's the bag?" he asks.

Vince touches both sides of the bag trying to feel what's inside.

"I just want to make sure it's not drugs or blood. I can't open that stuff here. That's gotta be done in a lab," says Vince.

I stay quiet and smile at Vince.

"Nope, seems like it's some sort of document or something small I can't feel," says Vince.

Vince looks at Kiki and me.

"You know, before we open anything, I might want to get my supervisor down here," says Vince.

Kiki watches me tighten my lips together, then looks down at her watch before looking back at Vince.

"I *really* gotta get outta here. I have a wardrobe consultation in ten minutes. Would it be too much trouble for you to just open that up for her really quick? I *really* need to go," says Kiki, smiling at Vince.

Vince looks down like he's thinking for a couple seconds. Then, he opens a drawer and sorts through it. He starts to rearrange a stapler, some pens, and then a box of paper clips.

"Yeah, yeah, no problem. Only cuz it's you," says Vince, smiling at Kiki, reaching far back into a drawer and pulling out a pair of scissors. He begins cutting across the edge of the envelope very slowly and looks inside.

"Hmmm. Officer Hector Cruz. I know who that is," says Vince, facing the card towards Kiki and me.

"So do I," I say, remembering him as the one who saved my job pulling Clown over.

I widen my eyes at Kiki, alerting her I found what I came for.

"Can you do me a huge favor and not let anyone know we were here? This needs to stay between you, me, and Gaby," says Kiki.

"Sure, no worries. You guys know where to find him? Cuz he's been put on leave," says Vince.

"Can you tell us?" says Kiki in a soft sweet voice.

Vince grabs a yellow Post-it note, scribbles on it, then hands it to me. I read Cruz's home address as Kiki leans over to cheek kiss Vince.

Leaving the property room, Kiki and I wave 'bye to Vince. As the door shuts, he holds his pointer finger up to his lips motioning for us to stay quiet.

"Good call on the police pin-up outfit," I say, winking at Kiki.

Thirty minutes after leaving the property room, I stand outside the front door of Officer Cruz's home with Kiki. "I can hear someone inside," whispers Kiki.

"What can you hear?" I whisper back.

"It sounds like a TV," starts Kiki. "Do you think we should be here?" she says, changing the subject and looking afraid.

"What do we have to lose? He obviously knows Laura," I say.

"But who cares? You have Clown in custody already," says Kiki.

"And Cruz's card in her pocket," I snap back.

"I'm giving him one more minute to open the door. If not, I think we should get out of here," says Kiki.

"What's wrong?" I ask, jiggling the front door handle, checking to see if it's locked.

"Don't do that," says Kiki frantically.

"What is your problem?" I ask.

"Vince said to be careful. He said Cruz is kind of shady," says Kiki.

"And you decide to tell me this now?" I say.

"You were gonna come here regardless," Kiki snaps back.

She's right. She knows me pretty well. "It still woulda been nice to know," I say.

"Can we go now?" asks Kiki.

"Gimme a second," I say, noticing the side gate to Cruz's home propped open on the other side of the closed attached garage door.

It takes me all but thirty seconds to slip through the side gate of Cruz's rather large, roughly three thousand square foot home. No wonder they call these houses McMansions.

Tuckford county is filled with them. Low-income families could afford them until the recession hit along with the subprime mortgage bust and they all went into foreclosure. I walk past a sliding glass door on the side of the house and glance in. Cruz is sitting at his couch facing away from me watching a big screen TV. He takes a sip of his beer can, which is so obviously not his first. At least a handful of beer cans litter the floor around his couch along with a pizza box and some packets of either parmesan cheese or red pepper flakes. Beer bottles line the standing bar area leading to his open air kitchen and on his dining table that sits in a room close to the TV room.

Cruz's house phone rings, but he doesn't move or answer it. A Larry King show blares from the TV and music blasts throughout the house. The phone stops ringing and Cruz's voicemail picks up, which I can't make out. Someone leaves a message.

As Cruz gets up from the couch, I lose sight of him as he makes his way towards the kitchen.

Kiki comes walking back towards the sliding glass door. "Get down," I whisper commandingly.

I strain to hear what Cruz is doing in the kitchen. But Larry King's voice on the television blasts out interview questions.

"Let's get out of here, Gaby. I'm scared," says Kiki.

"Hold on," I mouth to her.

Kiki shakes her head back and forth, disagreeing with me before walking away.

I rush back towards the side gate, following Kiki back to the pathway leading past Cruz's front door to get back to my car. Suddenly, the front door opens from behind us.

We stop in our tracks.

Should I run?

Stay calm. Breathe. Walk steady.

I turn to face the front door. Cruz looks right through me, not even recognizing who I am. He balances his unsteady body with his hand against his door jamb.

"Can I help you with something?" Cruz says, slurring his words. I stare at Cruz, seeing my stepfather's face in his. So many times I tried to speak to my stepfather, but I could never have a decent conversation with him. He was always so drunk, so belligerent, and so mean. I always wanted to ask him why he treated my mom the way he did and why he ruined every opportunity I had to spend time with her. But anytime I'd get the courage to, he'd look at me with those same glassy eyes, that smell on his breath, those unsteady feet, and I would walk away.

"I'm sorry, sir, we have the wrong house," I say, turning to leave and exhaling as I hear the front door slam shut.

16

RUSH REQUEST

Within twenty minutes of leaving Cruz's home, Kiki and I stand in the lobby at the Crime Lab with criminalist Miranda Jules.

"Miss Jules," I begin. "I know that you're not supposed to talk about these things until they're reviewed, but my office is going to be making a filing decision Monday. I came here to ask if you could share the results of your DNA analysis with me."

"Well, I do understand the time constraints you have for your filing decision," Miranda says. "However, it has always been my practice to wait until my work has been reviewed before I disclose it."

"How long is that going to take?"

"At least thirty-six hours."

"Does that include the weekend?"

"We're talking about business hours. I already rushed all the analysis for you. I'm not going to ask my supervisor to work the weekend to accommodate your office. We are, as you know, understaffed and in a major budget crisis right now," Miranda says.

"I understand that and I don't want to rush anyone," I say. "But our office needs to make a filing decision on whether or not the person we have in custody is actually the person who committed the crime."

"Well, Dylan seems to be sure you guys have the right guy," Miranda says. "In fact, when I spoke to him a little while ago, he didn't seem to care about knowing the results at all. He told me not to rush anything."

"I'm not speaking about Dylan," I say impatiently. "And Dylan's not making the filing decision in this case. I am, or at least I'm going to present the case in a staffing on Monday. And I'm trying to get prepared. I'm just asking you to let me know preliminarily what the results are. I'm not gonna hold you to it or even mention it, but I just personally want to know if we have the right person. I can't file a case until I believe I can prove it beyond a reasonable doubt."

I stare at Jules, wanting to rip off her glasses or grab her by the throat. It takes all of me to stay calm while I listen to her. She lowers her voice.

"Look," Miranda says curtly, "I know you're probably thinking there are other criminalists here in this laboratory that have no problem sharing this information with you. But like I said when we first met, that is not my procedure.

"There's a reason that I'm well respected in the community, by the laboratory, by the state licensing committee, criminal defense attorneys, and prosecutors. It's because I hold myself to higher standards. And what that means is that I follow the rules. I don't cut corners. Or do favors. I do my work."

Just twenty-four hours ago, this same woman seemed so much more helpful. I decide to remind her, since I can't keep my mouth shut.

"You were willing to do us a favor and rush the DNA in this case when Dylan was here. Did that have anything to do with it?" I ask.

"This has nothing to do with Dylan. I don't know what your problem is with me," Miranda says. "I did you a favor by rushing this case because you told me how important it was to you. I've been working on this case non-stop since yesterday. You showed me a picture of your victim and I did everything I could to help. But I'm not going to rush my supervisors and ask them to work through the weekend just to accommodate you."

"Of course you won't. Let's pretend I tell you it's important to Dylan. *Now* how do you feel about rushing it?" I ask in a sarcastic tone.

"Ms. Ruiz, this has nothing to do with Dylan," Miranda says.

"Don't tell me he asked you to delay this?"

"No, he hasn't."

"Which supervisor is going to be doing the administrative review?" I ask.

"I don't know because it hasn't been assigned yet," she replies.

I decide to raise my voice to get my point across.

"What do you mean it hasn't been assigned?" I ask. "I specifically asked this case be given priority. We have to make a filing decision by Monday. And I'm only asking you for some preliminary results."

Lloyd Stanley, the crime lab supervisor, opens the door, which leads to the main area of the Crime Lab. He peeks his head into the lobby.

"Is everything okay out there?" asks Lloyd.

"No, it's not," I say. "I'm trying to get some preliminary information on DNA results and Ms. Jules can't help me because they still need to be reviewed."

"Well, I'm the person who's going to be doing the review, so maybe I can answer some questions for you. Why don't we go down to the conference room?" says Lloyd.

"Thank you," I say, walking past and ignoring Miranda as I follow Lloyd into the Crime Lab with Kiki.

Kiki and I sit near each other at the same conference table I sat with Dylan yesterday. Lloyd sits down next to Miranda.

"What do you want to know?" Lloyd asks.

"Anything you can tell me. Let's start with the belt that was tied around her wrists. How many profiles were found on that?" I ask.

"I can answer that," Miranda says. "I've created a report based on how many different profiles there were. Other than Laura's DNA, there was one other person found on the actual belt. But the results need to go through administrative review. It's especially important in this case, which I'm sure Lloyd will agree with, because it needs to get uploaded into the DNA database."

Any unknown DNA profiles found on crime scene evidence are uploaded into the DNA database. This means that the DNA Miranda found on the belt is not Clown's. If it was his, she would know since we gave her his DNA sample.

"Something you need to understand from my standpoint is the importance of the technical review, especially in this case, because it's getting uploaded in the database. My findings need to be one hundred percent correct. Because uploading an inaccurate profile can subject some innocent person to prosecution if there was a match. This is why we need to stick to the rules," Miranda explains.

I think for a second how I've been subjected to all kinds of inaccurate matches lately, at least with online dating. This morning, I was matched with Bo, a five-foot-six man with a few extra pounds; he has three kids, completed up to high school, and owns a car. The database thought we were a good match because we both like dogs. If online dating websites had the same quality assurance as DNA, maybe I wouldn't be subjected to so much persecution. After all, I'm an innocent single female, too.

I look back at Miranda.

"There are strict regulations set by the state that require this lab to follow rules before the profile is uploaded," she says.

"I fully understand, Ms. Jules," I say. "I understand how the integrity of your laboratory is important. I know that you hold state regulations and your license with high regard. This lab and your work is your livelihood. I get it. And I want to respect that. So in order for you to upload that profile into the database and search it against other DNA profiles, that means one thing. You don't know whose DNA is on the belt. That means it's not Clown's."

Miranda stays silent. Kiki looks at me with big eyes.

"You're one smart prosecutor," says Lloyd, winking at me.

"What about the swabs that were taken from Laura's vagina? Do you know how many people she had sex with?"

"I produced a report on that, too. It appears the DNA of two separate men were found inside her vagina; one being a major profile and the other being a minor profile."

A major profile is a simple way of saying there's more DNA there. It probably means it's from someone who ejaculated a lot, recently. A minor profile is someone who was there further back in time, or ejaculated less than the major guy. Basically, Laura had sex with two guys recently. But for my purposes, all I care about is who last had sex with her at the motel and left her for dead. I got the hang of how Miranda would be willing to answer these questions where she would not be violating her ethical obligations. So I asked her questions in her own language, the scientific psychobabble that she wanted.

"Let me ask you this. Will either of the DNA profiles that you found inside Laura's vagina be uploaded into the DNA database, too?"

"Yes, one of them will be. The other one does not need to be."

Bingo. What Miranda just told me was that one of the vagina profiles belongs to Clown. The other one was unknown and that's why it needs to be uploaded into the database.

"Let me ask you one more question. Which profile will be uploaded into the database? The major or the minor one?"

Miranda stays quiet and glares at me. She doesn't want to answer my question.

"The major DNA profile will be uploaded into the database. We know who the minor belongs to," says Lloyd.

What Lloyd just told me was that whoever last had sex with Laura is not Clown; it's someone else.

"When will these profiles be uploaded into the database?" I ask.

"By the end of the day," says Lloyd.

"One last thing," I say. "Was there anything found on the flamingo vase?"

"Oh, that's what that thing is. I could tell by the body it was a bird. But I couldn't tell what kind with the head broken off," says Miranda laughing, finally lightening up. "There's nothing significant about the blood on the vase. It was Laura's along with traces of other people," Miranda says.

"What do you mean traces?" I ask.

"I wouldn't be concerned with the trace DNA. That could be people that just touched the vase at some point in the past. It could belong to the cleaning lady or another motel guest. Plus, that vase was lying on the floor, where people walk and shed skin cells or drip semen on the way to the bathroom. The trace DNA can be from any of those sources. Laura got assaulted in a dirty motel room and you're going to have a lot of DNA in there. But it's not all going to be forensically relevant.

"You should be focusing on the fingerprint on the vase Dylan told me you guys had. And I'm assuming that belongs to her boyfriend," says Miranda.

"You're right, that would be assuming," I say.

"Excuse me?" asks Miranda.

"Dylan didn't tell you?" I ask sarcastically.

"Tell me what?" Miranda asks.

"It's not his print," I say.

Silence fills the room and Miranda looks like I just told her she had cancer.

17

WHAT DO YOU KNOW

Later in the evening after leaving the Crime Lab, I groove to the rhythm sounds and Reggae music at the Island Bar. I dance close to Bill, my dating website match whom I met three hours ago for the first time after three weeks of exchanging boring emails and phone conversations. This is the part I hate about being single. Every Friday night, I force myself to go out on random dates, usually with men I meet online. I started doing this a year ago after coming to terms with the fact Dylan and I were probably over.

I reach down to make sure my pager is still on my hip attached to my low-cut jeans. I'm not supposed to drink alcohol or let anything get in the way of me and a dead body within one hour when I'm on the homicide pager. I feel the pager vibrating against my hip as Bill is grinding up on my leg.

"What was that?" he asks.

"I'm sorry. Remember, I told you I'm on call," I say.

"Oh, yeah. Do you gotta go?" asks Bill.

I wonder if it's Kiki, whom I had asked to page me while I'm on my date. She's my escape route if the date wasn't going well.

"Let me see who's calling. I'll be back."

I make my way through the bar, sliding through the Paris Hilton and Jersey Shore lookalikes in their tan wedge sandals and short skirts, and onto the sidewalk of the main highway. I instantly smell the salt in the air and hear the waves crashing over the loud voices of the drunken patrons.

I get a closer look at the pager and recognize Dylan's number. A part of me wants to turn around and go back into the bar and grind on Bill the rest of the night. Dylan still hadn't returned my calls since I left the Crime Lab. I feel as though he's blowing me off. Another part of me wants to walk down to the Cove and just zone out and ask for answers.

Just as my eyes start tearing up, I remember that I'm paid to answer the homicide pager, and this could be about an entirely different death having nothing to do with my relationship with Dylan. I pick up my cell phone and start dialing Dylan's number.

"This is Gaby Ruiz, I'm returning a call to the homicide pager," I say.

"So professional. You didn't recognize my number?" says Dylan playfully.

I stay silent.

"Gaby, it's Dylan."

"Hi, Dylan, what's up?" I say.

"Well, we have another homicide," he says. "Officer Cruz was found dead in his car parked in his garage that was torched. We're investigating it as an arson homicide. Some ground samples taken from the garage came back positive for igniter fluid."

"Are you serious?" I ask.

"Yeah, I am. This investigation just keeps getting better and better," says Dylan.

"Cruz was placed on administrative leave. We asked him to come in for a mandatory interview Monday afternoon regarding Laura's case. Then I got this call a few hours ago," he says.

"Dylan, why didn't you tell me about Cruz sooner?" I ask. "We have a staffing in three days. And why didn't you return my calls today? Laura's in a coma, Javier's case was dismissed, and now Cruz is dead? I mean, is this for real? Is it just me or is something strange going on?"

"What are you talking about?" Dylan says, exasperated. "Don't talk to me like I'm supposed to have all the answers. You know how this works. I can't work miracles. Why don't you go and ask your angels what the heck is going on if you think it's that easy? We found Cruz's card in Laura's pocket and I told you I was looking into it. The Leafwood Police Department forced him to go on administrative leave while we were investigating his connection to Laura.

"We asked him to come in and give a statement about why his card was found in Laura's pocket. Then he turns up dead. Now you're telling me things are strange. I don't know what the heck is going on. But what I do know is that I'm calling you because you're the on-call prosecutor and I have to," says Dylan angrily.

I hear a dial tone.

He hung up on me. Just as I'm fantasizing about calling him every cuss word I can think of, I see him calling me back.

"I'm sorry. I just needed to cool down," says Dylan.

"Dylan, why are you just calling me now and why didn't you call me earlier to let me know you had an interview set up with Cruz?" I ask. "I told you from the start I wanted to be involved in every part of this investigation. But instead, I'm finding out hours later that you were planning this interview. And now, you're calling to tell me that Cruz is dead.

"I don't know if you think I'm a joke or because I'm just a female prosecutor that you don't have to keep me in the loop. I'm sick of this. I've given you a lot of leeway. Do you realize that my job depends on this, my supervisor asks for updates, and Tanner sometimes calls her out on the carpet if she's not being kept in the loop?" I say frustrated.

"Gaby," says Dylan, trying to calm me.

"You might think it's just a fun game, but I don't. I don't want to get in trouble. And people are getting demoted left and right these days with the economy tanking. Tanner already told me I'm off the case as soon as we staff this thing. The least you can do is help me save face.

"I'm going to be asked questions on Monday like why should we file on Clown, was there anyone else involved, why shouldn't we be looking at Cruz. Now I have to get up to speed on all of this because you didn't have the professional courtesy to keep me in the loop," I say.

"You know what? If I friggin' knew what Cruz had to do with this, I'd be more motivated to invite you down to the station," Dylan says. "But his interview had to do with an internal investigation by the Police Administration. They were going to interview Cruz as an employee, not a suspect. You wouldn't be able to use his interview because it's forced and not voluntary.

"I'm confident Clown is our guy. Cruz's card being found in her pocket is a red herring. He was either in there sleeping with Laura or she had his card from some past investigation. I'm confident he didn't assault Laura in that room. I'm one hundred percent sure it's Clown."

"When were you going to talk to me about all the DNA findings?" I ask.

"Why don't you ask Ford? The Leafwood Police Department is still leading the investigation, both Laura's case and now Cruz's internal investigation. I'm working alongside these officers and don't really know who's in charge."

"Look, I'm trying," Dylan says. "I'm keeping you in the loop as much as I can. I'm now in charge of Cruz's homicide, because he's actually dead and possibly connected to a sex case. So it's the Special Homicide Team's jurisdiction. I can do more with this case now and direct what's investigated."

"I can't believe this. So where should I meet you?" I ask.

"At Cruz's home. 1123 Citrus Avenue. It's in Leafwood. Do you need directions?"

"I know where it is," I say without thinking. "I mean I'll GPS it," I say backtracking, not wanting Dylan to know about my visit to Cruz's house.

"Sorry," says Dylan, changing the subject.

"For what?"

"For everything," says Dylan.

"Don't worry about it. Thanks, though," I say.

"No really, I'm sorry. You're right. I should have called you back or let you know what was going on with Cruz. But I couldn't go over the Lieutenant's head. He decided how to handle the internal investigation and all."

"It's okay. Stop worrying about it. It's fine. I'm fine. Things are all good on my end. I'll see you in a bit," I say.

11:52 p.m. blinks in red on my dashboard. I park my car, get out, and start walking, feeling a sense of déjà vu. Once I get past the crime scene tape bordering not only Cruz's house but two houses on each side, I see Dylan walking towards me. The smell of his cologne and his big blue eyes never quit being my biggest weaknesses.

"Do you want a walk-through?" asks Dylan.

"Sure," I say.

"Go ahead and put these on," says Dylan, handing me a white cloth mask and a big yellow and black firefighter-looking coat.

"Standing in there more than a minute, the smoke really starts getting to you," he says.

I have never been in a place that had been burned. I always imagined that when buildings burn, they burn to the ground. But here, Cruz's garage is still intact, just completely charred, black, and wilted. The heaviness of the air and thickness of the garage begins to overwhelm me. My hot recycled breath inside the mask isn't much better than breathing in the barbecue-smelling garage.

The ceiling, an ashy grey and black color, looks like it is about to come crumbling down. The tools, gardening supplies, electrical wires, paint canisters, and automotive parts neatly line the wall units in the garage, but are charred and singed.

The dust still settling around and darkness throughout the garage makes it hard to focus in on anything. Firefighters and investigators walk in and out of the garage. Given everything is charred, it doesn't seem as important to preserve the crime scene. We creep our way a few yards to the Suburban.

Cruz lies on the slightly reclined seat like he is the rotting skeleton in the Pirates of the Caribbean ride at Disneyland perched up on top of a bed full of gold. But there is no gold; it is all dust, ash, and burned car seat. He looks peaceful, otherwise unrecognizable because of the burn and blackness to his face. His hands rest to his sides and he's sitting upright.

The window of his truck is down and all the doors are open. A cool nighttime breeze sends the smell of cow manure and charbroil seeping into my mask. The once tan interior of the SUV is now burned in sections. Firefighters in big yellow suits cut out samples of the floorboard carpet and fabric from the seats.

"The fire started right here," says Dylan, pointing at a black area on the ground near the corner of the garage.

"They are collecting samples to test them for lighter fluid or any sort of flammable liquids to see if that's what was used to ignite the fire. The preliminary results tested positive for lighter fluid, but they just need to confirm those samples. There was a can of fluid found on one of the shelves in here and it looks like a cigarette was lit in this area of the garage causing the fire.

"The fire started about ten feet from where Cruz was found. When the fire department arrived, his revolver was found next to the car door. Apparently he kept this gun unsecured in his nightstand. He has a bullet wound to his chest. That's all we have," Dylan says.

"Wow. What do you think happened?" I ask.

"I'm not jumping to any conclusions. I've learned my lesson not to. But I do know we'll get to the bottom of this. I know we'll need an answer by Monday as to what involvement he had with Laura. So that will be my next focus," Dylan says.

"Tell me more about the card found in the motel," I say.

"There's really nothing more than what I told you," Dylan says.

"Was he told why he was being put on admin leave?" I ask.

"He definitely knew we found the card in the motel. The Sergeant advised him that was the reason he was being put on leave. Speaking of which, this is the Sergeant right now," Dylan says, answering his phone and leaving the garage.

"Is it normal that the structure is intact like this?" I ask a firefighter standing near Cruz's body.

"Oh yeah, usually just all the smoke causes this blackness you're seeing throughout the garage. The flames jump around but are not touching a lot of the structure. This fire was very centered in the corner of the garage and the flames went straight up from where it started. It's the smoke inhalation and heat that causes all the destruction and causes people to die. People usually don't die because they're getting touched by the flames. But with a bullet wound like that," he says, pausing and pointing at Cruz, "he would've died before anything having to do with this fire," he says.

"Wow, I never realized most deaths occur from inhalation," I say, watching Dylan walking towards me, waving something in his hand.

"I just found the answer," he yells.

Between the smell of fire and male testosterone surrounding me, the circle I'm standing in near Cruz's truck alongside the firefighters and officers feels like a campfire meeting with Boy Scouts. I stand next to Dylan as he opens a small diary and starts reading it out loud.

"I wanted to say goodbye. I think it's best I end it this way. This will be the end of my career and I can't imagine life not being an officer. I'm sorry," reads Dylan, closing the diary.

"He had to be involved in Laura's assault," I say.

"I think you're wrong," says Dylan.

"Then why would he go to this extreme?" I ask.

"Being involved with Laura in prostitution would have damaged his career. It's understandable why he ended things. It would be humiliating," says Dylan.

"I think Cruz had more to hide than just a relationship with Laura," I say.

"What are you saying, Ms. Ruiz?" asks Ford.

"I'm saying that he's still a potential suspect who hasn't been ruled out in the motel assault. Can we make sure his blood is taken during the autopsy? I'd like to compare his DNA to the DNA found on the belt and inside Laura," I say.

"It was Clown's DNA inside Laura," says Dylan.

"Yeah, as the minor donor. There's a major donor still out there. I'm curious to see whether it's Cruz. There was also an unknown profile found on the belt. I'd like to see if he matches that," I say.

"He wouldn't be the match on the belt," says Dylan.

"How do you know that?" I say.

"Because that is an X-profile. It belongs to a woman," says Dylan.

"Clown is our guy and all of us standing here, including Dylan and the Leafwood Police Department, are in agreement that he's our guy. This agency is not going to spend resources looking at anyone else, including Officer Cruz. It's ridiculous that he would have killed this girl. Of course if you'd like, we can take a look at who that X-profile belongs to. I hear you may have been one of the last people to see Laura alive," says Ford threateningly.

It didn't take long for the brass to throw up a stone wall around me, especially because Officer Cruz was at the heart of the investigation now.

18

THE STAFFING

Dylan and I sit quietly on the thirteenth floor of the Tuckford County Prosecutor's Office. The adrenaline pumping from being on the power floor of this building numbs my early Monday blues. This floor houses most of the brainpower of the office. It is occupied by the appointed prosecutor and several special assistant prosecutors who advise her.

The moments right before a staffing are always unsettling for two people: the prosecutor who is presenting the case and the investigator helping. Basically, that means Dylan and me, since Detective Ford and the Leafwood Police Sergeant said they're not coming. There's a lot of pressure during a staffing because time is of the essence. Usually the case needs to get filed later the same morning. A staffing can leave you feeling entirely incompetent. But it's all for a good reason — so the bigwigs can make the proper filing decision.

The thirty minutes of hell during a staffing is basically a chance for the top prosecutors to nitpick every phase of the investigation and point out anything that has not been done. But it's all for good reason. These meetings provide an inordinate amount of experience and brainpower collectively in one room. It's invaluable when making the important decisions that come out of these type of meetings, like homicide charges and sentencing decisions. No investigation is perfect, so someone's feelings or ego are destined to get bruised during a staffing. I just hope it's not mine.

The prosecutor's plump secretary, Mary Eddington, walks out of her office towards me, smiling and holding a jar of candy. She sits down on a chair near Dylan and me.

"They should be done in there shortly. They're having another staffing. What is this one about, sweetie?" asks Mary.

"This is the case that I was prosecuting with the girl who lives in the trailer park where I host The Mamacita Club. She had been sexually abused by her stepfather. Remember that one?" I say.

"Yes, I do. Whatever happened with that case?" Mary asks.

"She was supposed to testify in that trial and she never showed up. I found her practically dead in a motel room, and it looks like her boyfriend who was pimping her may have done it. But the investigation is still ongoing, so it will be interesting to see what they decide," I say.

"Is this a staffing for a homicide, life case, or what should I put on the memo?" she asks.

"It definitely will have a punishment of fifteen years to life. But it's not a homicide," I reply. "Laura's not dead and we have the suspect booked on attempted murder charges right now, so I'll be asking for a decision on that. He's being arraigned this afternoon. It's just a matter of time before she dies. She's not even on life support anymore. I'm leaving on vacation in a week, so I wanted to get some direction before I leave."

"Honey, I'm so sorry," Mary says sympathetically. "I know you really tried to get that girl into your club."

"Thank you," I say. "It's been tough, but I just want to bring justice for her. I promised her that."

Mary's warm smile calms my nerves. I always wonder how much of her niceness over the years has been to help Mike Tanner build a rapport with me, something I've refused to do since I've worked here. When I was hired, Mary was Mike Tanner's secretary and she knew a lot about my mom's case.

I decided a long time ago not to give Tanner a chance to make amends, ever. But he doesn't seem to quit trying. I've been known to hold grudges, sometimes for years. Early on in my career, Mary made it a point to tell me that Mike Tanner spoke highly of my trial skills. He awarded me twice for top prosecutor of the office. I didn't say anything to him both years I walked on stage of the Annual Award Banquet to receive my awards. I didn't want any part of his efforts to make peace with me.

Mary Eddington still makes nice, warm, and friendly conversation every time I see her. And I think Tanner is just grateful she connects with me. I like Mary; women like her fill the void from the absence of my own mom.

"Oh, it looks like they're finishing up. Why don't you give them about five minutes and then go ahead and make your way into the conference room? I'll bring copies of your memo in and write Life Case and Possible Homicide Staffing on it. Good luck," says Mary warmly.

Dylan and I make our way into the conference room and sit next to each other in the plush leather chairs that surround a mahogany table. Several bigwig supervisors and the appointed Prosecutor Debra Miller stand around chatting about what sounds like the staffing that just ended. The panoramic view reminds me of the status of the thirteenth floor. It's rare to view the Castle from the same vantage point as the freeway all in the same room.

Stevie Sapp comes in and sits across from me. I almost want to vomit at the sight of her face, especially dreading what comments she'll have for me this time.

She doesn't waste any time to lay in. "I heard there was a *drive-by* shooting at the trailer park," says Stevie in her usual broken record voice, slowly emphasizing the words drive-by.

"There was," I say quickly and look down to my phone.

"This was the exact thing I was worried about. Has Vanderbilt spoken with you yet? And do we have any leads?" asks Stevie.

"No and no," I start. "It's probably the typical gang member drive-by. It just comes with the territory. And we've explained the danger to the girls. They still want to continue with the club for now," I say dismissively.

"This whole thing is concerning. Not to mention the pin-up thing you're doing. I just learned about that. And I must say, it's rather disturbing," says Stevie.

"That's a shame because it's helped us have some really good breakthroughs with the girls," I say.

"I just think you should find a theme that is a little more...how should I say this? A little more respectable than pin-up girls," she says.

"Like what? *Just Say No?* Do you think that campaign has really worked in the last twenty years?"

"Well, maybe not that, but my daughter's school uses the American Girl dolls and the slogan *It's Cool to Finish School.*"

"These girls are not upper-class, conservative beach city brats. They live in trailer parks. My club works because it's memorable to *them* and that's what *these* girls need. They're dropouts," I say.

"That's an interesting perspective you have. But it sounds rather risky. And it definitely looks risqué. Especially when you're wearing stuff like this," says Stevie, pointing towards the pin curls in my hair and the collar of my white polka dot blouse.

"We're not provocative pin-ups, we're professional ones. Our pin-up gear keeps the girls interested in the club because they can relate to this kind of stuff," I say, pointing to the red flower barrette near my ear holding up my pin curls.

"They don't relate to this kind of stuff," I say, pulling my shiny prosecutor badge out of my portfolio.

"And they certainly wouldn't understand that," I say, pointing to the ruffles on Stevie's white high collar Victorian shirt.

"But you're promoting promiscuity."

"Actually, we do the opposite."

"I can't imagine how," says Stevie balkingly, grinning at Dylan and shrugging one of her shoulders.

"We use the pin-ups to teach the girls about drugs, alcohol, sex, and abusive relationships," I say. "It's not any different from the rest of the costumes in our wardrobe. We have Hollywood starlets in there and even ones like Angelina Jolie and J-Lo."

"Angelina Jolie and J-Lo, huh?" says Dylan flirtingly.

"Yeah. Angelina's costume helps teach the girls about humanitarianism and social justice. J-Lo's good for Latina empowerment. Madonna's in there, too," I say.

"What on earth could Madonna teach?" says Stevie sarcastically.

"We use her songs *Papa Don't Preach* and *Touched Like a Virgin* to teach about sexual independence and teen pregnancy. We used the Eva Peron role she played in the musical Evita to help the girls understand about community service and cancer," I say righteously.

"The Evita concept is at least respectable. Much more than the pin-up selection of your wardrobe," says Stevie.

"What can I say? The pin-ups have been working. We've been having the girls pick a famous pin-up girl and research what she stands for, what she doesn't, and any poor choices she made along the way."

"Okay?" says Stevie, sarcastically.

"They help teach the girls how to make better choices."

"I'm still not getting it."

"Just the other day we debated whether the trampy styles and fetishes of pin-up queen Bettie Page demean women or empower them. We've also talked about Marilyn Monroe's sexcapades and drug overdose, and the fact Rita Hayworth was an alcoholic who married and divorced five times."

"And you're having success with this?" says Stevie disbelievingly, looking away from me towards an antique clock on a side table.

"Yep," I say. "The girls are going to be on a panel next month discussing pop culture. They'll be debating whether Katy Perry is a positive or negative role model for young women today. They've sold a hundred and fifty tickets so far at local high schools. These girls can relate to stuff like pin-up models because they're real life women with real life problems, not beach city plastic dolls," I say, looking down at Stevie's boob job, which she had three years ago.

"I guess I just would never allow my own girls in your club," Stevie says condescendingly. "The whole pin-up thing just seems like a major setback for women."

"What are you talking about? Pin-ups are a part of this country's history. We sent five million copies of Betty Grable's pin-up photo to GIs in World War II. It was something to distract them from the war they were fighting and a reason to come home."

"Exactly, during a *war*."

"The girls in this county are fighting a war here, too," I counter.

"Against who? Themselves?"

"Drugs, gangs, prostitution, bullying, broken homes, racism, I can go on and on. Every girl in The Mamacita Club has lost a friend to gang violence. Some of them have lost more than four people. They hear gunshots at night and don't feel safe living where they do. Some of them have used drugs and have been abused," I say.

"I still think pin-ups are counterproductive."

"If we used pin-ups to help the U.S. Military, why can't we use them to help the criminal justice system?"

"Those were for *men*. And *we're* better than that," says Stevie, pointing to the two of us, leaving Dylan out.

"By whose standards?"

"American female standards. *Our* standards," she says again, pointing at me and her.

"Maybe you should get out of your beach city bubble and visit countries like South America, where women's naked bodies grace billboards for things like everyday body lotion and reproductive health, not for casinos, strip clubs, and reality shows. Sculptures of voluptuous women are displayed in open plazas like Botero in South America," I say.

"Well, like I said, Vanderbilt will sort this whole thing out. Don't break your crayons over it if he says it's over. There are plenty of programs out there for these girls. You don't need to save the world. You picked a really tough crowd who doesn't even want to better themselves. No one forced them to drop out of school," Stevie says.

"How does our education system expect them to succeed when they live in places that aren't safe? They need a solid support system and mentorship. That's what The Mamacita Club is designed to do. No one else wants to help them," I say.

"I say that's better left to teachers. Our job is to focus on crime."

"Do you know what the best way to reduce the crime rate is?"

"Locking 'em up?" Stevie says rudely.

As Stevie rocks her aloofness back into her swivel chair, I rest my hands on the conference table and interlock my fingers tight enough so I can't punch her.

"No, Stevie," I say, matching her rude tone. "The most effective way to reduce the crime rate is to get kids to graduate high school."

"I've never heard that."

"The research is clear. And we're part of the equation. As Hillary Clinton said, 'It takes a village to raise a child.' We use these kids as witnesses in our cases, make them recall the horrifying memories of what they witnessed, then just send them on their merry way. We have an obligation to them. But most times we don't ever see them again. I just think we can make a difference if we try," I say.

"We help the community plenty. Every day, we lock up the bad guys and keep the streets safe. Going beyond that is what our social system is for. That's what Child Protective Services and social workers do. Why would you want to be a social worker when you went to school for so many years and have a law degree?" says Stevie.

"If the community knows there are people like us out there to help these kids, wouldn't they be more likely to come forward to testify or be part of the solution in bettering their community?"

"Sure, but that's not our job."

"I think you're wrong. I believe our responsibility extends beyond the courtroom," I say.

"All I can say is that I'm glad you're doing this charity work or whatever you want to call it and not me. I hope they appreciate all you're doing for them. Because after all the time and effort you put in, the impact I'd assume is rather small."

Stevie looks down at her watch then looks right back at me to add insult to injury.

"Maybe this whole thing will help move your focus in the direction of kids. Don't you want to have kids?"

The pressure in my head makes me feel like I'm about to explode.

"Nope. You can have them, I'll help them," I say.

My attempt to insult Stevie back, who just announced she's pregnant with her third child, seems to work. She looks away from me. My snide remark is a lie and a dig I like to use on people when they ask questions about me having kids. I don't know if I'm bothered more by Stevie's comments about having my own kids or her disdain at my club. Little does she know how much these girls have accepted me for who I am. Helping them has taught me about unconditional love. They've said things like, "This club has changed my life" and "I love you guys."

I want to tell Stevie that "She has a right to criticize who has a heart to help," but Stevie is such an unremarkable woman other than her pristine trial record, which doesn't count for much with me. She's an effective trial lawyer, but her view of the world is very narrow. She will never understand my passion, my calling, or the deal I have with my angels to help women. Only people like Angela, Riley, Kiki, and Mary really understand who I am and what I stand for.

Mary walks into the conference room and hands out the memo that I typed this morning. The room quiets down as everyone starts to read it.

Special Assistant Prosecutors Stevie Sapp and Mike Tanner, Division Managers Scott Crandall and Tom Cha, and the Appointed Prosecutor Debra Miller study the memo. Debra Miller was nominated and appointed by the governor ten years ago. She focuses her efforts on spending reduction, community outreach, and imposing harsh penalties for sex offenders, which the community is always on board with. Plus, she's a big supporter of The Mamacita Club.

Everyone continues to study the memo, sighing at different moments. I started the memo with a summary of the crime scene and the way Laura was found in the motel, then laid out all the evidence we have on the case, and what each witness said. Mike Tanner scans through the memo quickly and flips back and forth through the pages like he would have organized it differently.

Tanner flips to the last page. I concluded the memo with a long list. Each bullet point details in chronological order the crimes from Clown's past. It includes his two violent priors — one for carjacking another gang member at gunpoint, and one for breaking into a house. He served a total of six years in and out of state prison.

I know Tanner is interested in how bad of a guy he is. A lot of times filing decisions are driven by a defendant's criminal background. If a criminal defendant had the chance to reform himself and chose not to, we're less likely to cut him a break.

"Ms. Ruiz, I will let you have the floor. Why don't you tell us about the attempted murder to Laura?" says Tanner.

All eyes focus on me.

"This case started the moment investigator Dylan Mack from the Special Homicide Team and I stepped foot into a motel room in Leafwood. We went to Motel Leafwood around ten o'clock in the morning last Wednesday looking for Laura, who didn't show up to testify in an unrelated case I was handling. When Dylan and I walked into the motel room, it was pure horror. I have never seen anything like it in all the crime scenes I've been to. By all appearances, it seemed the motel room had been burglarized, and Laura had been raped and left for dead."

"What condition is she in now?" asks Stevie Sapp.

"She's sitting over at the Tuckford Memorial Hospital in a coma."

"Why are we here then? This isn't even a homicide case," says Stevie.

"It's just a matter of time before she dies," says Dylan.

"Don't her chances of pulling through increase every day that passes?" asks Stevie.

I smile at the idea of Laura pulling through.

"Don't forget, this is a defendant facing life. So it doesn't matter if she's dead for staffing purposes," says Tanner, snapping back at Stevie.

"She has a couple of doctors baffled, including the Director of the trauma unit, Dr. Lee. Since she hit the hospital doors, she has not spoken. But she's breathing and now she's off all feeding tubes. It's been five days," I say.

"Is that why you're involved? Because you assumed it would be a homicide?" asks Stevie, looking at Dylan.

"Exactly," says Dylan.

"What evidence do we have she was raped?" asks Tanner.

"The way she was found — naked, blindfolded, bound by her wrists, her panties around her ankles," says Dylan.

"But the VAT nurse didn't find any injuries consistent with rape," says Tanner.

This is the part of every staffing that becomes tense. You really can't sugarcoat things with skilled litigators like Mike Tanner. He's fearless, he sees through everything, and he's a relentless cross-examiner. And the other supervisors seem to like sitting back to watch the show when one of their own can tear apart an investigator or a young prosecutor like myself. I interject, wanting Tanner to get off Dylan's back. "Mr. Tanner, you're right, but oftentimes there are no injuries in rape cases. Remember, it's normal to be normal," I say, rattling off the typical doctor expert lingo they use while testifying in rape cases.

"Okay. Why would Clown ransack the room he rented?" Tanner asks.

"A ruse. To make it seem it was a random act, like a burglary gone bad," says Dylan.

"Why would he want to hurt Laura?" asks Tanner.

"For a couple possible reasons. Laura could have been trying to get away from him. It's common for gang member pimps to discipline their prostitutes. They want to teach them a lesson and teach other prostitutes what will happen if they try leaving the ring. It's pretty common for them to rape the prostitute then assault her like this," says Dylan.

"You talk about there being unknown DNA profiles, one from Laura's vaginal swab and another on the belt. Do we have any suspicion who those belong to?"

"As for the belt used to bound her, the DNA belongs to a female, but not Laura. I'm thinking it's either Bess's or Gaby's. Bess confirmed it was her belt and Laura borrowed it," says Dylan.

"Why would you think Gaby's DNA would be on the belt?" Tanner asks.

"I loosened the belt when I found her," I say.

Stevie looks up from focusing on the memo.

"Let me get this right. You think the lead prosecutor's DNA may be on the murder weapon?" asks Stevie.

Debra Miller and Mike Tanner glare at Stevie.

"Stevie, having trace DNA of medical personnel or officers on key pieces of evidence can happen," says Tanner.

"Not if it's properly handled and gloves are used," says Stevie.

I start to feel really hot all over my body.

"I was trying to save her life. I didn't have time to look for gloves," I say, carefully selecting my words and not even looking at Stevie.

"Let's move on from this point," says Debra Miller.

"What else are we looking into?" asks Tanner.

"The second profile on the vaginal swab. That belongs to a man, but we are still looking into that right now," says Dylan.

"It's not Clown?" asks Stevie.

"No, I'm guessing..." says Dylan before Tanner interrupts.

"I don't want this to be a guessing game of whose DNA is on any piece of evidence. Did we get buccal swabs from Gaby and Bess so we can match them against the DNA on the belt?" asks Tanner.

"No."

"That needs to be done immediately," says Tanner.

"I'll make sure that gets done," I say.

"Do you have any leads on the DNA from Laura's vaginal swabs? Those had an unknown profile, right?" asks Tanner.

"That's right. And no, we don't have any leads on those," says Dylan.

"Well, don't you think those are pretty important pieces of evidence? If your theory is she was raped and attacked, isn't it a logical conclusion that whoever raped her, also ransacked the room and attacked her?" asks Tanner.

"She was prostituting. That semen could've come from a number of men. There can be so many sources of the co-ejaculator. Neighbors heard people coming and going through the night. Personally, I don't think the semen tells us much in this case," says Dylan.

"Investigator Mack, is your theory that her boyfriend actually raped her and left her for dead? Or is your theory that he assaulted her to teach her a lesson and then staged a crime scene?" asks Tanner.

"I don't need to have a theory. What I do know is that all the evidence points to Clown. He was seen leaving the scene shortly after this happened, his phone was in the room he rented for her, he was pimping her out, she was probably trying to leave him, and he beat her. What more do you want? All the evidence points to him," says Dylan adamantly.

"Except the print that was found on the vase, which doesn't belong to him, isn't that right Investigator Mack?" asks Tanner rhetorically.

"Like you said, 'having traces of medical personnel or officers on key pieces of evidence can happen.' The print can belong to Gaby, Laura, a paramedic, or a tech. It could belong to me for all I know," Dylan snaps back sarcastically.

Silence fills the room.

"Who picked this guy up after he ran from here?" asks Tanner.

"You mean ran from here and tried to kidnap our victim's mother? Which by the way, according to Ed Vanderbilt, may result in liability to our office," says Stevie, intentionally reminding everyone how I dropped the ball.

"That's interesting you ask. That officer was found dead on Friday," I say.

"Any connection to this case?" asks Tanner.

"It depends who you ask," I begin. "I didn't write this in the memo, since I figured it wouldn't be a good thing to circulate. But it seems like a good time to talk about that right now. The officer that died was Officer Cruz from the Leafwood Police Department. It looks like he committed suicide after he realized his business card was found at the crime scene in Laura's pocket," I say.

"When were you going to tell us about Officer Cruz being connected?" asks Tanner, looking at Dylan.

Dylan stays quiet.

"Has the Special Homicide Team ruled Officer Cruz out as a potential suspect in Laura's assault?" asks Tanner.

"I have," says Dylan.

"Shouldn't he be one of our prime suspects?" Tanner asks.

Dylan stays quiet.

"How did we, or should I say how did *you*, rule it a suicide?" asks Tanner.

"There was a suicide note written in a diary he had in his night stand. He torched his own house garage and was found inside it lying in his parked car. He had a bullet wound to his chest, inflicted by his own gun," I say.

"What did the suicide note say?" Tanner asks.

Dylan takes out Cruz' diary from his briefcase, opens it and hands it to me. I begin reading it aloud.

I wanted to say good-bye. I think it's best I end it this way. This will be the end of my caReeR and I can't imagine life not being an officeR.

I stop. A wave of air drops from my throat to my stomach. I notice the purple writing. The capital R's.

I sit paralyzed.

I think about the note in my door, the rattling engine sound, and the drive-by shooting. Chills run down my arms.

"Gaby? Is something wrong?" asks Tanner.

I force myself to read on.

I'm soRRy.

"Why would an officer kill himself over something he didn't do?" asks Tanner.

"He probably knew he was going to be exposed for sleeping with a prostitute. He knew his card was found in the motel room and that he may be looked at as a suspect. An investigation alone would be career suicide. That doesn't mean he tried to kill her. No doubt, he probably slept with her. He'd get canned for that alone and it would expose the police department," says Dylan.

"Is there any other evidence pointing to Officer Cruz as a suspect in Laura's assault?" Tanner asks, looking at me, as if he distrusts anything Dylan says.

I hesitate. "Yes, there's one more thing," I say reluctantly, letting out a deep sigh.

"I received a threat note at my door the night of the drive-by shooting. It was written the same way as this suicide note. The ink is even the same," I say, still holding the diary and now trembling.

"The note mentioned a flamingo face and only the suspect would know a flamingo vase was used to assault Laura. Whoever delivered the note was in a car with a ticking noise and that's the same noise we heard during the drive-by. It's the same noise the housekeeper described at the motel," I say, thinking out loud and feeling relieved to get everything off my chest.

"Are you kidding me? What's Cruz's connection to Clown?" asks Tanner.

"That hasn't been determined yet," Dylan says.

"I don't know how you feel about what I'm going to ask you to do, Dylan," Tanner says sternly. "And I'm not in the business of running parallel investigations in the same case, but I've done it before and I'll do it again if I need to. I am not ruling Cruz out as a prime suspect in this case.

"I agree with you that there is a significant case on Clown and all the evidence points to him. I believe you had probable cause to arrest him and I understand why you submitted this case to my office for filing on Clown.

"However, we need to look into Cruz. There are some unanswered questions as to the DNA profiles that I want resolved by the preliminary hearing. I want to make sure that Bess's DNA is on the belt and I'm curious to see if it's Cruz's DNA on her vaginal slides.

"I want Clown's fingerprints rolled at 1:30 in court and a comparison done confirming that's not his print on the vase. I'd expect you to personally roll his prints, Dylan, with Gaby there.

"I will file the case, but you have ten days until the preliminary hearing to get these questions answered. If we don't have this DNA work back by then, we're not going forward on the case because I don't personally think you've ruled out Cruz as a prime suspect. Do you understand?" asks Tanner.

"If you really want Cruz's DNA and I only have ten days, I guess my department will be sending me to the Walled City," says Dylan.

"Why the Walled City?" asks Tanner.

"That's where his body was sent yesterday. His family wanted him buried there. That's where most of his family is," says Dylan.

"Was an autopsy done?" Tanner asks.

"No, the family didn't want one. And the department didn't think it was necessary. Blood wasn't even drawn. His body's on its way to the Walled City right now. The Leafwood PD helped arrange that. This is the first time I'm hearing about Cruz' connection to the threat note and the drive-by. I just don't know if my agency is going to send me for this kind of case. It's only an attempted murder," says Dylan.

"Today it is, but it sounds like it will be a homicide tomorrow, when Laura dies. Let me know if your department is not going to send you. If they don't, I'm not filing charges on Clown and you'll have to re-arrest him after you investigate it further and we figure out who this DNA belongs to," says Tanner.

"You can't release him. He's a runner. He'll be gone and you'll never find him," says Dylan.

"Like I said, I'm not going forward on him until we figure out Cruz' connection to all this. You have ten days. That's my final decision," says Tanner.

"You'll need to provide us with an attorney who speaks Spanish. We'll need to work with the police department over there and funeral home to get access to Cruz's body. I've done this before. It's a lot of work and we need someone who speaks Spanish," says Dylan.

"I don't need to do anything. This is something you need to figure out. And I'll tell you why," Tanner begins.

"Let's say Clown goes free and now the public knows that Cruz was inside that room and has something to do with a drive-by and threatening a prosecutor. We have evidence with DNA that we are still trying to figure out who it belongs to. Then it comes out that your department okayed his body to be shipped off to the Walled City with no autopsy and no blood taken. That is not going to look very good. I think that your Lieutenant might have an interest in your department getting to the bottom of Cruz' involvement and not forcing me to.

"If your agency doesn't want to give this case priority because it's not a homicide, tell your boss it will be. I can guarantee we'll be getting a call from Memorial Hospital within the next couple days when Laura is pronounced dead. And I don't think your Chief of Police wants any media attention for this, especially in a year she's running in an opposed election. That's just my take on things. But you let me know," says Tanner.

I decide to speak up, hoping to ease the tension.

"I'd like to make a suggestion. I can go. I speak Spanish," I say. "I'm scheduled to leave to a couple of countries near the Walled City in a week. I want to see this case through. Everybody knows how much I care about Laura. She was the girl I was trying to get into The Mamacita Club. But the office thought it would be a conflict and her mom really didn't want her joining, anyway.

"I'd be willing to head to the Walled City and help Dylan get the Cruz thing squared away. It's on the way. The countries are not that far from each other," I say.

"You'd miss your entire vacation for this?" asks Prosecutor Debra Miller.

"I didn't quite say that," I say, backtracking.

"After the Walled City, I'd still like to continue on with my vacation. I've been saving up for it for a while. I would actually wind up taking an extra week off if I went early. If the office can pay for me to get from the Walled City to my destination, I'd be fine with that. It shouldn't be more than a couple hundred dollars," I say.

"Done," Prosecutor Debra Miller says.

"Plus, I've always wanted to visit the Walled City. My mom traveled there with a family she nannied for when she was young. And she always spoke highly of it," I say reminiscently.

"Well, there you go," says Debra Miller.

"Now you have your Spanish-speaking attorney, Dylan. You just need to get yourself there. Assuming your agency approves you to go, let's get Clown arraigned today on the attempted murder of Laura Paula. Go ahead and file his violent priors as well. I'm not making any offers on this case yet. If we don't have this investigation squared away and Cruz ruled out by the preliminary hearing, I'm dropping the charges," says Tanner.

"I'll call my Lieutenant right now," says Dylan.

"The other thing, Dylan. I want Gaby involved in all stages of this investigation from this point on. She will be required to report back to me daily on the status. Do you hear me? I don't want my office to have to run a parallel investigation on this. I want you and the Leafwood Police Department to determine Cruz' level of involvement. Do you have any questions?" asks Tanner.

"No questions. I heard you loud and clear. I'll be heading to the Walled City. I hope I'm on a flight tomorrow and hopefully Gaby will be in the passenger seat next to me. I will try my best. I have until the preliminary hearing. I heard everything loud and clear," says Dylan.

"This meeting is over. Gaby, let Mary know whatever you need for the flight. I personally will handle this case until you return from your vacation. Have a nice trip and keep me updated," says Tanner.

Five minutes after the staffing concludes, I slam my office door.

"Are you comfortable with me taking a swab from you?" Dylan asks.

"Yeah. Why wouldn't I be?"

"You just seem a little annoyed."

Dylan takes out a plastic disposable envelope with a long brown stick with a white cotton swab at the end. He removes the plastic lid sealed around the swab and hands it to me. I have no idea what to do. I've prosecuted dozens of cases involving DNA and have had experts testify about the buccal swab, but I've never done one on myself. I hold it, looking at Dylan.

"Rub it six times in each side of your inner cheek."

I follow Dylan's instruction, wondering if this is what it feels like being accused of a crime.

Dylan re-caps the swab and hands me a second one, telling me to do the same thing.

"Are you okay?" asks Dylan.

"Is it just me or was it completely out of line for Stevie Sapp to suggest I did something wrong with the belt? I'm so irritated," I say.

Dylan stares at me and doesn't say anything.

"Why are you looking at me like that? Did I do something wrong?" I ask.

Dylan stays quiet.

"What was I supposed to do? Watch her lie there and do nothing? Go look for gloves? Let her circulation keep getting cut off from the belt?" I yell.

Dylan says nothing.

"Tell me, Dylan. What was I supposed to do? Did I do something wrong crawling into bed with her? She was dying.

I was trying to help her. Please don't tell me I did something wrong," I say dramatically, feeling myself start to tremble.

Dylan starts to say something and stops.

He walks over to me and puts his arms around me as I begin to shake. My eyes start to tear up as I think of my mom and how much I wish I could have saved her.

"Look, you're emotional. We can talk about this later," says Dylan.

"No. I want to talk about this now. What was I supposed to do?" I say demandingly.

I pull away from Dylan's grip and wipe my eyes.

"Assume that's your DNA on the belt. People are going to be concerned. Detective Ford was concerned when I told him female DNA was on the belt."

"Why would people be concerned? What are you saying? I loosened the belt," I assert.

"Stevie and Ford have a legitimate concern. It would be a huge thing for defense to use in their favor."

"What you're saying makes no sense, Dylan."

I stare at the ground in disbelief. I feel like I'm about to pass out.

"Ford wanted me to get a search warrant for your buccal swab and your fingerprints, which I also need to roll."

"Why would you need a warrant?"

"And he was really interested when he heard you were one of the last people to see Laura before she was assaulted," says Dylan accusingly.

"You're making me feel like I'm a suspect."

"This is why I didn't want to talk about this."

I take a deep breath. There's a knock at my office door.

"Come in!" I yell.

Mike Tanner pops his head into my office and looks at Dylan and me.

"Oh, I'm sorry. I just wanted to let you know that you need to talk to the Bureau so they can do a threat assessment on that note you received, Gaby. Don't sit on this any longer. We take these threats serious and I want you to feel safe. Whatever you need, we'll be here," says Tanner.

"Thanks Mike," Dylan says.

Tanner shuts the door looking at me, concerned.

"Are you going to be okay?" asks Dylan, tucking my hair behind my ear.

"I'll be fine. I need some fresh air and I need to get out of here and get this complaint filed," I say, regaining my composure.

19

EVERYONE WANTS SOMETHING

Department Nineteen is the place where arraignments for felony criminal complaints take place. I sit in the audience section alone, waiting for Dylan and watching the circus of the Monday afternoon arraignment calendar. An arraignment is the first appearance in court after a suspect is arrested for his crime. All the men who are being arraigned in Department Nineteen sit in orange jumpsuits in the first three rows of the audience section.

A government-paid criminal defender is standing like a teacher educating all these rejects. My jaded way of thinking knows they are all guilty, maybe not of everything they are charged with, but something. The truth usually lies somewhere in between a criminal complaint and their sad confession.

The criminal defender is telling them that this is the time and place for their arraignment. He explains that he's going to enter not guilty pleas on behalf of all of them. He's like a shepherd herding his sheep to the slaughterhouse. This is the first day of what will probably last at least a year spent in the criminal justice system between all the continuances, hearings, and motions.

Watching these young men, all wearing the same color outfit, reminds me of the danger in viewing all defendants in the same light, as outcasts. And when you begin to see people as outsiders and rejects, there's a risk they become expendable. Amongst the orange crowd, is Clown. He's so easy to spot with his bald head and his big squishy smile.

A well-put-together man, who looks like he just stepped out of his Mercedes or Audi, walks into the courtroom. He has "private beach city defense attorney" flashing from his forehead based on his expensive wardrobe alone. His light pink suit blazer and purple tie give him away. Men like him stumble upon the Tuckford sticks every now and again. They are either expanding their practice to Tuckford County from the wealthier beach cities, or they have roots in the Republican wealthiness, which is little known but quite prominent in Tuckford County.

He's obviously never appeared in this courthouse. I would have recognized him if he did. Now he looks confused, walking around the courtroom, looking at the calendar sitting at the podium near the exit door, and trying to figure out how things work in Department Nineteen. A part of me wants to help him out, but another part doesn't want to waste my breath on helping a defense attorney. He should be able to figure it out, anyway.

Courthouses are generally the same regardless of what county you're in. But each one has its own way of handling matters. In some cities, for example, inmates sit towards the front of the courtroom behind a big glass window. They are kept away from the public and away from the prosecutors. It seems a lot safer than how it's done in Tuckford County.

Here, the inmates are sitting in the general audience area of the courtroom. They move from a sally port that connects the courtrooms and leads to an elevator that takes the inmates downstairs to a holding cell, where they sit waiting for their court appearance. That holding cell connects to a tunnel leading to the Old Town Jail.

Inside the courtroom, the inmates constantly pass attorneys, practically brushing shoulders with them because of the small moving space inside the courtroom. Occasionally throughout the day, I hear a deputy yell, "Counsel, inmates coming through." It's basically code talk for "Get the hell out of the way because one of these bastards might shank you."

I've heard of a case where the inmate lunged at a prosecutor during trial in front of the jury. That alone would guarantee a guilty verdict. It's just a matter of time before somebody gets shanked in this courtroom, and I mean shanking as in stabbing. I've seen inmates bring sharp weapons to court, like it's show and tell day. They make them with whatever they can find in the jail. My hope is they bring them to defend themselves or attack other inmates and not me or any of my colleagues, even the defense attorneys I can't stand.

The man I've stereotyped a beach city defense attorney walks around the courtroom. His shirt and purple paisley tie make me wonder whether he's gay or straight. He walks straight up to me. His handsome face and smile erases my vision of him getting lunged at by an inmate.

Even a man like him in his early thirties, who most definitely has a trophy housewife, wouldn't deserve to be shanked. He's too cute and looks like my favorite actor, Matt Damon. But his cluelessness about his surroundings make him a prime target for shanking. He walks closer to me.

"Hi there, is this where the arraignments happen?" he asks.

"Yes. What arraignment are you here on?" I ask.

"Rodrigo Garcia, who also goes by Clown."

"Did you like how I put that as his AKA on the complaint?"

"You must be Gabriela Ruiz."

"How'd you know?"

"I read the complaint. And you signed it, charging my client with these horrific crimes. I'll forgive you for that. I'm Bruce Davis. I represent Mr. Garcia," he says, shaking my hand.

"Hi there. It's nice to meet you. Here's a copy of the initial police reports on the case. Are you ready to arraign him today?" I ask, handing Bruce some paperwork, noticing his left hand is ring-less.

"Thank you. I was retained on Friday and had a chance to speak to my client over the weekend. I've actually represented him before in his out of county cases, so I'm very familiar with him."

"Great, what would you like to do today?"

"How much time are you guys looking for?"

"A lot of time. Like double digits. But we're not making any offers today," I say.

"Do you seriously want double digits on this?"

"Yes. This guy is looking at life. Plus, he's gotten so many breaks in other counties. They just keep giving him chances. He needs to know that he's in "Big T," Tuckford County. And I'm not in the business of giving defendants a deal, especially when they've already been cut several breaks."

"Well, I know just a little about the case from speaking with him. Can you give me your version of the events?"

I hate when defense attorneys try and get me to chat about the facts of a case. Nine times out of ten they are just trying to figure out what my legal theory is or what parts of my case I think are problematic. Sometimes, things I say get twisted or misconstrued by them later on.

"You're just going to have to read the reports. I can tell you the victim is at the hospital right now about to die. If she does, we're going to be filing murder charges. I also need to fingerprint your client here in court."

"What's that for?"

"There was a print found on the murder weapon, a ceramic flamingo vase. My office just wants a confirmatory print."

"Confirming what?"

"Just to confirm it's not his."

"You're not sure if it's his?"

"That's not what I said. They are certain it's not his; they just want to double confirm."

"It doesn't surprise me that it's not my client's print. I was speaking with him over the weekend at the jail. I don't know how you guys work in this county but he has information you might want."

"What kind of information?"

"That depends on what you can do for him."

"That's not how it works here."

"Why don't you tell me how it works here?" asks Bruce, grinning at me.

"You give me the information first, or better yet, Clown gives me the information first. We make no promises to him in exchange. It's called a King for a Day interview."

"That's awfully greedy of you not to give him anything while he puts his life on the line and gives you information. Don't you think?"

"If he's serious, he'll talk. That's a decision he needs to make. And that's how it works in every single case. It's my office's policy. What information does he have that would even be worth it for me to talk to him?"

"The information is pretty good. In fact it's very good, if it's true."

"Give me some sort of indication what it is. I feel like I'm totally in the dark."

"It has to do with someone who may be involved in what you're charging my client with."

"Just so you know, I'm heading out of the country tomorrow so if he has anything to say, I would suggest he say it today."

"Is someone going to take over this case and do the preliminary hearing because we're not waiving time."

"Yeah, Mike Tanner, the Special Assistant Prosecutor of my office, will handle it. But a defendant who wants to play hard ball and not waive time just might be worth me cutting my trip short for."

"Wow, it must be pretty important for your Special Assistant Prosecutor to take over an attempted murder case. Or is there something about this case I need to know, like an officer being involved somehow?"

"You'll be given all the information you're entitled to when the investigation is complete. Is there anything else we need to talk about?"

"I'll talk to Clown right now and see what he wants to do. What happens if he wants to give up the information right now?"

"Investigator Mack should be over here any minute to roll his prints. We can talk to him then. There's a side room right here. But you and Clown need to understand that I'm making no promises today."

"What happens after that?"

"I evaluate the information with my boss. If we want to use it and he wants a deal, we can talk then about leniency. Let me see what else. Oh. I can't ever use anything he says today against him. So he's free to speak openly, even if he talks about other crimes he's committed. Just let him know, I have no tolerance for liars. If he lies on anything, even something small, he can forget about any deals, ever."

Snitches are inherently unreliable. Juries don't like them and have a hard time believing them. What's worse is that if I use them and they blow up in my face, my whole credibility is out the door. A lot of these convicted felons are natural liars; so even where there is some truth in what they say, there might be lies mixed in there, too. A good investigator will see through the lies and get the snitch to tell the whole truth.

"I'll talk to him right now and see what he wants to do," says Bruce.

The side room of Department Nineteen gives Dylan, Bruce, Clown, and I barely enough room to sit around a table. I read Clown the one-page King for a Day agreement that we signed, which tells him he's not getting anything for what he's about to tell us.

"We are tape-recording this conversation. It's my understanding that you have information you wanted to share with us, is that correct?" I ask, placing Dylan's small recorder on the table.

"Yes," says Clown.

"You understand that I am not making you any promises for this information. You are charged with assault. You are facing life on this case. Anything you say today won't ever be used against you, but you're not getting anything when you walk out this door today," I say, pointing to the cherry-colored wooden door that leads to the corridor outside the courtroom.

Clown shakes his head back and forth.

"So whatchu got?" asks Dylan.

Clown looks down and shifts his body weight, causing his wrist and ankle chains to clank.

"Man, I ain't talking. Just roll my prints," says Clown.

"You had something to tell us. Talk to us, man," says Dylan.

"Nah, forget it. I ain't talking," says Clown.

"I'm sick of this shit. You show up at the Prosecutor's Office wanting to talk to the Assistant Prosecutor, then you take off running. Does it have to do with me being here or something? What's your problem, dude?" asks Dylan.

Clown shakes his head back and forth. I don't blame him. As much as it's important to build a rapport with a victim on a sex case so they disclose information about what happened to them, it can be just as important to build a rapport with a suspect or possible informant. In general, they don't trust law enforcement, especially gang members. They know it's a big gamble to be a snitch and turn over information to police. Once they decide to do that, there's no turning back. It has to be worth it to them, like they are going to get a huge break in their own case.

Agreeing to speak with us is not for the weak-minded. Clown doesn't have to do this. And he knows it. It goes against all codes and rules, no matter whom you're giving up information on. Even if it's a police officer like Cruz he was going to expose, it wouldn't matter.

Dylan turns the tape recorder off and places his fingerprint kit on the table before opening it. Bruce motions with his finger at me to follow him outside the room.

Bruce and I stand in a tiny corridor separating the hallway from the courtroom. I'm close enough to him to smell his cologne, which I recognize being the same one Neil used to wear. I feel instantly repulsed.

"I'm sorry, I really thought he was ready to talk," says Bruce.

"This is a total waste of time," I say.

"I thought I was doing you guys a favor."

"You're not. You're wasting my time. I should be packing for my trip tomorrow. This is what I can't stand about defendants. They play with the system. Had you already explained to him that he wasn't getting anything today? He looked a little surprised when I mentioned that he's not walking out the door with anything today."

"I did. He said he was ready to do this. He even made a comment about being ready to debrief and get out of the gang."

"Yeah, right. This guy's in too deep. Just last week he's running a prostitution ring and he's got this huge letter L on his arm. Give me a break."

"I'm just telling you what he said."

"It seemed like he was expecting me to cut down his sentence or drop charges. I just don't like when defense attorneys give them false hopes."

"I told him you couldn't do anything today, but I also told him that in some cases, snitches get leniency, kickbacks from the police, or relocated through a witness protection program."

"And what did he say?"

"He understood. But I'm thinking he still was hoping for something today. I talked to him all weekend about this. He wanted to come forward. So I'm actually surprised. He was saying things like he was ready to get his life back in order. He said what happened to Laura really upset him. He's telling me he didn't do this," says Bruce.

"And you believe him?" I say sarcastically.

"Don't get me wrong. I hear these things all the time, but, yeah, I really believe him," Bruce says. "I've known him for a while and he just spoke differently about this one. I can't put my finger on it."

"Do you think him not talking had anything do with Dylan being in the room?" I ask.

"I don't think so. I just don't think he's wrapped his head completely around the idea of being a snitch."

"Tell me this," I say. "Can you give me any other information about what he was going to tell us?"

"I really don't want to do that. He's the one who needs to come forward and give that information. I don't want to put him in danger."

"I know, but you do have an obligation to give me any exculpatory information. If you have credibile evidence that he didn't commit those crimes, I need to know."

"That's not true. My clients tell me all the time they didn't do it and I don't tell the prosecutor. Are you forgetting there's something called attorney-client privilege?"

"Okay, but don't you think it's important to give me information that shows your client might be innocent?" I ask.

"Sure, but not when it's coming from my own client's mouth. Those communications are privileged and he has asked me not to say anything. I don't want him shanked in jail because he decided to talk to you guys. If the gang gets wind of him even thinking of talking with the prosecutor, I'm putting him in danger."

"I won't say anything."

"I know you probably won't. I've asked around about your reputation and you seem trustworthy. But Investigator Mack is in there. And I don't know much about him. Just think about it from my perspective."

"I can respect that. But I also want to make sure the right guy is prosecuted."

"Is there a reason you don't think he's the right guy? Do *you* need to turn over exculpatory evidence that my client may be innocent?" Bruce asks. "Because I certainly would hope *you're* not prosecuting someone you believe did not commit the crime. That would be a serious ethical violation and prosecutorial misconduct."

"You don't need to explain my duties or ethical responsibilites to me. I'm aware of them, thank you," I say.

"Are you always this defensive?"

"Yes, if someone talks about prosecutorial misconduct without something to substantiate it."

"Sorry," he says.

"Do you have anything left to discuss? I think this conversation is over. I'll be ready for the prelim in ten days.

I think it would be worth it to cut my vacation short to do a preliminary hearing against an attorney who's questioning my ethics."

"Oh c'mon. Lighten up. Look. He didn't tell me much, to be honest," he says.

"He really didn't mention anything specific. He said he wanted to tell you guys to look at someone else, but he didn't give details."

I study Bruce's eyes for any indication he has more information than he's giving me.

"Oh. One more thing. We would be happy to waive time until you get back from your vacation. I already discussed that with my client."

"No pressure, I'm fine with changing my flight."

"Honestly, my sense with Mr. Garcia is that he has a lot of information, but he's not ready to give it up. He's a gang member. I'll work on him while you're away. Maybe when you get back, he'll be ready to talk."

"Did he seem sorry for what happened to Laura?" I ask.

"He just said something about knowing he did wrong with her, but what happened at the motel was sick. He kept saying 'That is sick shit,' 'That is sick shit,' almost like he had seen the crime scene. He also kept saying, 'You don't do that to her.' Yesterday, before I left the jail visit, he said he knew who did this and he wanted you to know, too."

"So why isn't he talking?"

Bruce leans in close to me and lowers his voice.

"Because snitches get stitches," says Bruce.

"Let's get back inside and arraign him," I say before heading back into the courtroom.

20

LA CIUDAD AMURALLADA

As I sit on a lounge chair on top of our historic hotel outside the Walled City waiting for Dylan to finish showering in our room, I read the sign on the building next door. *Centro de Convensiones de la Ciudad Amurallada.* It's the Walled City's Convention Center. The vibrant-colored flags wave in front of it.

At a distance is the historic central area of the Walled City. It's called the Walled City because it's engulfed by a twenty-foot concrete and stone wall. Centuries ago, a fortress was built around the city to keep people in and invaders out. The walls shielded them from cannons and gunfire. But they couldn't protect them from illnesses that swept through the town. I guess that's one reason not to build walls around yourself. Mine are coming down slowly, but they're not down yet.

The cool breezes from the humid ninety degree weather cool me down as I sit in a purple, colorful, strapless cotton dress I specifically picked to bring on this trip. It flatters my petite frame and goes perfectly with my Carmen Miranda pin-up outfit I brought to help me get into the back rooms of the police department here.

"Hey there, it's lovely up here," says Dylan.

"Oh, you scared me."

"How did you find this hotel?"

"Just a little research and I love the historical feel of it," I say. "Mariposa, where my mom met Señor Santiago-Borges, was my first choice. But my office wouldn't foot the four hundred dollar per night rate. So this was the next best choice."

"Well, it's a great choice. Hey, check out that boat."

A dark brown-trimmed boat with black exterior and tall masts connected to white sails sits in the water outside the Convention Center. It's the pirate ship kind. Stairs up to the deck make it inviting enough to climb up if it was any closer to me.

"I wish we had time to tour the city and take a closer look at stuff like that, but I know we're here for work," I say.

"I'm sure we can make a little time for some adventure. I mean, we are in the Walled City. And it is your birthday," Dylan says. "Plus, I hear we need to get in tune with the schedule here. You have two choices here — history or sun. And since we're not going to be doing much sunbathing, we should learn about the history of this place. Let's take a stroll into town."

Walking through the Plaza feels like I've flashed back one hundred years. White, yellow, and tan-colored historic buildings line the cobblestone streets. Storefronts filled with clothing, handmade arts and crafts, bars, and music add to the vibrancy of an already lively city. The air suffocates me as I walk through the town perspiring. The loud music blares from all sides of me. Bands no more than fifty yards away from each other compete for the attention of tourists. A beautiful lady in a tight red skirt with a slit that travels up her thigh moves her hips to the rhythm. The red flower in her hair bun takes me back twenty-four years.

Growing up, my mom signed me up for dance classes to honor all the places she got to travel with the family she nannied for. I learned to dance Ballet Folklorico, Salsa, Tango, and Flamenco throughout Old Town. Before class, my mom would slick my hair back in a bun and fasten a big red flower next to my ear. In Ballet Folklorico, I got to play castanets, which are wooden shells tied to my fingers that I'd roll my nails over to clack pretty sounds on. I synchronized it with tap dancing heel-work patterns. Every Christmas I'd perform a dance recital at our local Catholic Church. One of my favorite pastimes was helping my mom sew on five thousand yellow, green, and red sequins on my China Poblana skirt.

I still remember the story my mom told me. The China Poblana comes from a legend that a Chinese princess was taken into slavery in Mexico. A rich family from another town bought her and adopted her into their family. The princess was known for her gentle manners, loving kindness, and helpfulness towards others. When she died, all the young girls in the village of Puebla wanted to be like her so they began dressing like her. All my costumes reflected the culture of different regions of Mexico.

My dance troupe was selected to perform at the Old Town Castle one year. So I worked hard to get my skirt finished for the show. One by one, I stitched the sequins along a sketch of an eagle perched on a cactus holding a serpent in its mouth on the front of the skirt. On the back, I sequined an Aztec calendar. It took me five months, every day after school, to turn my skirt into a sparkling Mexican wonderland of rich culture to perform at the Castle. The skirt was so heavy, we placed it on the floor and then I stepped into it before my mom pulled it up, hooked the metal eye, and cinched my waist tight with a green, white, and red satin band.

Watching the girl with the red flower in her hair dance around the cobblestone street makes me realize why my mom loved the Walled City so much. The life, the passion, and the love for the rich culture here is undeniable. It's a life that is different from anything I've seen back home.

People from all around the world along with locals fill the streets vending beautiful pearl, silver, and colorful stoned necklaces, rings, and bracelets laid out on blankets. The blare of music in the distance and warm breezes add to the feel of a vacation for me.

Dylan pulls my hand and yanks me up to the sidewalk as a horse-drawn carriage clip clops down the narrow street.

"You were almost run over by a horse. Imagine that on your gravestone, death by horse carriage," says Dylan.

"I think it would be a perfect way to go out. To die in the beauty of this culture would be a blessing," I say.

"The police station should be right up here," says Dylan.

The police station blends right into the narrow streets and side shops of the Walled City. The white painted splashed walls and dark wooded reception desk represents the traditional style of this entire city.

"Hello, ma'am. Is Officer Nuñez here? We have an appointment with him," I say in Spanish.

While watching her speak to Officer Nuñez on the phone, I'm reminded that the Walled City has some of the most beautiful women. Even this policewoman, with her hair slicked back and dressed in her dark green police uniform and hat, has an elegance that's rare to see in the female officers at home.

She hangs her phone up. We continue speaking in Spanish.

"He'll be down in a few minutes," she says.

"Put these on," she says as she hands us the badges.

"They are asking us to put these visitor badges on," I tell Dylan in English, handing him one.

"One more thing, ma'am. Do you know an officer named Santiago-Borges?" I ask the woman.

"Yes, I know who he is. He works with politicians. Why do you ask for him?" she asks.

"He met my mother many years ago when she visited here in the Walled City and I was just curious," I say.

"What is your mother's name?"

"Anita Ruiz. But she passed away. I was just curious to see what happened to him. He had a special place in her heart. I at least know that," I say. "She was in love with him."

"Oh, they were in love," she says affirmatively.

"I don't know if he was," I reply.

She starts laughing and winks at Dylan, who has no clue what we're saying. But he still smiles back politely.

"I don't think one experiences love alone. It is something they both must have felt for each other," she says.

I can't help but want to persist in a debate about all the one-sided love affairs I've had. But her phone rings.

I fill Dylan in on our conversation. He pokes at my side trying to tickle me and we look at each other and laugh.

She hangs up the phone. "That was Officer Nuñez. He asked that I take you upstairs. Please follow me," she says.

Within seconds, we are whisked to the top of a staircase inside the police station. I can instantly connect with what my mom must have found attractive in Officer Santiago-Borges if he looks anything like Nuñez. Officer Nuñez's light skin, dark hair, fuzzy eyebrows, fine features, and deep sexy Spanish accent send me into a trance.

There's something about a hard-working blue collar man with a uniform on that is extremely sexy and even more so when he is speaking in his native tongue, something I can't help but fantasize about it entering my mouth.

"Dylan, do you have the name of the mortuary where Señor Hector Cruz was sent to?" I ask.

"Yes, I have it here in my phone," says Dylan.

After exchanging some playful Spanish banter with Officer Nuñez, he pulls up on his computer six different addresses of the mortuary locations throughout the Walled City, one being close by.

"Will you be able to assist us in contacting the mortuary and locating Señor Cruz's body?" I ask in Spanish.

"Yes, we are prepared to assist you in that way. We have orders to work with you. Whatever you need, we are here for you. I will contact them now; however, I will say one thing. I can't make any guarantees the mortuary will cooperate with us, but I will try. We may have to get a letter from a judge. How much time do you have?" Officer Nuñez asks.

"However much time you need. This place wouldn't be so bad to stay in," I say.

Giving him one of my biggest and warmest smiles, which comes so naturally to those who win my affection, has Nuñez making eyes with me and me back before he picks up his telephone and starts dialing the mortuary.

There's something about being in another country that makes me want to sample the thirty-one flavors in men, right now being the Latino flavor. I was once told by Sister Olivia at a Catholic Church camp Nana sent me to after my mom died, that dating is like thirty-one flavors. You should taste a little sample of each of the flavors before you decide which one you want for the rest of your life. I feel like I'm eternally sampling the flavors and have yet to pick the one.

When I was young, I had the same gripe. I'd ask my thirteen-year-old camp girlfriends, "How will I know when I taste the right flavor?" I even asked Sister Olivia, "What if you never find the flavor you're looking for or what if your favorite flavor is Neapolitan? That has three flavors I like to swirl around in my bowl until the vanilla, strawberry, and chocolate melts down into one puke-colored ice cream that tastes like pistachio."

Sister Olivia looked at me and called over Sister Frances, the nun that was supervising the girls' division of the camp.

Sister Frances took me into a separate room and sat me down. "Gaby, have you thought about your future? Have you considered that it is possible that the Lord is calling you to the convent? This is a special calling that doesn't come to many girls. Perhaps it is for you and it is something you should think about," Sister Frances said.

Then she gave me a gold chain and told me to wear it and pray daily and think about whether I felt the calling. The only calling I was feeling at that time was for my thirteen-year-old crush Justin Vargas, who took me behind the bleacher stands after I agreed to show him my boobs.

Officer Nuñez hangs up his phone. "Señor Cruz has arrived into the Walled City. He came here on a direct flight and arrived yesterday. He is at the mortuary and there is a funeral that will take place the day after tomorrow near the Plaza. There is a beautiful church there. That is where the mass will be and he will be buried locally.

"The problem is that the funeral home will not allow us access to his body without an order from the court. Just like I suspected. This shouldn't be hard to do, but it will take me about a day to get. I arranged an appointment for tomorrow at four o'clock with the mortuary. Hopefully, I can help you get the order by then," says Officer Nuñez.

"Thank you so much," I say.

"You're welcome," Nuñez says. Looking me straight in the eyes, I'm lost in a dream of sneaking out of my hotel at night to move my hips against Nuñez's body in sync with the musical rhythms I haven't stopped hearing since I arrived in this beautiful city.

"Why don't you return tomorrow at three o'clock in the afternoon and we will head over there?" says Nuñez.

Our hotel becomes Dylan's and my safe haven from the sweltering humidity and sun of this city. The cool room we walk into after visiting the police station sends me into a frenzy.

"I love this city," I say.

"What do you like most about it other than Officer Nuñez?" says Dylan, lounging on the bed looking at me while I walk to the vanity area.

"Stop it. I like meeting people like Officer Nuñez, the passion, the culture, the history. Life is so simple here. I think they have it right. Why do we work so hard back at home?"

"Yeah, you have a point. They may have the easy and good life figured out," Dylan says. "I think you're falling for Officer Nuñez. I saw you making eyes at him."

"There's something about the men here that captures my attention. I think it's just because they're different from what I'm used to."

"I didn't know you liked Hispanic men."

"I have no preference. The men here seem a lot more simple than the ones I've dated."

I open my suitcase up and take out my beauty case, placing it on the bathroom counter, an area completely open to our beds. Watching Dylan's eyes follow me in the mirror in front of me gets me wondering how I'm going to have any privacy getting ready. I brush my hair, massaging my scalp with each stroke.

"The grass is not always greener on the other side. A lot of Hispanic men are womanizers and controlling. You should know this with your culture."

"So are Americans. Look at Neil. I guess that's what I'm attracted to."

"You know what I think your problem is?"

"I don't want to know. I'd rather live in ignorance. I'm kidding, tell me," I say.

"That you just have too many standards, too many requirements. You need to figure out what is important to you. What you want in a man and what you're willing to compromise. When you meet a man, see if he has those things you like or dislike and let that be your starting point. The problem is that you follow your heart too much and you only pay attention to who you're physically attracted to. It leaves you unsatisfied at the end, because that initial attraction goes away."

"Really, I've never thought about it in that way. I don't want to settle and don't think I should."

"Is that why you're not settling with me?" he asks.

I stop brushing my hair and look directly at Dylan's reflection in the mirror.

"You haven't even tried to make that happen," I say.

"What are you talking about? I've tried so many times. I feel like you just are looking the other way, in another direction that's not towards me."

"It doesn't seem like you want to move things between us along," I say.

"What gives you that impression?"

"You don't call. You don't pursue. I don't feel cherished by you, Dylan."

"Even if I did those things for you, it wouldn't be enough for you."

"What makes you think that?"

"I know that," he says. "Because you haven't been a part of this relationship. You have been looking at it from the outside in, like you're watching and waiting for me to screw up. I don't know how you feel about me and sometimes in the past when we dated, you weren't affectionate with me. I'd get confused."

"I don't know how to respond to that, Dylan. A part of me wanted to fight for you, but a part of me felt rejected by you because you let so much time go by and you never tried to win me back. I get freaked out by the idea of being serious with you or any attachment. I don't want to be abandoned or cheated on at the end of us."

"That's a risk we both take, any couple takes. Love is worth the risk. I don't see it that way. I've always thought you were worth the risk," he says.

Dylan's cell phone ringing interrupts a conversation that had to happen. The tension between Dylan and me had come to the boiling point where something needed to give way, like a volcano waiting to erupt. Sometimes I need things spelled out for me in a straightforward and honest way so I know where I stand on the spectrum, especially in Dylan's heart.

"Thanks for that information," says Dylan before clicking his phone off.

"Dammit," he says.

"What's going on?" I ask.

"That was Linda Dean from the Fingerprint Office," says Dylan, getting off the bed and walking towards me.

"And?" I say.

"The print on the vase didn't match Clown, Laura or any of us who were in the room, including you, me and the technician who collected it."

"Are you kidding me?" I say, turning around to face Dylan. "It's gotta be Cruz."

"You think so?" Dylan asks.

"We gotta get Cruz's DNA and thumbprint. I'm not leaving the Walled City until that happens. And I don't care how long it takes. The rest of my trip will have to wait."

"I think you just want to stay in the Walled City with me a little longer and feel me grind against you in the bars like this," he says.

Dylan's deep and come-and-make-love-to-me voice still makes my inner thighs tense up. Holding my hip bone as we stand facing each other, Dylan uses his hand to put pressure against me. Moving his hand to the small of my back, he tickles me and sways me back and forth, in sync to the rhythm of the music on the radio alarm clock. Wrapping my arms around Dylan's neck and following his lead to the music, I enjoy the fun moment and realize for the first time he can dance.

I feel his hardness against my pelvis as he thrusts closer into me, pulling my hair back freeing my neck for soft nibbles behind my ear. Between the music playing softly in the background and the smell of his cologne, I feel wetness and throbbing in my lace panties. It sends me into an orgasmic outer space. I wonder if it's the humidity of the Walled City that just hit me or what I know is about to happen next.

"Do you think we can get in trouble for this?" I ask, lying next to Dylan naked and rubbing his chest lightly with my fresh manicured nails.

"Does it matter?" asks Dylan.

"I just don't want to lose my job. 'Prosecutor on the case sleeping with the investigator in the Walled City when they are sent on assignment there' doesn't sound very good. I'm just curious."

"Probably. I'm sure I'd get scolded for it before my boss gives me a high-five."

"Of course, it's always a double standard. You will be getting the pat on the back, while I'm losing my job and getting my Bar license suspended."

"Hey, if it comes to that point, where anyone cares, it means we've solved the case. I'd love to wrap this case up."

"Why did you listen to me when I said it had to be Cruz?"

"I was thinking the print on the vase had to be Laura's or the tech's. Plus, seeing Clown on Monday wanting to give up some information made me question things. I know he didn't tell us anything, but the fact that he was ready to tells me he has something he wants to say."

"Good. Don't worry. We'll find out who did this to Laura. I'm going to take a stroll down to the water. You stay here napping; you look a little worn out," I say, winking at Dylan.

21

INTERNATIONAL SIGNS

Thirty minutes after leaving the hotel room, I walk alongside the old boats docked in the harbor outside the Convention Center. The boats are no longer used for travel. They are remnants of historic times, used as a means for bringing goods to this seaside town. Nicer boats and elegant restaurants line the opposite side of the harbor where speedboats dart across the water without any speed limits. The city in the distance is made up mostly of apartment towers, which give it a more modern feel.

Wishing I could slip into one of these boats and sail away, I notice a young girl playing on the bow of a boat, hanging her feet off the sides. Watching her laughing and play sword fighting into the air, I get closer to the edge of the walkway, looking around and notice she's alone. The whole boat is empty.

Realizing she's no older than eight years old, I begin to yell at her in Spanish, telling her to get down from the boat and that she's going to fall. When she ignores me, I switch to English. Between several attempts to warn her, I get a better look at her while still standing on the dock. She seems in a trance, her eyes stare blankly into the wind. She's blind. Childish and playing in an innocent way, giggling and moving around in one spot, sticking the sword I imagine in her hand, she's completely at ease.

Walking onto the boat and hearing the creaking from the boat makes me think it's not as sturdy as it looks from the land. This thing is old and not something I'd get paid to sail away on. I walk up to the girl thinking I'll grab her by both of her shoulders so she doesn't fall into the water. Thinking I'll sneak up on her like a cat from behind hoping to take a hold of it before it hops or pounces away, I move up on her from behind.

Just as I'm about to grab her arms, she turns around and the look of death and demon eyes stare knives into mine. "Leave me alone," she screams. I jump and fall back, startled, with my heart pounding out of my chest about a thousand beats a minute. Her beautiful curly hair turns to straight long hair and her once playful smile turns to the stare of a cold ice princess. She is gone, disappeared.

A splash from down below brings the lukewarm bay water onto my face. I run to the ledge of the boat in the same spot she was sitting and feel an enormous sense of warmth. I can see a dolphin or something down below scurrying in the water, looking like it was about to make a jump into the air. A beautiful mermaid-looking dolphin in amazing coral and aquamarine colors shimmies out of the water.

"Gabriela." A beautiful voice soothes my excitement.

"Don't ever disturb the inner child in someone, but most importantly never let it be disturbed within you. It is bad luck. What you perceive as danger in your life, may be someone else's joy. Live and let live. If you allow yourself to be guided by this principle, you will learn to let go and not control. That is important for your life, too.

"You're not on a timeline; you don't need to force things to happen. The Universe will make them happen for you. The boat you sit on may look beautiful to you from the outside, but once you step onto it, you realize it is rocky, unstable, and creaking. It feels unsafe to you, but it feels safe to me, Giselle. Let me live and I will let you live. If you do, you will have peace in your life and serenity in your mind," she says before disappearing into the water.

Hands grasp onto my shoulders, startling me again.

"Silly, what are you doing on this boat? There's a rope closing it off. You probably shouldn't be on it. The police are going to arrest you," says Dylan, grabbing my arms from behind.

"Dylan, do you believe in magic?"

"Well, sort of," he replies. "Guess who just called me? Officer Nuñez. He said he was able to work some magic and track down your mom's ex-lover. Apparently, he lives with a politician in one of the fancy buildings that faces the sea. He's one of his bodyguards. He remembered your mom and said he'd love to meet you."

"Wow."

"Are you okay? You look like you just saw a ghost."

"I'm fine. When can we meet him?"

"He's dining right now at Trece Mares, one of the best restaurants here in the Walled City. He's willing to meet with us there after he's done, for a drink or coffee. Plus, he's interested in hearing about our investigation."

"Perfect, let's get back to the hotel so I can shower."

Trece Mares, one of the best places to eat in the Walled City, has a quaint feel to it with framed pictures and art on the walls. Young beautiful local women sit dining with older men who look like tourists. I study one woman who looks about twenty years old with long brown hair. She sits elegantly with her legs crossed as she gushes across the table at her date; her extreme enthusiasm gives her away as a sex worker. Prostitution is legal and rampant throughout the Walled City. Most of it is organized by former drug cartels.

The bar with six stools is our haven out of the way from the couples that have taken over a makeshift dance floor in front of a band. The music in the Walled City is the best I've heard around the world because the rhythm, bongos, and flutes whistle Spanish love songs in a melody I've never heard before.

"What has the Walled City changed for you?" Dylan asks, staring into my eyes like he never has before.

"My perspective of love."

"Really. In what way?"

"I've learned that maybe I'm looking in all the wrong places or maybe my standards are all wrong," I say.

"What do you mean? I thought you didn't want to lower your standards?" says Dylan.

"I'm not lowering them," I say. "I'm just talking about the things I once thought were important maybe are not. Take this couple, for example."

A girl in a light pink cocktail dress with ruffles, looking like my best friend growing up, spins in circles as her Spanish lover embraces her tightly in his arms nibbling on her neck.

"This Guatemalan girl, for example, looks like she's completely enjoying herself. Her partner doesn't have a full head of hair and is not the best-looking man here, but she acts like she's the luckiest girl in the Walled City. He's singing into her ear and she's happy."

"How do you know she's not just a sex worker?" Dylan asks.

"Her body language. It's genuine, not like that girl," I say, pointing to the twenty year old. "Plus they have wedding rings on," I say.

"How do you know she's Guatemalan?" asks Dylan.

"Guatemalans just know how to enjoy themselves and they dance well. Plus, she looks like my best friend growing up who was Guatemalan, so I'm presuming."

"You know who I think the luckiest person is in this place?" he says.

"Who, me?" I say.

"No, me."

"Aw. Thank you. I couldn't think of a better place or with better company to spend my birthday than right here with you," I say.

Our lips brush up against each other and he flutters his nose against mine in an Eskimo kiss that feels like a feather.

"Señora Ruiz?" a deep male Spanish speaking voice says.

"Yes," I reply back in Spanish.

I turn around to greet Señor Luis Santiago-Borges. I introduce him to Dylan and translate their small talk back and forth. Señor Borges and I continue speaking in Spanish.

"Your beauty is as striking as your mother's," he says.

"My mother wrote wonderful things about you in her diary," I say, taking out a vintage Polaroid headshot of my mom all dolled up with her hair in pin-curls, wearing a black feather boa.

"I wish I had the opportunity to say the same about you, but I knew your mother before you were born," Señor Borges says.

He studies the photo. "Wow, that takes me way back. I always told her she looked like Ava Gardner. She was a beautiful woman," he says fondly. "I remember how she loved the models and actresses. When I was working security at the hotel, we met here. She was so excited spotting the stars that were in town.

"What has brought you to the Walled City?" asks Señor Borges.

"We are here investigating an attempted murder that happened in our county. One of our potential suspects came here in a body bag. We are trying to get his DNA and thumbprint," I say. "Plus, for me, it was an opportunity to come to a town that had a special place in my mom's heart. It makes me feel close to her."

"Please tell me how your mother is."

"She passed away."

"My dear, I'm sorry to hear that. Was she sick?"

"No, she was not sick."

"An accident?"

"No, it wasn't an accident."

"Well, she was a woman who had a passion for life. I'm sorry to persist. But I loved your mother and I'm curious what happened to her. I've dreamed about her for many years. Every day I see something that reminds me of her. Her favorite number was three. She even said she wanted three kids because that was her favorite number. I remember she wanted to buy one of the blue houses here because that was her favorite color, and there are not many of the vibrant blue casitas here in the Walled City," says Señor Borges.

"Aw, you remember so many little details," I say.

"Because she has lived in my heart and dwells in my mind every day. Like the ghosts in El Monasterio. Have you had a chance to visit that hotel?"

Remembering I read in a travel book on the plane that the Monastery Hotel used to be a morgue, I notice his eyes are becoming glassy.

"I'm sorry, I've had several glasses of wine. I'd like to buy you two a drink," says Señor Borges.

"That is beautiful that my mother lives in your mind and your heart. It proves to me that all the men are romantic here. That is what I love about this place."

"It is not just the men here that fall in love. Women dwell in the minds and hearts of men everywhere. Here, we are just more able to express it. This man here has eyes for you," he says, pointing at Dylan. "I was watching you two from across the room. I don't need to know the both of you to know that you are in love with each other."

Dylan and I start giggling almost on cue. I begin to wonder if Dylan understands some Spanish. Two glasses of red wine make their way in front of us at the bar.

"Cheers to love," I say.

Clinking our glasses together sends me into a memory I have of my mother, who loved to toast her glass of wine. "Salud," she would say, until the day my stepfather ripped a wine glass from her hand during a toast. He thought smashing the glass against the wall would teach her to make eye contact with him during their toasts. A piece of glass hit my mom in the eye before my stepfather punched her in the side of the head.

"Excuse me. I'll be right back," I say discreetly.

Running to the bathroom and wetting my face with cold water was something I did as a child when my mom would get hit. Today, it still stops a bad memory from swelling my mind. Within seconds, I'm in the bathroom of Trece Mares and the cool water on my face makes me feel better. I reapply my powder and lipstick to refresh myself before rejoining Dylan and Señor Borges, who are now outside on the cobblestoned street.

"Are you okay?" asks Dylan.

"Yes, why?" I reply.

"Because you looked like a deer in headlights before you left," says Dylan.

"It's nothing," I say.

Learning to live with the death of my mom and the nightmare of her life with my stepfather is something I've learned to cope with and sweep under the carpet. I've learned to shoo away the spirits that lurk in my mind and heart.

"Señor, how have you coped with my mother dwelling in your thoughts?" I ask.

"Señorita, I loved your mother," he says. "I welcome her spirit every day. I ask that she appear in my heart and mind every morning that I wake up. She comes invited. I would never turn her away. This is what you must learn to do, also. There are bad spirits and there are good ones. You must learn to welcome the good ones. The more you allow them into your heart, they shoo away the bad. Trust me. It is the same with love. When you let those good people, lovers, family, and friends love you and come into your life, they help to shoo away the ones that are not good for you, the bad ones.

"It's the same thing with your mother. Try to welcome her spirit into your life. You seem like you try to shoo away what is painful and hard for you to understand. You are a beautiful woman, and you must try to welcome the good memories of your mother. She will help you send away those bad memories, like the one you had a couple of minutes ago."

"That's all it takes?" I ask.

"Your mother taught me to fill your heart and life with love and passion. Be open-minded to these things and you will be guided through life. She believed that the Universe has a plan for you already inscribed in here, your heart. Let it be. Calm yourself and slow down; that is what your mother taught me. I hope that she somehow was able to feel calm before she passed. And if she could not, all the more important it is for you to do that in her honor. She would have wanted that for you. She was a beautiful woman. Please though, I need to know what happened to her."

"I will tell you in a letter if it is okay. I have a hard time talking about it, even though it happened twenty years ago."

"Of course, of course. I don't want to upset you. Please take my card. Promise me you will write me and tell me what happened to her. Do you have any sisters or brothers?"

"I will explain when I write. But no, I'm an only child. Thank you for caring about my mother. It means a lot to me to know that she experienced true love."

"We were in love, he says. "Tell me what I can do for you here in the Walled City. How can I help with your investigation?"

"We may need your help tomorrow if we have a problem at the mortuary, but I think Officer Nuñez has everything covered. The police have been a big help to us, thank you," I say.

"Good, I'm happy to hear that. I'm glad I got a chance to meet you while you were here. I'm going to leave you two lovebirds alone to enjoy the night here in the Walled City. Please take advantage of the time you have in this place and anyplace you find yourself together or in the company of those that love you. We have a short time here on this Earth. Hug those a little tighter that you love and live every day like it's your last. Because you never know what tomorrow brings," Señor Borges says before stepping up into a horse-driven carriage.

"I'll be waiting for that letter," he says before being whisked away.

22

THE MORTUARY

The first funeral I went to was my mom's. This is the second time I've stood at a mortuary looking into the casket of a dead person. Standing at the mortuary with Dylan makes me feel like dying again. Officer Cruz's body disintegrates as I stare at him and my mom appears inside the coffin.

When my nana walked me up to her coffin at her funeral, my mom looked like she was sleeping and her eyes would open at any moment. She looked a lot older than just the week earlier when I saw her alive. It was probably all the makeup they put on her. The mortician did a terrible job. The makeup was chalky and didn't match her warm skin tones. It was a bad attempt at hiding the marks on her face. I couldn't remember which ones my stepfather made. There were so many times mom's face was puffy, her eyes were swollen, and she had dark circles under her eyes; for the most part, I thought they were all natural.

As I stared at my mom in her casket, I hoped I died, too. I wanted to crawl into her casket and wondered if there would be enough room for me to fit inside with her. I just didn't want to live without her and I felt so bad about not saving her. I never told anyone how bad I felt that day, especially not Nana. I was afraid of getting in trouble. Nana was so angry that my stepfather hadn't been arrested yet. She was frustrated at how slow police were working on the investigation. She squeezed my hand and said, "We really need an attorney in the family."

Later that day I told Nana I wanted to be an attorney. I figured they protected women like my mom from bad things happening to them, and that's what I wanted to do if I couldn't go with her to heaven.

I stare back at Officer Cruz, who looks like he's about one hundred years old. The flames from the fire really wilted his whole body and his skin looks leathery. Dylan starts with Cruz's hands. One by one, he clips the fingernails from each hand. Then he moves to his head and pulls off several follicles of hair from the base of his head.

Inside Cruz's mouth, Dylan swabs all around the inside of his mouth, collecting cells. Dylan does the same in the ear and nose area of Cruz. Dylan looks at Cruz's fingers. Then he opens his briefcase. He sets up his casting materials next to Cruz's casket to take a mold of his thumb.

It looks like Cruz is grasping tightly onto something. The rigor mortis is fully developed. His hand is clenched tightly and his fingers look wrinkled and hardened. Dylan takes some wet cloths and begins to clean Cruz's thumb with a wet towelette before he starts to dry it. Then, he wipes a black fingerprint powder to the thumb with a brush, struggling to keep Cruz's fingers separated. The thumb returns back to his fingers, like an instant reaction every time Dylan pulls it away for the casting.

Once he gets a stable grip on Cruz's thumb, Dylan sets the casting material around it on top of the black powder. We sit for fifteen minutes, before Dylan begins to peel off the casting material.

"This isn't looking good. The cast didn't come out that well. It's really hard to separate his fingers to get a good working space here. His hand is clenched so tight," says Dylan.

"Miss Ruiz. I know you are trying to get this impression. But the mortuary is closing. It's five o'clock," says Officer Nuñez in Spanish.

"Do you think we could come back tomorrow to get another impression?" I ask.

"To tell you the truth, I don't think they are going to let us back in. We were lucky to get in today. But let me go ask," says Nuñez walking away.

"Dylan, we need that thumb. We can't leave without it and they're closing. This is our last chance," I say, wondering if I should have worn my Celia Cruz outfit instead of this Evita one.

"What do you want me to do, cut it off?" asks Dylan.

"Yes, if you have to. "What do you think this is for?" I say, pointing to a scalpel in Dylan's molding kit.

"Stop!" says Dylan.

"We wouldn't even need the whole hand. Just the thumb. And we'd only have to sliver off the pad of it where his thumbprint is. That's only skin. It's not even bone or nail!" I whisper excitedly.

"No, we can't do that!" says Dylan.

"They used to chop off hands before they had these types of things," I say, pointing to Dylan's molding kit.

"I'm not doing it. We can get his print from his internal police file," says Dylan.

"What if he somehow destroyed that, too? Make me one promise. If I slice it off, you will transport it back," I say.

"You won't do it," says Dylan playfully.

"Promise me," I say seriously, hearing someone walking towards us. I hear Officer Nuñez' voice.

"They will not allow us to return. The funeral for this gentleman is tomorrow and the burial is immediately afterwards. It would require us to get another court order. And that might delay the funeral or require us to dig up the body once he's buried," says Nuñez.

I translate for Dylan.

"Okay. Would you be able to ask them if we can stay here another hour to finish up?" I ask nervously, smiling at Officer Nuñez.

"Yes, of course," says Officer Nuñez, turning to walk away.

"Well?" I whisper to Dylan.

"I'll check it in with my suitcase," says Dylan.

I remove the scalpel from Dylan's briefcase and thank God I won't be on the same flight back with him tomorrow.

23

HONEYMOON PHASE

I lay alone surrounded by darkness in my bed at the historic hotel wishing Dylan hadn't left this morning. All I can hear is heavy panting and bed creaks coming from the room next door. I close my eyes in utter disgust. And I pull the blankets over my shoulders and up to cover my ears. I wrap my body into a ball. I knew I should have asked for another room when I saw my hotel neighbor, aka "Señor Crazy," at the bar last night. He had one of the cleaning ladies from my hotel pinned up against a brick wall. She was obviously not into him and looked completely bored as he demanded kisses from her. When I pointed it out to Dylan, he sized her up as a sex worker.

"No," a faint female voice says.

The bed creaking and moans stop suddenly.

I remove the blankets from my ears to listen closer.

"Don't say 'no' to me," Señor Crazy responds sternly in Spanish.

A loud slapping sound followed by a shuffling sound in Crazy's room moves towards the wall closest to my headboard. I try to make out muffled words of what has to be the sex worker.

What is she saying? Does she need help? Does he have his hand over her mouth?

I pull the blankets back up over my ears and purse my lips tightly, curling back up into a ball with my head down. My heart starts beating fast and the rushing sound of blood flowing through my ears makes my head buzz and feel warm.

Twenty years later, I'm still accustomed to blocking out fights or tension from the room next door. I became so good at doing it as a kid hearing my parents fight, it still feels like a natural thing to do today. My stomach starts to clench up.

I hear a loud laugh from the sex worker. And the knot in my stomach starts to loosen up and my beating heart calms down. The alarm clock on my night stand reads: 1:52. I can't believe I'm up this late. I glance over at the phone wondering if I should call the front desk to complain about the noise, but they're not going to be up.

A loud thump against the wall with more muffled moans startles me again.

I think hard frantically. *Should I call Dylan? No, who knows where he'll be. Should I call Señor Borges? No. He's probably sleeping. Should I call Officer Nuñez? No. Mom, what should I do?*

I pick up the phone and dial the front desk. It rings nine times before I hang up. I hear two more thumps to the wall and then dead silence.

The neighbor in the motel room next to Laura heard thumps the night she was assaulted. I heard thumps after my mom pleaded for me to call police the night she died.

I cover my head with the blankets again. Tears warm my cheeks as I think about my mom and how I didn't do anything to try and save her.

Pick up the phone, Gaby, call the police. Walk next door, Gaby, and help the lady.

"Please, no!" I hear in a low woman's Spanish-speaking voice.

I look back at the list of numbers on the phone. Bell desk, laundry, housekeeping, restaurant. I go through each one, letting each ring eight to nine times before I hang up to dial the next. No one answers. I move down the contact list to *Policía* and hesitate a couple seconds before pushing that button. It seems to ring forever, before I hear a loud knock at my door.

I throw the phone receiver down onto my bed, step into my slippers, and throw my hotel room robe on. I grab a letter opener from the desk, stick it in my pocket, and open my door.

The cleaning lady sex worker stands at my door. Her lipstick is smeared above her upper lip and her black eye makeup smudged under her eyes makes her look like a racoon. It matches her black dishelved hair. She looked much prettier last night at the bar.

We speak to eachother in Spanish.

"Do you need help, Miss?" I ask.

"Yes please. Can I come in?" says the sex worker desperately.

"Yes, of course. Come in," I say, watching her close the door quickly behind her.

She makes her way into my room and towards the sink. She removes her black lacy top and studies the red scratches down her back in the mirror.

They look just like ones I'd see on my mom. She starts wincing in pain from the sight of her back.

"Look at this," she says pointing to the scratches on her back. "Asshole!" she says angrily.

I move to the sink and begin soaking up a washcloth with cool water.

"Do you want me to call the police?" I ask.

"No, no," she says adamantly.

"Why not?" I ask curiously.

"Because they can't help me," she says.

I let out a sigh feeling hopeless as I wring out the towel. The white hotel wash cloth stains with red blood every time I pat her back with it.

The lady looks at me fondly in the mirror, like this is the first time anyone has touched her to help her instead of hurt her.

Her smile turns to fright when a knock at the door startles us both.

"Shhh," she whispers with her finger up to her mouth.

"Who is it?" she yells.

"Me," Señor Crazy yells in Spanish.

The sex worker's scared look turns to anger and she motions for me to move into the closet.

"No. Why?" I ask.

"Please. Trust me," she says sternly.

"What is he going to do?" I ask.

"Please," she says insistingly.

Another loud knock at the door startles us. "Open the door!" Señor Crazy yells in Spanish.

I give in, following her direction towards the closet. I crouch down and she throws some clothes over my head.

I peek through the clothes and lock eyes with her. "Miss, don't go with him," I whisper fiercely.

"Don't worry," she says assuringly, closing the closet door.

I sit in the darkness and listen to her heels click towards the door she opens. They speak in Spanish.

"What are you doing here?" Señor Crazy says.

"What do you want?" she asks rudely.

"Who's here?" he says.

"No one. Don't worry," she says dismissingly.

"Let's go," he says.

"No. I'm going to sleep here," she says aggressively.

The silence goes for too long. It reminds me of all the times my house would go mute. It happened right before I would hear a head or rib being punched by my stepfather. I start to shake, curled up in a ball.

Then I stop, forcing myself to listen closer.

"Leave me alone!" she screams dramatically. Loud clicks from her heels, then swirling sounds come from the bed as screams muffle. But they sound like male screams this time. And I could be an expert on sounds of struggle. It's all based on personal experience. One. Two. Three. Four. I count and count and count, keeping my eyes shut tightly.

The slaps and Spanish curse words the sex worker is shrieking at Señor Crazy finally brings me back into real time.

What do I do? I feel down to my pocket and feel the metal letter opener. I tighten my fist around it.

I hear a loud knock at the door and release my grip. I return to calm, hearing footsteps moving towards the door.

"Who is it?" asks Señor Crazy.

"The police," yells a man in Spanish.

The door creaks open.   "Good evening," Señor Crazy says.

"Open the door all the way Sir," says the policeman.

I relax the tension in my body hearing the door open.

"Miss, do you need help?" the policeman continues in Spanish.

"No, no," she says.

I cringe in disbelief.

"Are you sure?" the policeman asks.

I want to scream.   I can't believe she's not taking his help.

"Yes, yes, thank you," she says casually.

"Did you call the police?" the policeman asks.   "Look at the telephone," the policeman says.   I remember my last call to the police and leaving the receiver off the hook.

"I'm sorry. It was an accident," she says.

"You don't want him arrested?" the officer asks.

"No, no," she pleads.

"Fine," says the officer.

I stay silent in the closet listening to the police officer leave.   Then I hear Señor Crazy and the sex worker make their way out of my room.   I come out of the closet, turn off the lights, and crawl back into bed.   I drift off to sleep remembering all the times my mom and stepdad would make up with each other.   It was like they were honeymooning all over again after a big fight.   We'd always get to go to the seafood restaurant after they made up.   We ate so many times at that place.   It was my stepdad's way of making it up to us.

This sex worker is no different.   I called the police and she didn't want him arrested.   I pleaded for her not to go and she ignored me.   I treated her wounds and she still left with him. *How can I save someone when they can't even save themself?*

Two gunshots ring out from Señor Crazy's room. And I go numb.

24

THE LETTER

Dear Señor Luis Santiago-Borges,

This might be the hardest thing I've done in a while, but it was such a pleasure to meet you in the Walled City. We were able to take care of what we needed to do. Dylan returned home and I am now traveling alone. Thank you very much for taking the time to meet with me. It means a lot to know that my mother had a true love. I always wonder if I will ever find love the way I imagined it to be. But it seems that love is what's in your heart and dwells in your mind. Maybe it can be right in front of us. If you are too busy to stop and love those that love you, life and love will just pass you by.

After my mother returned from the Walled City, she had me and started dating my stepfather. I don't know anything about my real father. I have my mother's diary that I found and kept after she passed away. She married my stepfather thinking it would be the right thing to do; especially because she had me. She knew that you would never come to the States and she couldn't go back to the Walled City, so she settled.

As best as I can remember, she and my stepfather had a violent relationship. He abused her. He hit her often. My mom never went to police but instead stayed with him.

One day it got so bad. He chased her throughout the house and she was screaming for me to call the police. I covered my ears and stayed quiet when I was hiding under my blankets in bed, trembling and crying, praying for it to stop. I felt frozen and paralyzed. He stabbed her twenty times and she died. My stepfather is serving life in prison. I have not seen him since his trial. I don't know if I'll ever see him again.

I blame myself over and over again because I could have saved her. I didn't call the police. I didn't help her when she came in my room begging. I've never forgiven myself for that. I hope you can. I'm sorry. I'm sorry I didn't save her. Thank you again for your kind words, and I wish you a life filled with love and passion.

xo,
Gaby Ruiz

P.S. Thank you for putting me up in Mariposa Hotel my last night in the Walled City after the shooting.

25

FORGIVENESS DOOR

Beloved Gaby,

We have a big red door here in the Walled City. You probably walked right past it while you were here. It is called the Forgiveness Door. It is your responsibility to forgive yourself. This door reminds you that once you walk through it, you will be forgiven. But that is a myth, because it is not that simple. You must forgive yourself. It's not your fault, you couldn't have done anything.

It sounds like your mother stayed in a relationship that was dangerous and only she could have saved herself. In domestic abuse cases, this happens a lot. It's a difficult thing to change. You must believe this. Your mother would not have wanted you to spend the rest of your life beating yourself up over this. You cannot realize your full potential in life, which I believe is much more than you know, until you forgive yourself.

Thank you for sharing what happened to your mother. I'm very, very sorry you had to experience this. And I can only imagine how hard it was for you to understand as a child. But the one thing that you can do to make amends with your mother is to forgive yourself. Please do this for yourself, the world, and the Universe.

Besos,
Señor Luis Santiago-Borges

P.S. I'm sorry once again for what happened at the historic hotel. This client and worker had a long history of problems before she killed him then herself. We believe she grew tired of the abuse. Domestic violence and sex trafficking is just as much a problem in the Walled City as it is in your own backyard. I hope it didn't ruin the rest of your trip. It would be wonderful to see you and Dylan in the Walled City one day again soon. I would be delighted to know it was for your wedding. You make a very beautiful couple. Please send him my best.

26

MAMACITA MASON JAR

Two days after sipping on red wine and dancing on my vacation, I rest my feet on my office desk waiting for Kiki. She's bringing the applications for new girls who have signed up for The Mamacita Club. I close my eyes and drift back to the Walled City.

I jerk up from my seat when the dark-haired girl on the edge of the boat pops back into my head. The boat didn't have any sails. It was stagnant. It was not sailing. It was sitting on the side of the waterway, like it was trapped. I start scribbling on a blank piece of scrap paper. *Fear. What does this boat mean? Why does it keep popping into my life?*

I unscrew the mason jar I have on my desk and toss in my scrap, seeing a vision of a ship behind the "Mamacita Mason Jar" label on it.

As Kiki walks into my office, I yell at her. "Shut the door."

I open the side drawer of my desk and see the envelope I've collected with all the girls' Mamacita Mason Jar notes. I grab the envelope and start pouring out all the crinkled pieces of paper. I watch them roll out onto my desk.

"What are you doing?" asks Kiki.

"Go through these with me. I need to see what's on them."

"Why did you keep these things? We told the girls that we were throwing them away. I thought the whole point was to write down stuff you didn't want anyone else to know. Some of my stuff is probably in there. That's embarassing."

"I just hope something's in here."

Kiki sits down, I divide up two piles, and one by one we start opening them.

"Listen to this one. This has to be yours," says Kiki.

"Dylan is not that into me. I'm nervous about giving the class today. I hope I can make a difference for these girls," Kiki says, laughing.

"I wrote that the night of the drive-by. I got what I wanted. He wants to be with me. And now I don't know what to do. I've wanted so much to find love when all along, it's been right in front of me. Why can't I just love him back?" I ask.

"You love him, a lot, Gaby. Don't forget that," Kiki says. "You wanted him and you waited for him, but that was a long time ago. You gave him a chance. You might have moved on when you realized he wasn't reciprocating the way you deserve. Don't think for a second that men don't regret their phobia of falling in love. Love will give him another chance, just maybe not with you. If he learned anything, he'll grab it and embrace it the next time he's faced with it. Hopefully, his experience with you taught him not to be such an idiot the next time he falls for someone," she says.

"I just hate being that one girl that got away. We had a great time in the Walled City, but I'm not convinced it will last."

"This is Christina's writing," I say.

I can tell by her curly writing. I would see her write things on the chalkboard in the Airstream.

"*Threats and death stare me in the face. The same reflection as Laura's mirror,*" I read.

"Oh, my gosh," I say excitedly.

"Look, here's another one," says Kiki.

"*Mother, the Club, the Kiss of Judas... misplaced blame,*" reads Kiki.

"What does that mean?" asks Kiki.

"Judas was the biblical figure for betrayal. Haven't you heard of the Kiss of Judas? It represents a complete betrayal to someone," I say.

"What do you mean?" Kiki asks.

"I don't think Christina's mom ever wanted her to join the Club. She had the same reaction as Laura's mom. Maybe she thinks of it as a betrayal. I'm not sure, but that's the only thing that's coming to mind," I say.

"That's all I have here. What's that one?" says Kiki curiously, pointing to one stuck under the envelope.

"These have to be Christina's," I say, unfolding two notes wrapped together. The first note is filled with Christina's doodles.

I read the second note. Chills throughout my body set in.

Within twenty minutes of reading Christina's Mamacita Mason Jar writings, Kiki and I walk through Lacy Park. This park is one of the most beautiful parks in Tuckford County. It's one of the few that doesn't have gang members flocking and graffiti decorating the walls. Rather, the homeless and drug-addicted population of Old Town color this park. If you look beyond the transients, the dogs they keep on leashes and their tents, you will see the beauty of the park. Lacy Park carries the feel of walking through Central Park in New York City. It's amazing how many little gems there are within ten minutes from my office.

This park is my favorite place to ride my bike during lunch breaks. There's a two mile loop around two lakes. It's a good way to escape the heat. The lush trees and water keep it cool. Sometimes during the summer, the lakes have paddleboats gliding on them. On weekends, the park hosts things like a Mariachi Festival, summer nights, and music in the park.

I released Kanga in this lake. When I was six years old, my mom bought a duck home for me at Easter. Kanga was pooping all over our yard, so my stepfather took it out on my mom. I thought giving up Kanga would stop my stepfather from hitting her. But the beatings never seemed to stop.

It was during one of my lunchtime bike rides that my angels helped me find the murder weapon in one of my cases. A Native American maiden walked out and stopped me as I was riding. She was yelling out some word I couldn't understand, "Mazawaka," and pointing towards the lake. Riley later explained that the word meant "gun."

Within twenty-four hours I had the Old Town Dive Team searching for the gun, but the water visibility was so low they couldn't find anything. When I pulled favors from all my contacts to have the lake drained, there was a forty-five caliber Smith & Wesson sitting in the same spot the Indian maiden had pointed to. I later learned that nearby the lake, there was a former site of a Native American Indian tribe that lived on the land two thousand years ago. I guess their spirits had a message for me that day.

Kiki and I walk towards the picnic benches close to the beautiful lake and sit down to wait for Christina, who agreed to meet with us when I spoke to her just ten minutes ago.

"Have you heard from Dylan?" Kiki asks.

Kiki's black hair shines from the reflection of the sun. Her dark skin glistens. It's barely nine in the morning and the heat is already feeling warm against my tan shoulders.

"Yes, he texted me a little while ago," I reply.

"Did you respond?"

"Not yet."

"Why didn't you tell him to come down here?"

"Remember he can't, cuz of Christina being a runaway."

"Oh yeah, I forgot."

Christina, being a reported runaway, causes a huge liability when a police officer like Dylan makes contact with her. Police need to report runaways to social services and take them home or even to Juvenile Hall. I can do more for these girls by building a rapport with them and encouraging them to make better choices than by calling police on them. If I report them to social services, they'll lose trust in me and run away, anyway.

Christina comes walking towards me from the passenger side of a white car.

"Hey Christina, thanks for coming to meet us. How are you?" I ask.

"I'm fine," she says.

"Who'd you come with?"

"My mom."

I don't know which is worse, Christina hanging around with her mom or her bottom bitch.

Her mom, who sometimes stays with Christina's grandmother at the Leafwood RV Park, uses drugs and tried to sell Christina to a man in the past.

"I thought you were supposed to be living with your grandma," I say, before reminding myself to keep my mouth shut.

"I was, but I don't feel safe at the trailer park anymore. That drive-by shooting really scared me. I thought I was gonna die. I'm strapped now, worrying what's gonna happen next. You wanna see my gun?" asks Christina starting to open her purse.

"No, but thanks for telling me. I was afraid, too, that night. I was so relieved when I saw you get up. Why don't you sit down? We wanted to ask you some questions about that drive-by."

"Like what? Who did that to us?" says Christina, sitting across from me.

"Yeah. Stuff like that."

"It had to be Clown."

"But Clown was locked up. It couldn't be him," I say. "Look, I don't know if you're trying to cover for someone, but we need to know the truth," I say.

"I am telling the truth," Christina says adamantly.

"Christina, I read what you wrote in your Mamacita Mason Jar notes, that you were getting threats after what happened to Laura. Tell me about that," I say.

"I don't want to be involved."

"Christina, Laura's in a coma. She can't talk. You need to tell us what you know," I say.

"I don't know what you're talking about," says Christina.

"Tell me who was threatening you," I say.

"I don't know who it was."

"Why did you say Clown did the drive-by?"

"I don't know. I'm thinking it has to be someone from Lincoln. They want to come and kill me."

"Why do they want to kill you?" I ask.

"Someone was calling my cell phone and saying I better keep it out of my mouth. She called me a snitch."

"Did she identify herself?"

"No."

"Did she explain what she meant?"

"No."

"What do you think she meant?"

"To keep my mouth shut about everything."

"What's everything?"

"Clown pimping Laura out. An officer she was messing with."

"Tell me about the officer Laura was messing with."

"Well, he would come by once in awhile and she took care of him. He never had to pay though. He would get favors for free because he had something worked out with Clown."

"He never arrested Laura?"

"No, no way. He'd never do that."

"Who do you think the lady calling you is?"

"Maybe Laura's boss."

"I thought Clown was her pimp."

"He is, but more as protection. She has a boss lady. I know that for sure, she just never told me who it was."

"Why do you think Lincoln's shooting at us?"

"Because who else would it be? Laura wanted to leave the ring. Then that thing happened with her in the motel. She was taken care of and now they're trying to take care of me. That's how they play. Clown knew I was close to Laura."

"Did you see who was inside in car?"

Christina looks down.

"No," she says nervously.

"Christina, I know you were looking right inside the car when you were out there. Are you sure you didn't get a look?"

"I didn't. I couldn't see who was in there. It happened so fast."

"I know, but you were right there. I thought maybe you got a look."

"I didn't," Christina says, putting her head down and shaking it back and forth.

"I swear, Miss Gaby, I couldn't see," Christina starts to cry.

I wish I could order her to answer my question, but I'm not in a courtroom and she hasn't taken an oath to tell the truth. I'm out on the street, where court rules and judge's orders don't seem to matter. Life out on the street is hard enough for girls like Christina. They are just trying to get by day to day. They live by their own rules and if they don't want to answer something, they don't. They have their own safety to worry about.

The best I can do is appeal to Christina to do the right thing and tell me. Even though she knows more, I can't force her to tell me, just like I couldn't force Clown.

"Someone's trying to send you a message, Christina. It's important for you to tell me who that might be. If not, I can't help you."

"I think they're trying to send a message to you, Miss Gaby."

"What do you mean to *me*?"

"They don't like what you're doing."

"What am I doing?"

"You're helping girls like me and Laura stay off the street. Laura was starting to change. She really wanted to join The Mamacita Club and made me give her all my books after I read them. Bess and my mom think the club is all BS. They want it shut down. Bess wouldn't let Laura join because she didn't want us hanging around," she says.

"Did she think you were involved in the prostitution stuff too?" I ask.

"I don't know what that woman thought. But she certainly doesn't like me. I've never told you this, but I'm the one that called police on Javier," she says.

"I always wondered if it was you," I say.

"I think my mom told Bess it was me," she says.

"So why am I the target?" I ask, changing the subject.

"The club is making a difference. You're making it harder for the ring to do their job. They don't want me talking to people like you."

"How do you know that?"

"Because the lady said that on the phone. I told her I was going to tell you what was going on. And she said she was going to take care of you."

"Did she say what she was going to do?"

"No. She just said 'Don't worry about her, I'm going to take care of her.'"

"Do you think they're here right now?"

"No. But I'd watch my back if I were you, Miss Gaby."

"Did that officer that Laura was sleeping with know how close you and Laura were?"

"Yeah, I've met him. I've hung out with them."

"Tell me this, Christina. What's the name of the officer Laura was sleeping with?"

"I ain't telling you his name."

"Christina, why are you going with your mom?" I say, changing the subject.

"What are my other options? The guy I'm with now beat me up for no reason. He used to treat me good, but it ain't worth him slapping me around, even though he buys me things. Sleeping with him is one thing, but abusing me is another."

I stay quiet. What do I tell a seventeen year-old girl who openly admits that she uses her body to get by on a day-to-day basis? It takes all of me to keep my mouth shut, but I do. Because I need Christina to help me. I need girls like her and Laura to be willing to come forward and lay down the law for these men so they stop taking advantage of young women like Christina.

"Christina, can I ask you something?" I say.

"Yeah, sure."

"Why would a pimp kill his source of income?"

"What are you saying? Why would a pimp kill a hooker like Laura?"

"Well, yeah."

"Let me tell you something," she says. "These men prey on girls that have issues. They look for girls whose parents don't care about them or have parents that are drug addicts, alcoholics, gamblers, gang members, or in prison. They look for girls like me. When I was eight years old, I still remember my mom taking me to the bathroom in a fast food restaurant on the way to the mountains. When I came out, she was gone. I waited for three days before social services picked me up. I didn't see my mom again for seven years.

"These men know who the girls are that have issues. They take advantage of us. If you're asking me why a man would kill a girl like Laura, somebody who's making them money? I've been beaten up before when I'm trying to get away from a guy. They'll come and stalk you, beat you up, and even leave you for dead if you try and leave them. Especially these gang members. They're all pimping out girls because prostitution is hard to uncover," says Christina truthfully.

Christina is right. No one involved is going to snitch to police. Plus, it's easy to get away with. When police stop a girl with her pimp, it's easy for her to pass him off as her boyfriend. Sex workers are a lucrative commodity for a gang and they carry less liability. They aren't easily detectible by police, such as guns, stolen merchandise, or drugs.

But the real problems start when the girl tries to get away from her pimp. These gang members will stick other gang members on them just to control their bitches. They even post things online about assaulting the sex workers that leave. People tell the girls you can stop doing this, but it's not true. Aside from getting the gang on them, pimps will threaten their sex workers and even kill them; all to show other girls what will happen if they try to leave.

"What else can you tell me about the cop that was sleeping with Laura?" I ask.

"I can tell you this. Laura told me her mom and the cop were close," she says.

"Did she say in what way?" I ask.

"She never wanted to talk about it," she says.

"Did Laura ever tell you if this cop threatened her?"

Christina stays quiet, looking down towards the metallic bench connected to the picnic table we are sitting at.

"He never threatened her, but he was aggressive sometimes. She mentioned he did things."

"Like what?"

"Tie her up."

"With what?"

"Anything he could find. Things around the motel room or even his uniform. He would take off his shirt and tie it around her," Christina says.

"What do you mean motel room?" I ask.

"Clown rented her motel rooms and sometimes Laura would be with three or four men that would come through the room. Clown would wait for her downstairs in his car and make sure she was safe. If Laura ever had a problem, she could call him and he'd be right there," she says.

"Did you actually see Clown waiting or did Laura tell you about it?" I ask.

"I saw it happen. They were trying to get me involved."

"Did Laura say how the cop would tie her up?"

"He'd just have her put her hands together above her head and tie her wrists together," Christina says. "I mean, nothing that hurt or anything. Laura never had bruises. She was cool with it. It just seemed like he wanted to domino, I mean, what's that word? Dominatrix?"

"Dominate?"

"Yeah, that. She would say that word."

I stare at Christina, who looks so young, but knows way too much about Laura and prostitution, that I'm convinced she has started hooking or is about to.

"Christina, why are you going with your mom? She's not a safe person to be with."

"I feel safer with her than with the men I've been living with lately. And I'm done living with my grandma at the trailer park. In fact, I'm heading over there right now to pick up the rest of my stuff."

"You deserve more, Christina," I say. "I want you to believe that. Your mom is no example and not a good person for you to be with. She hasn't proven to you that she's changed. A few months ago, she was trying to sell you to a man. You're better off staying with your grandma.

"You're a beautiful girl and you have so much potential. The poetry you write is amazing. You could do something with your life. It's your choice. But please think hard before you decide to stay with your mom. That's only going to land you in the wrong place at the wrong time.

"I care a lot about you and this is the only reason I'm telling you this. Your mom has a drug problem. She can't take care of you and you don't need to be taking care of her. You should be following your dreams, finishing school, and being the counselor you want to be. There's other options out there for you. When you're ready, you can call me or Angela and stay at the Airstream."

"I know," Christina replies. "You've always said that to me."

"I'm going to try and stay out of your business. But what I need you to do for me is show up to court the day after tomorrow and testify about Laura getting pimped out by Clown and the things she told you. We'll be in Department

Nineteen at one-thirty in the afternoon. If you don't show up, I'm sending out a search crew for you," I say.

"I'll show up. Someone like Clown, he's going to keep doing what he's doing, pimping out young girls. That's why I'll show up," Christina says.

"I need you to tell me one more thing," I say, reaching into my pocket and taking out the crumpled Mamacita Mason Jar note. I unfold it and study it again.

You'Re next. You'Re choice. Bullet, blade, oR flamingo vase?

It's identical to the one I received at my door.

"How'd you find that? I thought your threw those away?" says Christina.

"Why didn't you say anything?" I ask.

"I was afraid," says Christina.

"Where'd you get this?" I ask.

It was in my door jamb at my grandma's," she says.

"Who do you think left it?" I ask.

"The same person who did the drive-by. I found it the same day," she says nervously.

Christina pulls a crumpled piece of paper from her purse. "And this one was left at my grandma's yesterday," says Christina, whose eyes are filling up with tears.

I open it and read the purple ink.

You and Gaby aRe next.

27

UNRAVELED

A couple hours after leaving Lacy Park, I head home in the beast. My cell phone rings.

"Hi, Gaby, this is Officer Vince Saunter, Kiki's friend from the property room. I'm not sure if you're aware, but there's quite a stir going on at Leafwood RV Park. Your Airstream was just towed. Apparently some calls came in starting around five o'clock. Leafwood PD was dispatched out there and a flatbed was sent out there. I thought I'd give you a call, since I know how expensive it can be to store something like that and pay tow fees. You know?" says Vince.

"Do you know who requested the tow?" I ask.

"Hmmm. It should say right here. It looks like the name Bess Sanchez is showing as the initial caller in the 911 log," says Vince.

"I know exactly who that is," I say disgustedly.

I pull off the freeway ramp and head to Leafwood RV Park. The possibility that Bess could have been involved with jeopardizing The Mamacita Club appalls me. Bess is going to have to answer why she did this. The thought of her being involved in any of this, especially when I fought for her daughter and tried to get Laura help is beyond me. Bess needs to explain all of this – why she's upset at me and why she doesn't want my motorhome there. And if she doesn't explain, I will make her explain. This conversation is long overdue. She must have a problem with me personally. But I need to play this right. I want to find out what she knows about Cruz. And maybe she could give me some information about Laura's boss lady.

I pull into the Leafwood RV park. The space the Airstream was parked at is empty. Tire marks in the dirt are the only thing left. I drive towards Bess's trailer and see that her television is on inside her mobile home. Before making a sharp turn towards her home, I turn my lights and engine off and roll my Celica past Bess's space to the next home.

I step on my brakes and let my car glide until it comes to a stop. I open my door, denting it against a clay pot holding a small cactus near some rocks. I shut my door and look at my watch. 8:50 p.m. I make my way up to Bess's home. I usually try to avoid confrontation, but I'm not letting this one go. She's messing with The Mamacita Club.

I knock at Bess's door and hear a rocking type chair squeaking before I hear footsteps creaking on a floor getting louder and louder. The front door opens.

"Yes, may I help you?" asks Bess nonchalantly.

"Hi, Mrs. Sanchez, may I speak with you for a minute," I say firmly.

"Sure, what's going on?" says Bess calmly. "Come on in."

"I'm fine out here. Did you have my Airstream towed?" I ask excitedly.

"No, of course not," says Bess.

Knowing Bess is lying makes me even more angry.

"Well, why don't you explain why your name is on the dispatch log as the person who first called the police," I say.

"It was the neighbors who have been complaining. They have been asking that I call ever since the drive-by, so I finally did. Plus Mr. Vanderbilt from your office told us to report any concerns we had directly with the police. It was becoming a nuisance. Children were starting to play around it and it blocks the view of traffic," says Bess.

A teapot starts whistling loudly inside Bess's home.

"Come in, Ms. Ruiz. I need to turn the tea down," says Bess, motioning me to come inside her mobile home.

I follow her in and stand alone in her living room, desperately waiting for her to return from the kitchen so I can examine her more.

"Bess, do you have a problem with me?" I yell towards the kitchen, knowing her answer alone will tell me everything. "I mean, do you have a problem with me helping your daughter or the other girls here at the park?" I ask.

"No, no, not at all. I didn't understand what you were doing before, but I understand now," says Bess. "I'm making myself some tea. Would you like some?" Bess yells from the kitchen.

"I'm fine," I say back, disbelieving Bess.

I take a couple deep breaths and start to relax.

Bess's living room looks exactly the same way I remembered it. Never knowing if she realized Dylan and I had been in her house the day Clown was arrested, I decide I certainly am not going to bring up that subject again. The same books I gave to Christina for the program still sit in the bookshelf. Christina *did* give them to Laura. *The Alchemist.* I loved reading that book and remember how abstract it was to the girls who read it at The Mamacita Club, but I knew they would relate to it someday. The idea of always looking for something, some trunk of gold that wasn't ever there, would at some point hit them. I feel like I'm still searching for that gold, but am slowly coming to terms with the fact that it's right in front of me.

I move closer to the bookshelf, hearing Bess pouring water. The books lay horizontally on the shelf, stacked up in one straight pile one on top of the other. Wanting to read that first line of *The Alchemist*, I reach for it and pull it from the shelf.

The top of a glass jar exposes itself behind the stack of books. *Oh, my gosh.* My arms tense up and I freeze. There's no way that could be what it looks like. A million thoughts run through my head. I remain entirely silent and try to hear where Bess is.

I pretend not to have noticed what I just saw, but look one last time to make sure it is what I think it is. Trembles through my body start from my chest, move up to my face and take over my lower extremities.

The small head of a flamingo rests to the side of the jar. The bright pink and cream colors of the ceramic are as remarkable as the matching vase inside the motel room Laura was found.

I think back to the letter that rested near my peephole, threatening my life with a bullet, blade, or flamingo vase.

"Have you read that book before," says Bess in a whisper. I feel her warm breath on the side of my head.

I turn around and open *The Alchemist.* "I've always loved this book," I say nervously.

"What did you like about it?" asks Bess, suspiciously.

"Just the idea of magic, adventure, a journey, the idea of coming back to something familiar and grounded in love," I respond quickly.

"I believe there is no such thing," says Bess sternly. "At least those things were taken away from me," says Bess. "My family, my daughter, my life. All taken away," says Bess moving closer to me.

The look of anger in her eyes tells me everything I need to know. I begin to back away from the bookshelf and move toward the front door, fearing for the first time that Bess may really be capable of something like murder.

Before I have a chance to decide whether to make a run for it, Bess takes out a sharp pocket knife from her apron pocket. "My life was taken away by you," says Bess, staring evily into my eyes. My sight blurs as I catch the shimmer from the blade. I see my mom with a stab wound through her chest.

My vision sharpens once Bess grabs the hair on the back of my head. Bending me back over her rocking chair, I lose my balance and land on my tailbone, losing any chance to grab my Lady Smith. Dammit, I think, fearing the worst if Bess gets to it. She holds her pocket knife up to my throat.

"Please, Bess, you don't have to do this," I plead, staring into her eyes, which are blankly staring through me. It's that same blank stare my mom had in that photo.

Mom, please help me, please save me. A violent kick at Bess's front door startles us both. Christina stands in the doorway of Bess's home, with her arms extended holding a gun, ordering Bess to let me go. Everything around me goes blurry and I begin to faint.

28

SURE SIGNS

I take the day off to recuperate from Bess trying to kill me last night. Down at the Cove, I inhale the smell of salt water and realize more than ever how lucky I am to be alive. It brings me the peace that I need to call upon the Universe.

I sit breathing, in and out, in a rhythm and pace that slows down everything around. Laura comes walking towards me, wearing a white flowing dress with her hair pinned up to its sides by white and yellow flower hair fasteners. Her smile calms me and she sits next to me on the rocks.

"When I first met you, I thought there was nothing you could do for me, ever. I didn't care if another day went by that I never saw you or spoke with you again," Laura says.

"But my gut told me that I needed to trust you, that I needed to put my faith in you, because I had nothing to lose. What drew me to you was your sense of hope, your belief in leaps of faith, and your fearlessness. You seemed like you could make my dreams come true, especially to help me get out of the ugliness of where I live and do well in school. That's why I believed in you and wanted to join The Mamacita Club.

"But the best part was that you believed in me. That's what you should continue to do every week over and over again; keep helping young girls like me. I may not make it through, but the next girl will, I promise. There will be another girl like me who wants to join The Mamacita Club and needs your help, and you will help her as you wanted to help me.

"None of this is your fault. I could never play on the edge of the boat like the girl you saw in the Walled City. You don't have to worry about disturbing me. You did what you could do. There's nothing more you can do. Let me go.

"I ask you one thing, though. Make sure my mother is held responsible for what she did to me. She tried to take my life and she tried to take yours. She has a black heart. The case will be difficult, but know in your heart that she is the one who took my life. You will be able to prove the case with the little evidence you have. Just promise me that you will do this for me," Laura says while getting up.

"Laura, tell me how I can prove this, tell me. I need something more for the case. I need you to testify. Please don't leave, please. I need to save you," I scream, feeling my legs trapped.

I struggle to get myself up but my legs aren't responding to what I'm trying to do. They are limp, they feel heavy. Laura walks away from me coolly, not looking back, with a cigarette in her hand, smoking, inhaling long slow breaths, one after another.

She continues walking along the rocks, then flicks her cigarette into the water, causing the whole ocean to roar up in an orange flame, before she disappears in the distance.

I sit alone, watching the flames dance on the ocean at the Cove.

The day after watching the flames dance on the ocean, I hold Laura's hand at the hospital and rub her cheek. I whisper to her that I hope she can keep fighting through recovery and someday, tell us what happened. Her eyes flutter when I sit by her, alone in her hospital room. She focuses in and out with her eyes. I tell her that I know her mom was involved and she smiles. I tell her how her mom was about to kill me, too, but Christina, who was visiting her grandma, heard me screaming and came to the front door.

I encourage her to join The Mamacita Club when she turns eighteen so she can tell her story to other young girls. I ask her to stay strong and pull through this for the case. But I also tell her that if the fight is too hard, I will be there to help her die, too. I tell her that it's okay to die. This gives me a sense of peace, where I no longer feel I'm trying to control her destiny.

The doctors thought Laura was a lost cause, but it's been three weeks since she's been off her life support and she's still alive. She was in a coma for weeks, but now she is able to eat food even though it's spoon-fed. She can shake her head up and down and answer questions. She can acknowledge pain and sensation and moan, but she still can't speak. Laura has no family left, and her mom is now in custody for assaulting me. She's going to be an orphan. But Laura pulled through herself.

Laura looks peaceful, and I stare at her a few times just to make sure she's still breathing. After crying myself to sleep last night thinking she might not pull through, I know I need to stop trying to save her and constantly be in control. I decided to surrender and let nature work its course. I feel free, but still hopeful Laura will pull through. I stay focused on Laura's breathing, thinking she could die at any moment. But for the first time, I feel that I'd be okay with it.

Today, I hope that if Laura dies, it's in my presence. My mom used to say that people who are dying wait for their loved ones to be by their side before they take their last breath. Too bad my mom didn't have her choice of who she would take her last breath with. I know she would have picked me, Señor Borges, Nana, and our cat Penny.

Laura opens her eyes and stares right at me, squeezing my hand. She starts studying my face, eyes, and a tear that starts falling down my face. "Christina saved you," says Laura.

"Laura," I say hopefully.

The warmth from her fingers radiates through my arm as I shake my head trying to figure out if what I just saw and heard was real. These would be Laura's first words.

"Yes, she did. You're right. I was working so hard trying to save Christina. But at the end, she saved me," I say.

Thirty mintues after visiting Laura at the hospital, I sit across from Angela inside the Airstream. While she recites her usual angel babble, I cut Angela's deck of tarot cards in three. She flips over the Eight of Swords. A woman is handcuffed and blindfolded, surrounded by swords.

"Well. Are you feeling trapped today?" asks Angela.

"Yes, and frustrated. All the signs were all there. The Mamacita Mason Jar. I kept getting clues from the Universe and just ignored them. The ship sailing in the distance when I was at the Cove, the ship I saw inside the Mamacita Mason Jar, the ship I saw in the Walled City all clueing me in to the scraps of paper inside the Mamacita Mason Jar. We could've found those scraps, spoken to Christina and solved this case weeks ago if I just paid attention to them, and that frustrates me," I say.

I look down at the tarot card with Angela.

"She's trapped in a prison of her own making. Her thoughts and beliefs are keeping her stuck. That's what you're doing. The energy of the Eight of Swords can be frustrating because *you* are the one who holds the key. Her hands are cuffed together but to nothing else. All she has to do is remove her blindfold to find the key. And then she can free herself," says Angela.

"Why do I do this to myself?" I ask.

"Sometimes, when you are too busy with life, and you rush through your days, ignore those around you, or what the Universe is handing you, you waste time and energy. It's not the worst thing you can do, but it's good to slow things down. Things don't need to be figured out immediately.

"If you had discovered the Mamacita Mason Jar clue the first time it came to you at the Cove, you may have realized what was on those scraps of paper and spoken to Christina sooner. But you never would have visited the Walled City. Do you understand what I'm saying to you?" asks Angela.

"I would have never met Señor Santiago-Borges. I would have never experienced the beautiful Walled City, the people, the culture, the passion. I would have never learned the wisdom of my mom and how she lived and loved from the perspective of someone who knew her in a different time. And Dylan and I wouldn't have realized our love. Is this what you mean?" I ask.

"Precisely," Angela replies. "Things happen for a reason. Love happens and fails for a reason. People come into your life with a purpose, whether it means to give you a nugget of information to answer a pressing question for the day or for your life. You must never ever question why you ignored these signs. It happened for a reason and you must just let go and trust that the Universe has a plan for you.

"What we do know is that your angels are still sending you signs and clues to help you with your cases. So that's a good thing. It tells me you're not abusing them. Keep your eye out and ask the Universe for more signs and clues about love, Dylan, and how to prove Bess's involvement," Angela says.

"Where do I look? I'm stuck. That flamingo face I saw in Bess's home was gone by the time police searched for it. But I know for sure it was there. We can't even use it, anyway, since I was snooping in her bookshelf without a warrant," I say.

"Well, keep snooping and stay curious. You have an intuition you haven't been in tune with. Remember back to when you were a kid. Children have strong intuitions. They are so creative, passionate, excited, and imaginative. They have a sense of wonder. Just because you grow legs and unpleasant emotional experiences over the years doesn't mean you should lose that.

"You need to make room in your mind and heart for these things again so healthy feelings can energize you and help you grow and become happy again. It's so easy to get bogged down in your head and analyze everything, breaking the flow of what our gut, our hearts, and what the Universe is telling us," says Angela.

"I think I know what you're saying. I shouldn't disturb my inner child. I need to stop bothering that young playful girl I saw sitting at the edge of the boat playing in the Walled City," I say.

"Exactly."

I look back down at the tarot card.

"Why do I feel so afraid?" I ask.

"Because you don't know how to free yourself and break this case. But you can't think your way out of this frustration. Especially if you use the same thoughts, logic, and reasoning as you did when you first got into this investigation. The more you struggle, the more stuck you become," she says.

Looking at the blindfold and tied hands reminds me of how we found Laura in the motel room.

"This card gives you clues to solve this case and loosen the knots you have in your own life. You hold the key."

"Laura was found tied and blindfolded this same way," I say.

"But the question is, do you think she could have saved herself?" Angela asks.

I take a deep breath in and let it out. I think of Laura, my mom, and the sex worker in the Walled City.

"I don't know anymore," I say hopelessly.

"Gaby, prostitution and domestic violence are forms of slavery. Mentally, the women are stuck in a jail. They've been so brainwashed and demeaned," Angela says.

"I just feel like if I only..." I start before Angela interrupts me.

"Stop! If you only what? Saved them? Helped them? Gaby, don't you get it? They would need to have a mental breakthrough themselves to escape. Just like you need a breakthrough to let go and forgive yourself over what happened to your mom," Angela says.

"I know. I realized that in the Walled City. I just need to believe it now. And I need to figure out how I can link Bess to Laura's assault," I say.

"Stay as fearless as you can and let the Universe guide you. Isn't it enough for you to go forward with your case? I mean, knowing in your heart what happened and finding that flamingo face?"

"No, we need solid evidence to prove her mom was involved. Dylan's even questioning whether I really saw the flamingo face. I need something else. I have nothing."

"You promised her justice. Your mission has always been to save women, and Laura is one of us."

"I know, but I need some evidence linking her mom," I say.

"Keep looking for signs. The Universe seems to be working in your favor right now. The answers will come. Just be patient. Tell me more about the flames you saw on the ocean," Angela says.

"It was this enormous eruption of flames on the ocean. It was beautiful actually."

"Were you afraid?"

"No. I knew the flames wouldn't hurt me. I was up on the rocks and knew I wasn't in danger."

"What happened right after the flames stopped?"

"All the water was completely drained from the ocean. I could see all kinds of marine life. Then the dry land started filling back up with water."

"Hmmm. Like a regression followed by a transgression. What happened right before the flames came?" says Angela inquisitively.

"Laura tossed her cigarette into the ocean."

"Hmmm," says Angela curiously. "Don't ignore the signs that are right in front of you and don't be too wrapped up in your head to miss these things. Comb through the evidence. The devil is in the details," Angela says.

"I'll see what I can do," I say, standing up and grabbing my purse from the backside of my chair.

"And remember something," says Angela.

"What's that?" I ask.

"We can't solve problems by using the same kind of thinking we used when we created them."

"Right. Albert Einstein. Eight of Swords," I say, leaving the Angel's Den.

Thirty minutes after Angela's angel reading at the Airstream, I sit at my desk still contemplating what to do about Bess. She's sitting in custody for assaulting me but that won't bring justice for Laura. I pick up my desk phone and call Dylan.

"We need to dig deeper into Bess's involvement in the motel assault," I say.

"Gaby, I don't know where else to look. Are you sure you even saw that flamingo face at her house?" asks Dylan.

"I can't believe you're still questioning that," I say.

"I just know sometimes you black out or have flashbacks, so I wanted to make sure," says Dylan.

I purse my lips tightly, forcing myself to stay quiet and think before speaking.

"Yes, I saw it, Dylan," I say indignantly.

"It's just that it wasn't there and...," Dylan starts before stopping himself. "We don't have anything else at this point, Gaby," he continues matter-of-factly.

"Bess's DNA was found on the belt," I say dramatically.

"From the beginning, she always said it was hers. Laura borrowed it."

"Did you check the size of the belt?"

"I don't remember," says Dylan.

"Did you compare her prints?" I ask.

"We're doing that right now. Gaby, what is this all about?" Dylan asks.

"Clown used to sit downstairs at the motel in his car waiting for Laura to get done hooking. I'm wondering if that's the information he keeps wanting to give us. Maybe he walked up to the room afterwards and saw the mess," I say.

"If the print's not hers, I'm not looking any further. We've got her in custody for assaulting you anyway," Dylan says firmly.

"But a part of the murder weapon was found in Bess's house," I snap back.

Dylan sighs. "So where should I start?" Dylan asks defeatedly. "All this stuff you're telling me seems like a stretch."

"How about we start with this? I know there was a cigarette on the landing outside the motel room along with a soda bottle. Can you get those looked at for DNA? And put a rush on the prints?"

"C'mon Gaby, that stuff is trash. Do you know how many motel guests come and go through that landing. We have no idea how old that stuff is. I'll check on the fingerprint and we can go from there."

"You saw how good of a cleaning job that housekeeper was doing when we first got there. She was sweeping the landing, so that stuff couldn't have been sitting there that long."

"I'm not doing it. You call Miranda Jules and convince her."

"She likes *you*. She'll do it for *you*. She doesn't like me. If Bess's DNA is on either of those items, that means she's lying about not being there. What's the harm?"

"There is no harm. It's just a big waste of time. It costs a lot of money. Plus we're still waiting on the fingerprint comparison."

"Dylan, Bess smokes," I say dramatically.

"And I'm sure a lot of guests at that motel do, too."

"Does it require you to actually lift a finger and do more work, write one more report, make one more arrest, testify in one more trial? Is that what this is about? That you don't need to lock one more person up?"

"Stop, Gaby."

"Or is it because it would force you to work with me for a little bit longer? Is that what this is about? Or does it have to do with Miranda Jules? Or does it have to do with you not believing I saw the flamingo face inside Bess's house. Well, forget it. I'll call Miranda myself," I say.

"Gaby, stop. I don't care about doing more investigation on the case. I care about the case almost as much as you. I want to get the right person just as much as you. I just don't see the point in looking at this anymore."

"I'll order it then."

"You can't."

"Why not?"

"Because I'm the investigator on the case; you're just the prosecutor. She's going to call me for approval, anyway. There's been no arrest for Bess on Laura's incident, so the case is not with your agency yet. That's just how it works."

"Don't ever talk to me again, Dylan Mack."

"Gaby, stop. If it's that important to you, I'll look into it. Calm down. I'll run with it like any other lead. I'll call Miranda, swing by the Fingerprint Office, and I'll be at your office in an hour to prepare for Clown's preliminary hearing," says Dylan.

29

TRUSTING GUT

Getting ready for Clown's preliminary hearing, I reread the Fingerprint Office's report. Dylan reviews his reports.

"I can't believe this," I say.

"What are you reading?" he asks.

I look up from the report I'm holding.

"That the thumbprint on the vase matches that disgusting thumb skin we brought back from the Walled City," I say.

"You mean the thumb skin that *I* brought."

"Yes, that *you* brought. But *I* sliced," I say jokingly.

"I still can't believe you did that," says Dylan.

"I've always told you, you do things your way and I'll do them my way," I say.

Dylan and I laugh.

"In all seriousness Dylan, I'm glad we're only proceeding on the pimping charges against Clown," I say. "But I still don't get what the connection is between Bess, Clown and

Cruz. And why Cruz was threatening me and Christina in the first place," I say.

My phone rings and I pick up.

"This is a collect call from an inmate at a correction facility. To accept the call, press one. To not accept the call, press two," says an automated operator. I press one, even though my office says we're not supposed to accept collect calls.

"This is Gaby," I say, putting the call on speaker phone and holding my finger up to my lips, signaling Dylan to stay quiet.

"Ms. Ruiz, this is Javier. I want to give you some information. I know who did this to Laura and it's not Rodrigo. It's not Deputy Cruz either. And I swear on your life," says Javier.

"I don't believe one word you're telling me until you go on tape with this," I say.

"Ain't doing it," says Javier.

"Then why'd you call? You must want something from me," I say.

"Fine. I'll do it , but you gotta let me out," he says.

"I can't. You gotta tell me what you know first, then we go from there. It's standard procedure," I say. "Plus, why should I believe you anyway? Like you said, you just want to get out," I say.

"That's not the only reason," he says. "I messed up with Laura. I know it. But I ain't no child molestor. And that's what's on my back in here. There's more to it. And you need to know that," he says.

"Why would I let you out Javier? So you can go and do this to someone else?" I say.

"I've changed. Gimme a chance. I saw an article in jail today in the paper on your club and how you give people a chance. I seen what you are doing for the girls is making a difference. I wish I had someone who believed in me back then. Even if you only change one out of ten, that one can go and help ten more. I seen Laura change after she met you. She started thinking more about her life. I want to tell people about my mistakes if it could help them change," Javier says.

I stay quiet, imagining the Tuckford Press in the hands of inmates wearing orange jumpsuits sitting on the toilet inside a jail cell.

"Hang on for a second," I say, pushing the hold button.

I look at Dylan.

"What am I supposed to do?" I say.

"I say offer him immunity. Look, we really don't have a case with Laura in the condition she's in. See if at least he'll bite on something and see if he'll talk," Dylan says.

"My office is never gonna give this guy immunity. He had sex with her," I say.

"Yeah, but look at it this way. We don't have enough evidence either way without Laura. What we do want is to find out what he has. Especially if it's related to Bess. We don't have anything to lose by at least offering him a deal," Dylan says.

"I'll need to get all kinds of approval to even speak with him," I say.

"You have authority to give him immunity. I've seen other prosecutors do it."

"Not in this county."

"No. But in other ones."

I think back to Tanner's training on jailhouse snitches and his words of advice: "Gang members, sex offenders, pimps, and drug dealers can never be trusted. A good snitch can make your case but a bad one will break it. Trust your gut."

I look down at the phone and watch the red hold button flashing. Then I think of Laura and look at *The Mamacita Club* screensaver traveling across my computer monitor.

"How would anyone ever find out that I gave him immunity, anyway?" I say defiantly.

"Now that's my girl talking. Your office would only find out if we used him to testify against. We have nothing to lose," Dylan says.

"Don't ask permission. Beg for forgiveness later?" I say.

Dylan shakes his head up and down, agreeing.

"You know this could cost me my job," I say.

"Or the investigation on Bess, if we don't hear him out."

"True, but Javier has a motive to lie to get out of trouble," I say.

"Don't forget we're still waiting for DNA. I'm submitting the cigarette and soda bottle tomorrow. This guy's not going to lie. He has something to say," Dylan says.

My gut tells me to take a leap of faith and trust that Javier might be the key to solving Laura's case.

"Do you have your tape recorder?" I ask.

Dylan takes out a small microcassette recorder from his suit pocket, pushes the record button, and places it near my desk phone.

I depress the hold button on my phone and get Javier back on the line.

30

BRIDGE TO CLOSURE

I never thought a day like today would ever come. I'm sitting in court elbow to elbow with Mike Tanner, a man I've despised for nineteen years. I've learned that the Universe works in strange ways and I'm not about to question it right now. If there is one place I would choose to sit next to him, it's here, as co-counsel during the trial of People versus Bess Sanchez. Bess is charged with attempted murder of her daughter Laura. Just four months ago, I got that jail call from Javier. He filled in the gaps we needed.

Javier came clean about Bess trying to kill Laura. He knew the whole time Bess was Laura's boss, selling her for sex. And she allowed him to have sex with her too. Clown provided the protection, hanging out in his Lincoln while Laura was servicing her clients. Bess was even selling Laura to Deputy Cruz. It all made sense why Bess never wanted Laura joining The Mamacita Club.

Javier knew the whole time Bess planned to take care of Laura, but did nothing about it. He only had to gain from it since he was facing unlawful sex charges. It wasn't until Javier discovered that Bess was sexually involved with Deputy Cruz, that he decided to come forward and tell us everything.

It didn't take long before Tanner reminded me Javier couldn't testify against Bess because of the spousal privilege, but Tanner didn't make a big deal about me cutting Javier a 12 year deal. Javier helped us connect the dots and I think Tanner wanted to cut me a break. From the day I spoke to Javier, Dylan worked the case tirelessly and that was just what we needed. He treated Bess like she was a brand new suspect. And he never again questioned me about seeing the flamingo face inside her home.

Judge Samuel Hoffman's courtroom is packed with attorneys, Laura, her friends from The Mamacita Club, and Dylan. No one sits on Bess's side of the courtroom, except a media journalist taking notes. Bess and her attorney, douche bag defense attorney Collin Fox, sit on the opposite side of Tanner and me.

Fox and I went to law school together. During a night out in my first year, I confided things in him I wish I never had. It was late and I had one too many bourbons at the local pub. The best part of that night was that I had the sense not to sleep with him. He tried to make out with me when we got back to my car, but I was smart enough to put a stop to that. I didn't want to get arrested for lewd conduct, plus he had bad breath. He could fill a car with the stench of his halitosis just from breathing. There was no way I was going to make out with him. Neither Fox nor I felt the need to disclose this to Tanner or Judge Hoffman during pretrial motions.

This is the first time in my career I've sat as co-counsel in a trial. I had to because Fox put me on the defense witness list after trying to have me recused from the case. He argued I was a material witness who found Laura's body, cut Cruz's thumb off, and had the Mamacita Mason Jar notes in my chain of custody. These reasons were defense tactics that Mr. "I'm a loser defense attorney" tried to use to get me off a case he otherwise knew I would kick his butt in.

Tanner fixed the problem by assigning the case to himself, then asked me to be co-counsel. It was his way of saying, "We'll show you," to Fox. But also, I think Tanner did it to get me on his good side. He knew Laura's case was way too important for me to turn down the opportunity to work with him. So I accepted and Judge Hoffman approved.

Tanner and I agreed he's going to do the opening statement and closing argument. I'm going to be called as the first witness to describe Javier's case, finding Laura's body, and striking a 12 year deal with Javier to give us information about Bess. Tanner agreed that I'll do Laura's and all the experts' direct examination. I like the idea of handling all the scientific stuff, especially the gory finger testimony.

I also get to cross-examine Bess if she testifies, which Tanner thinks is a long shot since any skilled defense attorney should be able to talk their client out of testifying. But I think the odds are good, since it's douche bag Fox we're talking about.

One by one, the jurors pass us on their way up to the jury box. Four of them smile at me. Two are holding big coffee mugs. The jurors are fresh for a Monday morning.

They look like kids arriving for their first day at school. Judge Hoffman takes the bench.

"Remain seated, come to order, court is now in session," says the deputy.

"Good morning, everyone," Judge Hoffman begins. "We are about to start trial in the case of the People versus Bess Sanchez. The defendant is here represented by her attorney Collin Fox. The People are represented by Special Assistant Prosecutor Mike Tanner and Assistant Prosecutor Gaby Ruiz. All members of our jury panel have taken their seats along with the two alternates. This morning is the start of our trial where we will hear opening statements and testimony from our witnesses. Mr. Tanner, would you like to give an opening statement on behalf of the People?"

"I certainly would. Thank you," says Mike Tanner, standing up and looking as impeccable as always.

He walks up through the well, which is the area right in front of the jury box leading up to the judge's bench. It's poor etiquette to "enter the well" without asking the judge for permission and could be considered a violation of court rules. But Judge Hoffman gave Tanner and Fox permission to enter before trial started.

"Ladies and gentlemen of the jury. Good morning," Tanner begins. "This case is about power, control, and murder. Back on July sixth, this defendant sitting right here at the counsel table, Bess Sanchez, did the most despicable thing any mother could ever imagine. She attempted to carry out the brutal murder of her seventeen-year-old daughter Laura. Then she sat back for months watching police investigate Laura's boyfriend as the primary suspect.

"Laura was struck over the head with this ceramic vase by this woman. And why did she do this, you might ask? It was to control Laura. It was to teach her a lesson. It was to silence her. And it did, but only temporarily.

"Sometimes the Universe and medicine work in strange ways. No one expected Laura to survive, much less fight to get out of her coma. But she did and she sits here in court, in her wheelchair, because just one person believed in her; that is Assistant Prosecutor Gabriela Ruiz, whom I'm honored to call my co-counsel. Laura also is here today because of her determination to survive, fight, and see that the right person is brought to justice, Bess Sanchez. Thank you."

There're not many times I've been in the spotlight to answer questions about my personal life. One of these times was when I was hired at the Prosecutor's Office and asked about the most personal information like if I ever used drugs, committed a crime, or lied about anything significant. I had to disclose things I did when I was nineteen years old, like getting a Tinkerbell tramp stamp tattooed on my lower back and posing in a yellow polka dot bikini on top of a bigrig as the pin-up girl for a trucking magazine.

Now is another time I'm feeling exposed as I sit in the witness stand on cross-examination.

Tanner thought we should get this over with, so I agreed to be the first witness and now I'm regretting it. Douche bag Fox stands up to start cross-examination. The audience section of the courtroom is filled. Judge Hoffman and his clerk, deputy, and court reporter's eyes are on me.

Nothing can fully prepare you to be the focus of the defense case. I realize most of it is for show, especially when the defense has nothing else to go on. I'm accused of how I tainted everyone as an overzealous prosecutor. Blah blah blah.

I wasn't surprised when Fox cross-examined me about the Mamacita Mason Jar scribbles from the girls and why I didn't tell anyone sooner about my suspicion Clown wasn't involved. None of this cross-examination seems to bother me until the part about my mom comes up.

"Isn't it true, Ms. Ruiz, that your mother was killed by your stepfather when you were twelve years old and you witnessed the entire thing?" asks Fox.

I stare straight at Fox's grey and mint green tie that sits against his perfectly pressed white shirt. His navy blue suit pants are tight around his crotch making me think he's trying to show off something that isn't there. His pants being too short leads me to believe he was way too excited to wear his new suit before sending it to the tailor.

"Yes, that is true, sir. But what does my mom have to do with this case?" I ask.

"Just answer my question," says Fox.

"I did. Do you have another one?" I snap back.

"Ms. Ruiz, I know this may be sensitive material to discuss, but I'm going to ask you to just answer the questions that are asked and not to pose any questions back to defense counsel. Do you understand?" says Judge Hoffman.

"I'm sorry, Your Honor," I say.

"Proceed, counsel," says Judge Hoffman, looking towards Fox.

"You'd agree that in this case, one parent has allegedly tried to kill a member of her family, correct?" asks Fox.

"That's what your client did."

"That is similar to what happened to you, isn't that right?" asks Fox.

"In what way?"

"One of your parents killed another family member," says Fox.

"It's completely different.   Plus, this trial is about Mrs. Sanchez trying to kill Laura," I say.

"Ms. Ruiz, I'm going to ask you again.   Isn't it true that one of your stepparents killed your other parent?" asks Fox.

"Yes, my stepfather killed my mom," I say.

"Were you upset over what you witnessed when you were a child?"

"Who wouldn't be?" I say sarcastically.

"Exactly.   And I would imagine you were upset at your stepfather for a long time after that."

"I was."

"Have you seen your stepfather since he was convicted?"

I look at Tanner, then Judge Hoffman, hoping one of them will object. They look away from me.

"No, Mr. Fox, I haven't."

"Do you plan to?"

"Objection, relevance," says Tanner.

"Sustained," says Judge Hoffman.

"That experience affected you so much that you made a promise to yourself that you would protect women.   Isn't that true?"

"I did. And your point?"

"My point is that you will go to any length, bend the rules, step outside the line to carry out that mission, isn't that true?"

"Like what specifically are you talking about?" I ask.

"Like going all the way to the Walled City to cut off a man's thumb? Not to mention the same man, whose print was on the murder weapon," says Fox.

"That was part of what needed to be done. And for the record, I only sliced off the skin pad of his thumb."

"You disfigured a body for purposes of your investigation?" asks Fox dramatically.

"If you want to talk about disfiguring, let's talk about Laura. She received a gash to her thumb during the assault *and* had to have her thumb amputated right here in Tuckford County because your client tied a belt around her wrists so tight she developed gangrene," I snap back.

"Your Honor, I'm going to move to strike that answer," says Fox.

"Overruled."

"Mr. Fox, some get an eye for an eye, others get a thumb for a thumb," I say, causing the whole courtroom to erupt in laughter.

"You're quite witty, Ms. Ruiz. Speaking of thumbs, your thumbprint was in fact found on Officer Cruz's front door handle the night he turned up dead," says Fox.

"It was," I respond reluctantly, regretting I jiggled his front door handle when Kiki and I visited his home.

"You were one of the last people to see Cruz alive just like you were one of the last to see Laura before the assault, isn't that true?" Fox.

I agree with Fox disgustedly.

"How long have you been a prosecutor?" asks Fox slyly.

"Six years."

"How many cases have you tried during that time?"

"Around forty."

"In how many of those have you slept with the lead investigator?"

"Objection," says Tanner, stepping in to try and save me.

"Sustained," says Judge Hoffman.

I wish I had my nine millimeter Glock right now.

"You said that you went up to Room 333, is that true?" asks Fox.

"Yes, that's where we found Laura," I say.

"In fact, before you found her, you pinged a location at the intersection of where Motel Leafwood was, isn't that true?" says Fox.

"It is," I say.

"How did you know to go to Room 333?" says Fox.

"I just had a feeling," I say, starting to worry that Fox knows something about my powers.

"Is that how you investigate cases, based on feelings?" says Fox.

"Objection, relevance," says Tanner.

"Sustained. Move on and ask a more relevant question," says Judge Hoffman, saving me.

"When you gained access to Room 333, you saw what I believed you described as the most horrific scene you've ever seen. Is that correct?" asks Fox.

"It was," I say.

"Let's revisit that scene," says Fox, picking up an exhibit that looks like a photo.

"Your Honor, may I approach the witness?" asks Fox.

I start feeling really warm. I look down at my hands that are starting to shake like they are becoming possessed. I start counting my fingers to make sure they're all there, something I used to do as a kid when I was afraid. 1, 2, 3, 4, 5, 6, 7.

"May I ask why he's approaching?" asks Tanner, standing up.

"To show her a photograph of the motel room," says Fox, waving the photo in his hand like he's trying to show the jury.

Tanner looks at me. I'm sure I look like a deer in headlights. My breathing feels really shallow and goose bumps travel from my tailbone all the way up over my shoulders and through my arms heading to my fingertips. My arms, biceps, and fingers all of a sudden freeze.

"Objection, Your Honor," says Tanner.

"On what gound?" says douche bag.

"Relevance and foundation," says Tanner.

"What is the relevance of this, counsel?" asks Judge Hoffman.

"This is the crime scene that Ms. Ruiz is a percipient witness of. I should be able to examine her about her personal observations she made," says Fox.

"He should do this with the crime scene technician who took the photo," says Tanner, looking at me.

"Your objection is overruled," says Hoffman.

Fox walks right up to me and places a photo face down in front of me.

"I just placed People's Exhibit One right next to you. I would like you to turn that photo over, take a look at it, and tell me whether you recognize what's depicted in it," says Fox.

Before reaching for the photo, I stare at its blank backside, remembering the photo that Tanner showed me when I testified in my stepfather's trial. And I start to freeze.

"Ms. Ruiz, did you hear the instruction?" asks Judge Hoffman.

I shake my head up and down in agreement.

"I'm going to object again, to showing this witness the photograph," says Tanner.

"Overruled. I'm going to order you to follow Mr. Fox's instruction and turn the photo over to look at it," says Judge Hoffman.

Just as I start to reach for the photo, I hear Tanner again.

"Your Honor, I'm objecting again," he says.

"On what grounds this time?" asks Judge Hoffman frustratedly.

"Beyond the scope. This photo belongs to the People. I intentionally did not use any photos with this witness. And defense should have brought their own photos if they wanted to use them during cross-examination," says Tanner.

"Counsel?" says Judge Hoffman inquisitively, looking at Fox.

"I didn't bring any. And would need about an hour to go print them. I only have them on a CD," says Fox.

"You should have prepared your own exhibits for trial, Mr. Fox. I'm going to sustain the People's objection, but I'm also going to allow you some time to go print your photos," says Judge Hoffman.

I hear the jurors start to sigh and shift their bodies in the jury box. I look up at Tanner and smile at him, before mouthing the words, *it's okay*. Then, I turn towards Judge Hoffman.

"Your Honor, I'm fine. If it's okay with the People, I'll look at the photograph," I say.

"That's fine with me," says Tanner.

"Very well, go ahead," says Judge Hoffman.

I turn over the picture and stare at Laura's naked body on the motel bed, then turn it back down. I can't help but remember my mom's silk kimono in the photo I was ordered to look at during her trial. That picture will stay burned into my memory forever.

Tears roll down my cheeks and I reach for a tissue sniffling and wiping my tears. I look down and cry as silently as I know how to, trying to remember if I'm supposed to answer a question.

The jury starts to reach for the tissue boxes that are sitting on the railing of the jury box.

I finally come up for air to answer more of Fox's nonsense questions about the crime scene.

"How long have you been running The Mamacita Club out of your motorhome?"

"Since my first marriage ended."

"First? How many marriages have you had?"

"The same number you can probably count up to."

"Answer the question, Ms. Ruiz," directs Judge Hoffman.

"One, so far. But I'm shooting for three like J-Lo, hoping it won't turn into five like Rita Hayworth," I say, receiving a smile from one of the divorced women on the jury panel.

"Speaking of her, aren't you also known as the Pin-Up Prosecutor?"

"That's one of my nicknames."

"How many do you have?"

"It depends what day of the week you're talking about. Or what pin-up costume I'm in. Or if I'm in court versus The Mamacita Club out at the Airstream. I've been called Latina, Carmen Miranda, J-Lo, Eight of Swords, Bruja, Trailer Hillbilly, Rockabilly, Grace Under Pressure, Gang Banger, Bulldog Stick-It-To-Em Lawyer, the Closer. I can go on and on."

"What's your favorite?"

"Mamacita," I say.

"And let the record reflect, the witness has a red flower in her hair that's pulled back and she has red lipstick on. Let the record reflect all of that. Just out of curiosity, how would you say *spicy* in Spanish? Caliente?" says Judge Hoffman.

"Picante. Caliente. It's all the same as Mamacita," I say, smiling at Judge Hoffman.

"Hot, spicy, and Mamacita in what way, Assistant Prosecutor Mrs.... I mean Ms. Ruiz?" says Fox emphasizing the fact I'm not a Mrs.

"My friends call me Mamacita. I like to salsa dance and I'm Latina. It's a term of endearment. I'm different to them. We all need that unexpected friend in your close circle. Someone who's just different. That's who I am and what I like about being Mamacita," I say, giggling inside wondering if Fox's friends call him *Hal* for his halitosis.

"I believe you were quoted in the Tuckford Press stating that you wear pinstripes by day and pin-ups by night. Can you explain exactly what that means?"

"It speaks for itself. There's nothing to explain."

"Do you also dress in garters, stockings, and other provocative things at night?"

"That's none of your business, but when I'm around the girls, of course not. We're professionals. We just wanted to pick fun alter egos. The girls dress up, too. We encourage them to be creative; it's all a sign that they're in recovery."

"And let me get this right. You choose pin-up models as your alter ego?"

"It works with the girls and helps to teach them things."

"Like what? How to become a prostitute and wind up blindfolded, tied up, and almost dead in a motel room?"

Just as I'm about to stand up and personally walk up to Fox and kick him in the balls, I think twice. Taking a deep breath in and letting it out, I smile politely. I can be a lady when I need to. Plus, poor Fox has no clue how to serve his community, our youth, or even his bad breath. The only thing he knows how to serve is himself.

"Mr. Fox. You and I both know that Laura should have joined The Mamacita Club. But your client didn't let her," I say sternly.

"Isn't the real truth that your office didn't allow her into your club because it was a conflict of interest?"

"Everyone in the criminal justice system could have dealt with that. A judge could have ordered her into my club or her stepfather Javier and my office could have waived any conflict; but we couldn't even get to that point, because she was a minor. And your client said no thanks. Laura was trying to change. She wanted to join The Mamacita Club and even told Clown and Bess the night she was assaulted that she wanted to stop prostituting. Clown was actually going to let her go. Bess, on the other hand, had a different plan," I say.

"And you believe that Clown was going to let her go?"

"I have seen some of the most selfish people motivate the people around them to make better choices than they did."

"Wow, that's pretty liberal of you, Ms. Ruiz, wouldn't you say?"

"It's the truth."

"Following that logic and assuming you believe my client is guilty, wouldn't it be possible she acted in a heat of passion, upset at Laura wanting to stop?"

"That's up for the jury to decide, but my personal opinion is absolutely not. Hours before this happened, Laura told your client that she was going to testify against Javier and stop prostituting. Your client wasn't trying to motivate Laura to make better choices. She was trying to control her and spent hours planning it."

"I'm showing you Defense Exhibit Number 20. Am I reading this article correctly that a certified angel reader works at The Mamacita Club?"

"Yeah, that's Angela. She's amazing. She's certified in Angel Therapy."

"So she's like those fortune tellers with a crystal ball?"

"No, she gets her messages from angels, not plastic balls."

"What's her pin-up?"

"Angel Gabriel."

"Gabriel? I thought your club was all women?"

"It is. There's some dispute whether Gabriel is a male or female. In Judaism, Gabriel may have been thought to be a female angel. Angels in general don't have a gender."

"Interesting. There's an angel in the Airstream. But what's more interesting is how seriously you take this. Do you have an angel?" says Fox laughing.

"Angels are like buttholes, Mr. Fox; we all have them," I say, causing the courtroom to erupt in laughter as Judge Hoffman glares at me pounding his gavel on his desk.

"You didn't answer my question. Do you have an angel?"

"Objection, relevance," says Tanner agressively.

"Overruled," says Tanner.

"Yes," I respond.

"How does your angel communicate with you?" says Fox inquisitively.

"Angels are like gut intuitions — everyone's got them, just not everyone listens to them," I say genuinely.

"Did you get an intuition before that drive-by happened?" asks Fox.

"Maybe so. I *was* dressed like a mob wife that night," I say nervously, speaking before thinking.

"Excuse me? The Mafia is in the Airstream now? Explain that to us, Ms. Ruiz," says Fox dramatically.

"We were learning about crimes and how sometimes the whole family enables it. Gang members in this county have their girlfriends and wives hold drugs and guns when police pull them over. It's similar to mob wives. When they're in jail, gang members have women bring drugs into the facilities. Through jail calls, they use women to arrange drug deals and murder hits. Look at your client and how she tried to kill her own daughter for Javier who was in jail facing serious charges," I say firmly.

"Is it possible your gang-banging mob outfit provoked the drive-by shooting that night?"

"No, I was in a long red dress, not a jersey, knee high socks, and Nike Cortez," I counter as Fox returns to the podium and flips through his notes.

"Ma'am, isn't it true that you were dressed the other night in a pin-up like Lady Justice?"

"It wasn't Lady Justice, it was Eight of Swords. I was at the Airstream talking to girls about domestic violence."

"You had a blindfold and a sword with you. Isn't that what Lady Justice looks like?"

"Yeah, *and* Eight of Swords."

"Call it what you want. Eight of Swords or Lady Justice. But that's how Laura was found. You realize that don't you?"

"Yes, I found her."

"You didn't blindfold her yourself, did you?"

"Objection," says Tanner.

"Overruled," says Judge Hoffman.

I look at Judge Hoffman and squint my eyes so hard it almost gives me a headache.

"I don't know what you're trying to insinuate, Mr. Fox. But whatever it is, it is completely inappropriate. I'm going to allow Ms. Ruiz to answer this question, but I want you move on," says Judge Hoffman.

I shift my glare to Fox.

"Laura was blindfolded with a sock and tied up with a belt with rhinestones that had your client's DNA all over it. She looked like Lady Eight of Swords, an image I didn't even know existed until after I found Laura. And my blindfold is made of Japanese silk, not a dirty man's sock."

"Did you find your silk blindfold in a sex store along with the rest of your pin-up costumes?"

"No!" I scream, looking straight at Fox without flinching amidst the tears rolling down my face.

"Is it something from your past that causes you to want to adopt an alter-ego?" Fox asks.

Fox knows about my past from that one night I confided in him and as tempted as I am to bring up his attempt to make out with me and his halitosis breath, I stop and compose myself.

"I think we all wish we could be something different," I say.

"And you encourage the girls you mentor to become pin-up models?"

"No, I encourage them to learn from the models."

"What on earth could these girls learn from pin-up models?"

"I don't know what you're suggesting. But I think we could all learn from them. Especially how to fix our pasts. I wish I could go back and help my mom the day she died. But the truth is that we're all human, we're not perfect, and we make mistakes. But we can learn from them. That's what the girls learn from the pin-up models. How to fix our pasts. The same thing the girls have taught me," I say, trying my best to keep my calm.

"Have you thought of dressing up as a police pin-up or just being yourself, as a prosecutor pin-up to teach these girls how to obey the law?"

"I'm trying to build a rapport with these girls, not a wall. And that doesn't happen overnight. Or by throwing a police badge in their face. They've had negative experiences with police. Does that make any sense to you, Mr. Fox? Because if it doesn't, maybe you should think about getting out there and serving your community. Especially before you criticize the way I'm doing it," I say, before Fox shys away from asking his next question and tells Judge Hoffman he's done.

After a quick ten minute recess, Tanner doesn't waste any time standing up to start his redirect examination on me, the part I like the most.

"Ma'am, you mentioned earlier that one of your pin-up costumes is Trailer Hillbilly. Do you realize that some of our jurors live in mobile home parks?"

"Yes, I grew up in one, too," I say, thinking back to jury selection when I had to allieviate Tanner's concerns about trailer park residents being appropriate jurors.

"Just out of curiosity, what lesson are you trying to teach the girls with your Trailer Hillbilly pin-up?"

"Trailer Hillbilly teaches us about stereotypes. There's all kinds of jokes about trailer park trash that these girls are subjected to every day. We use the pin-up as a way to teach tolerance. Stereotyping and jokes lead to bullying. Most of these girls have been bullied or wind up bullying themselves. So Trailer Park Hillbilly is a big part of The Mamacita Club."

"What about Carmen Miranda?"

"It's a pin-up I use to identify with them, like my J-Lo one. Many of our girls are Latina and don't have a positive role model in their lives. Plus, with economic times being hard, people blame lower class citizens or illegal immigrants for their problems, most of whom are Latinos in this county. It's the same type of discrimination that led to things like the Holocaust and other race wars."

"What about Angel Gabriel?" Tanner asks.

"Aside from being a certified angel reader, Angela uses that pin-up to teach the girls we all have angels. It gives them a sense of hope, something they have very little of. We also use Angel Gabriel to teach tolerance for homosexuality and the dangers of sex discrimination, like the discussion earlier about Angel Gabriel being female or male; it shouldn't matter. Young people everywhere struggle with identity issues. Kids are bullied over this. We teach them to be comfortable in their own skin and accept everyone regardless of their sexual preference," I say.

"It seems like The Mamacita Club is like your family. Is that an accurate characterization?" Tanner asks.

"It's the closest thing I have to a family," I reply.

"And what about Eight of Swords that you were recently wearing? What were you trying to show the girls with that?"

"Just that we women are blind when we're subjected to violence. I teach the women that they just need to remove their own blindfold and find the key to the lives and the home they want to have. I encourage them to dig deep and listen to their guts and hearts, because they hold the answers," I say.

"Can you tell the jury a little more about what you mean when you say victims of violence are blind?" Tanner asks.

"Objection, relevance," says Fox, starting to stand up.

"Overruled.   You opened this door with your questioning," says Judge Hoffman, smiling at Tanner.

"The girls all know about my mom," I say.   "I've discussed with them how she had her own blindfold on, not realizing how dangerous the situation was that she stayed in. And the mistakes she made putting herself in harm's way. So I use my mom as an example of a victim who could have removed her own blindfold to find the key to free herself. She just didn't do it soon enough."

I stay strong, being Grace Under Pressure, but hear a couple jurors grabbing tissues out of the box.

"And just a couple more questions," Tanner says.   "Fox asked if you got your silk blindfold from a sex store. Can you please tell the jury where you got it from?"

"Objection, relevance," blurts out Fox.

"Overruled; you opened the door on this," says Judge Hoffman.

"It was my mom's. It came as part of a set I bought her with a silk Japanese kimono that she was found murdered in. That, her diary, and some photos are the only things I have left of her."

"Can you tell the jury what personally inspired your pin-up theme."

"My mom loved pin-up models. Her favorites were the Vargas Girls. She loved old-time classic movies like *It's a Wonderful Life* and actresses like Rita Hayworth and Betty Grable. Growing up, I loved to watch her put her powder and lipstick on when my stepfather wasn't around. She was so beautiful and always wanted to put her hair in pin-curls, but my stepfather never let her."

"Did you bring a photo with you today?"

"I did."

"Why'd you bring it?"

"Objection, Your Honor. I haven't seen this photo before," says Fox.

"He opened the door on cross-examination asking her questions about her pin-up costumes. The photo supports what she's told this jury," Tanner says.

"Overruled. Go ahead and answer," says Judge Hoffman.

"I've always carried it with me. This is the last picture my mom took."

"Your Honor, may I publish the photo Ms. Ruiz has with her to to the jury?" asks Tanner.

"It will need to be admitted into evidence as an exhibit," says Fox.

"No, it won't, Mr. Fox. And yes, you may put it on the screen," says Judge Hoffman.

After I give Tanner the photo, he publishes the most beautiful picture of my mom, in pin-curls, dark hair, and glamorous. I smile at her as she projects life-size in the courtroom.

"Where was this photo taken?" Tanner asks.

"Here in Tuckford County," I say.

"Under what circumstances?" Tanner asks.

"One day, when my stepfather was at work, my mom got all dolled up, put her hair in pin-curls, and put on this fancy dress. It was around the holidays and we went to the local market where they had an old-fashioned photo booth with a vintage photographer. The man even had a black boa that he let her wear. It was the prettiest I had ever seen my mom. She gave me the photo to hold so my stepfather wouldn't see it.

"When we got home, we snuck back in and my mom went to the bathroom to undress; but she forgot to take her makeup off. When she came out, my stepfather, who was drunk, became suspicious about where she had been. I ran to my room while my stepfather chased my mom around the house, accusing her of sleeping around.

"My mom came into my room pleading with me to show the photo to my stepfather so he would believe her. But I stayed under my covers and never let go of the photo. My stepfather came in and dragged her into the next room, where he killed her. I still wonder every day if she'd still be alive if I just showed him the photo."

"Why didn't you?"

I hesitate, thinking hard why I didn't, before answering. "I think I was mad at her," I say truthfully.

"For what?"

"Making me do something I didn't want to," I say regretfully.

"You didn't want to help save her?"

I look down and clasp my fingers together in my lap to catch a few teardrops. Then, I look up towards my mom's photo, still being projected. "I was twelve and scared. I wanted her to save herself. And save me," I say timidly, beginning to understand my past for the first time.

"Thank you. Nothing further," says Tanner, picking up his notepad and walking away from the podium, glaring at Fox.

I hear my mom's voice. "Gaby, I'm sorry I didn't protect you. And I didn't protect us. I didn't make the life for you that you deserved. But you can.

"This case is not about what happened to me. This case is about Mrs. Sanchez, who tried to kill her daughter. You have done nothing wrong. Let it go. You have a greater mission in life to do what you need to do. And one of those things is waiting for you outside. Dry your eyes and get along. I love you," says my mom.

There's nothing more annoying than watching a defense attorney who tries to shift the whole focus on one thing, and it's me in this case. It's a beginner criminal defense tactic and Fox decided to make it about my personal life. It's all because he knew how sensitive my mom's case still is to me.

The death of my mom and the helplessness I still feel from time to time for not saving her is sometimes debilitating. All the glimmers of hope and progress in dealing with her death, including my trip to the Walled City and meeting Señor Luis Santiago-Borges, seem to be erased. These are little reminders that I have not fully coped with my mom's death.

I walk down the corridor of the courthouse. My cell phone rings and the caller ID says it's Christina's cell phone. I pick up, but the phone disconnects.

I see Dylan walking towards me on the sidewalk. He gives me a big hug and warm smile.

"Are you okay?" says Dylan.

"I'm just shaken up a little," I say, still startled from my testimony.

"I heard he was trying to suggest you were somehow involved in what happened to Laura and Cruz," says Dylan.

"He has no idea the pain I carry for being the last person to see them. It's like he wanted to remind me that I could have done something to help them," I say sadly, thinking of everything I could have done to help my mom. "I'm wondering what the jury is thinking of all this," I say.

"They're not buying any of the defense. I'm proud of you," says Dylan fondly.

"For what?" I say.

"For standing up for yourself and not letting that A-hole Fox have his way with you. Word spreads quickly through the court and police department. Everyone thought you came across great. Really sympathetic. Good job, Gaby."

"Have you heard from Christina at all about coming to testify? She hasn't been to The Mamacita Club in the past week and she just called, but the line disconnected," I say.

"No one's heard from her, including her mom, who thinks she's back to her old ways. We really don't need her to convict Bess, though. Personally, I think she's playing games and just doesn't want to come to court," says Dylan.

"I know. But I don't want to be the last person to see her alive, too," I say.

"I know, but let's focus on getting this trial done. Then we can worry about that," says Dylan.

31

LEGAL MYTHS

There's nothing more exciting about a trial than when a defendant takes the stand.   Bess Sanchez walks with the deputy following close behind her towards the witness stand, where I was just two weeks ago when the trial started.   The entire courtroom, packed with attorneys, two media journalists, and Dylan Mack, sounds like it's humming.   Mike Tanner looks at me with wide-open eyes like he's not ready for this to happen.   But I am.   Bess is unshackled because the jury is not supposed to know she's in custody.   It's all a myth. The jury has to expect that a woman who tried to kill her daughter is locked up.

Another one of these legal myths is how Bess gets to dress herself.   She's dressed in a short-sleeved maroon knit sweater.   Her striped silk shirt pops out of her sweater near her neckline.   A neat bow made of the same silk stripes sits tied around her neck.   Her brown three-quarter-length skirt rests below her knees.   What a joke.   She looks like a schoolteacher.   This disgrace of a woman gets to wear whatever she wants to try and make the jury like her and appear that she could have never hurt Laura.

It's as much of a myth as her presumption of innocence. The jurors are supposed to presume she's innocent at the start of the trial. But the reality is that she did something to wind up in the defendant's chair. The more evidence the jurors hear at trial, that presumption slowly gets erased. It's a BS lie that she's innocent, but that's where the presumption starts.

Bess makes her way past the jury box and steps up into the witness stand. "Please remain standing, Mrs. Sanchez, and raise your right hand. Do you swear to tell the truth, the whole truth and nothing but the truth so help you God," says the courtroom clerk.

"I do," says Bess.

Of all the legal myths, this is the biggest one of all. I expect Bess Sanchez to lie her way through her entire testimony.

"Mr. Fox, you are free to examine your client," says Judge Hoffman.

"Mrs. Sanchez, please tell the jury what happened on the night Laura went missing through the following day when you were notified about the crime," says Fox.

I stand up, wanting to object to this question because it calls for a long narration. But Mike Tanner grabs onto my arm and pulls me back down into my chair.

"Hold on, let's see what's happening here," whispers Tanner.

And then I remember something. It's extremely rare to see a defense attorney ask such an open-ended question. It happens when either the attorney has no clue what he's doing or he doesn't want to suborn perjury. If a defense attorney knows the witness is about to lie, they ethically can't participate in the questioning. So they'll ask some open-ended question like Fox just did, then sit back and let the defendant rattle off her lies. It's another legal myth, because the jury doesn't know what's going on. But the judge and the prosecutor know exactly what's happening.

As if she rehearsed it in the mirror for the past four months while sitting in jail, Bess turns towards the jury and begins to tell them her BS story.

After the fifteen minute break Judge Hoffman gave us after we listened to Bess Sanchez's ridiculous story of how she had nothing to do with assaulting Laura and that it was all Officer Cruz's fault, the jury files back into the still packed courtroom and takes their seats.

"The People may now cross-examine the witness," says Judge Hoffman.

"Ma'am, what do you do for a living?" I say, jumping up from my seat. It's important for a prosecutor to stand up immediately and ask *something*. It could be anything and it should be a question no one cares about. It catches the witness off-guard, not knowing what to expect next. And it should be a question they will know the answer to. It's just as important to jump around in topics when you're cross-examining. It forces them to start thinking about when they need to lie or tell the truth. Designed to intimidate and confuse a witness, these are tactics I learned from one of Mike Tanner's trainings on "Hostile Witnesses and How to Order Them to Answer."

"I work with a cleaning service," says Bess.

"Do you recall hearing testimony from the Custodian of Records from your phone company?" I ask.

"Yes."

"So you'd agree that five calls were placed from your cell phone to Officer Cruz's phone the day of the assault. Correct?" I ask.

"Yes, I heard that testimony," Bess says.

"Yet, you want this jury to believe you had nothing to do with Officer Cruz?" I ask.

Bess stays quiet.

"Ma'am, did you hear my question?"

Bess doesn't answer.

"I'm going to object. This question is argumentative," says Fox.

"Overruled. Mrs. Sanchez, I'm ordering you to answer the question," says Judge Hoffman.

"It's not how it looks," says Bess.

"Then maybe you can explain why your daughter says you were her "boss" and that you worked out deals with Clown to pimp her out, you allowed Javier to sleep with her, and you even rented her out to Officer Cruz."

"I don't know what you're taking about" says Bess.

"Ma'am, you went to the motel room to hurt Laura so she would not be able to testify against Javier, didn't you?" I ask.

"I didn't go to that motel."

"Are you certain you never went to that motel?"

"Absolutely. Officer Cruz did this. It's his fingerprint on the vase, not mine," says Bess.

This is the most damning evidence against our case and Bess and douchebag Fox haven't missed one opportunity to remind us. So I change the subject.

"Do you smoke, ma'am?"

"Yes."

"What brand of cigarettes?"

"Newports."

"Regular or light?"

"Light."

"Ma'am, your DNA was found on a cigarette outside the landing near room 333. You're aware of that, aren't you?"

"That's what they said, but I wasn't there."

"Do you know what kind of cigarette was found?"

"No."

"If that was a cigarette *you* were smoking, is it fair to say that you'd expect it to be a Newport Light?"

Bess stays quiet.

"Answer the question, ma'am," says Judge Hoffman.

"Yes, I suppose."

"Suppose? What are you supposing?"

"Objection, argumentative, relevance," says Fox.

"Sustained. Move on, counsel," says Judge Hoffman.

"Were you Laura's boss?" I ask.

"Laura was prostituting. When I first found out, I wanted her to stop. Javier and I tried to help her."

"So then at what point did you decide to join in and make a profit from it?" I ask rhetorically.

"Nevermind answering that," say. "Where was Javier at the time you were trying to 'help' Laura on July sixth?"

"He was locked up. He couldn't help me."

"Did Laura upset you by coming forward about Javier's sexual abuse?"

"That was a concern at the time, but that's not why I did it."

"That's not why you did *what?*" I ask, loving it when defendants don't think before they speak.

"This had nothing to do with Javier."

"Ma'am, what is your waist size?"

"Ten."

"And in belts?"

"The same, ten."

"What waist size is Laura?"

"I think a two. The same in belt size."

"Showing you People's Exhibit number twenty, do you see this white belt with black stones on it in this clear plastic bag?" I ask.

"Yes."

"Whose belt is that?"

Bess stays quiet.

"Please answer the question," says Judge Hoffman.

"I told the police it was mine," says Bess.

"If it was yours, what size should it be?"

"Well, I'm a ten."

"Do you know what size this belt is that I'm holding?"

Bess stays quiet.

"Ma'am, I'm going to order you to answer the question. If you don't know the answer, please let us know. But you need to answer the question," says Judge Hoffman.

"It's my belt, so it's probably a ten," says Bess.

"Your Honor, may I publish the size of this belt?" I ask.

"Sure, and just for the record, what size is it?" asks Judge Hoffman.

"It's a two," I say, smiling at Hoffman.

"I guess if the belt doesn't fit, you must convict," I say, triggering laughter throughout the courtroom.

"Ms. Ruiz, please save your commentary for closing argument," says Judge Hoffman.

"I apologize, Your Honor. Mrs. Sanchez, you tied Laura up with her own belt, didn't you?"

Bess stays quiet and looks down.

"You ransacked the room and make it look like it was a random sex assault, didn't you?"

"I didn't."

"I'm showing you what's been marked as People's Exhibit forty," I say, putting a news article dated July seventh on the projection screen.

"Can you read the news heading for the jury, please?"

"*Girl's body found in motel room.*"

"Now please read the second line of the article."

"Objection, hearsay. The article speaks for itself," says Fox.

"Overruled. Mrs. Sanchez, please read it."

"*When she was found, 'her hands were tied with a belt, her underwear was around her ankles, and the whole room was ransacked,' said Bess Sanchez, the mother of the seventeen-year-old girl.*"

"Did you tell the reporter that?"

"Yes."

"Why?"

"Because that's what happened."

"When did you speak to the reporter?"

"In the late afternoon the day Laura was found."

"Did you ever see the motel room?"

"No."

"Then *who* told you the room had been ransacked, *her underwear was around her ankles,* and she was found tied with a belt?"

Bess stays quiet.

"Answer the question, ma'am," says Judge Hoffman.

Bess looks down.

"You can't answer that question because police never told you these things. You only knew those things because you did them."

"I didn't."

"You were the one who tied her up.

"Stop."

"You ransacked the room to make it look like a random assault."

"That's not true."

"You tried to murder your daughter the morning she was supposed to testify against Javier."

"I didn't."

"She wasn't supposed to tell, was she? You tried to murder your daughter because she wanted out of your prostitution ring, isn't that true?"

"Objection, argumentative," says Fox.

"Overruled. Answer the question, ma'am," says Judge Hoffman.

"I just wanted my problems to go away."

"Did you ever tell Javier what you were going to do?"

"No, I didn't tell him anything."

"What nickname did Javier call you?" I ask.

"B-B."

"What did you call him?"

"Javi."

"Your Honor, at this time I would like to play a jail call of a conversation between this witness and Javier Sanchez."

"Go ahead," says Judge Hoffman.

I hit the play button on the recorder and hear a man's voice.

"Hey B-B, it's Javi," says Javier.

"Hey Javi. I'm glad you called me. I can't talk right now, but I'm gonna carry out that mission tomorrow morning. Don't worry, I'll get it done," says Bess.

I stop the recorder.

"Ma'am, is that your voice?"

"I don't know," says Bess.

"Would it refresh your memory to see a copy of the phone log showing the number Javier called?"

"No."

"Your Honor, for the record, the call was made to the same number this witness testified was hers."

"So noted," says Judge Hoffman, smiling at me.

"Mrs. Sanchez, it is still your testimony that you never went to the motel room?"

"Yes."

"I'm showing you a report from the Crime Lab that indicates the type of cigarette inspected, People's Exhibit number nineteen. Have you seen that before?"

"I don't think so."

"Would it surprise you that the cigarette found on the landing outside Room 333 was a Newport Light?"

"Objection, discovery. I haven't seen this report," says Fox.

"It was provided to counsel back on August third. I have proof with Mr. Fox's signature," I say, holding up a discovery receipt.

"I'll withdraw my objection," says Fox defeatedly.

"Answer the question, Mrs. Sanchez. Would it surprise you it was a Newport Light?" says Judge Hoffman.

"No, Your Honor. I was there," Bess says quietly.

The courtroom turns to complete silence. There're times when a witness or defendant will say something when they're on the stand that everyone seems to know there's been a major breakthrough. But I just need to make sure I heard right.

"I'm sorry, ma'am. Did you just say that you were at Motel Leafwood the morning Laura was killed?" I ask.

"I was there but I didn't hurt Laura," says Bess.

"Let me get this right. One hour ago, you told this jury that never in your life had you stepped foot at Motel Leafwood."

"Yes, that's what I said before."

"But now you're saying you were there?"

"I was there, I smoked that. But I didn't hurt her."

The worst thing a witness can do for their own credibility is to lie in front of the jury. When witnesses lie to police, the jury will give them a break, but when they do it in open court from the witness stand, that's a whole different type of lie. It's living proof that the person can't be trusted.

"Thank you, Mrs. Sanchez, for telling the truth. Because I was flabbergasted at how a cigarette you smoked could have wound up somewhere you were claiming to never have been. I'm sure this jury was wondering the same thing," I say.

"Objection, argumentative," says Fox.

"Move on, counsel," Hoffman says to me, following with what looks like a wink. It's hard to tell if he's winking or just blinking because of his black pirate-looking eye patch.

"So which is it, Mrs. Sanchez? Did you hurt Laura because she wanted to stop prostituting? Or, did you do it to stop Laura from testifying against Javier?"

"I just wanted all my problems to go away."

"Why did you involve Deputy Cruz in all of this?" I ask.

"I don't understand what you mean."

"Ma'am, I know you were in involved with Deputy Cruz. You were sleeping with him and allowing him to sleep with your daughter. What did you have over him for him to do a drive-by shooting at *my* motorhome that I parked in *your* trailer park to help women like you and your daughter? That's what I mean. You went that far, to get a Deputy involved, to make Javier's case go away and cover up what you did to Laura," I say aggressively.

The entire courtroom quiets as Bess glares at me. Her entire demeanor changes.

"You don't belong in my trailer park. You don't have the right to be involved with my daughter. I told you that from the beginning. You just don't get it, do you?" Bess says dramatically.

"Ma'am, look at Laura out there. She sits in a wheelchair. The doctors don't know if she'll ever walk again."

"Yes, I know."

"Was *this* worth making all your problems go away?" I say, shoving a photo on the projector so it pops up on the big white screen behind her. Laura is lying in her hospital bed with her head shaved and thumb black from the gangrene.

"Objection, argumentative," says Fox.

"Overruled," says Hoffman.

Bess stays quiet.

I rip the photo off the projector as quickly as I shove another one on it.

"Or was this worth it?" I say, straightening the photo.

Dylan took this one with his phone when Laura was lying in the bed inside the motel. Her head was bloody and she was still blindfolded and bound with the belt. In the picture, I'm starting to loosen the sock around her eyes when we were waiting for paramedics to arrive.

Bess begins to sob on the witness stand, shaking her head back and forth. She reminds me of myself when Tanner showed me the picture of my dead mom on the stand. But this time is different. Bess *is* responsible for this. She is a Mamacita who murders. I'm not. I couldn't save my mom.

"Objection, argumentative. The prosecutor is badgering the witness," says Fox.

"Overruled," says Judge Hoffman, turning to Bess.

"I'm going to order you to answer the question," says Judge Hoffman.

"I wanted Javier's case to go away. I resented her. I resented all of it. I allowed him to sleep with her. After she met you, she began moving away from my control. She threatened me that she was going to testify and tell everything. She wanted to stop prostituting. She was going to tell you.

"I'm her boss. I say where she can go and who she can sleep with. And that included Officer Cruz. He was her last client of the night. I knew Clown would be waiting downstairs and he'd be the first one you guys would go looking for. He wasn't my concern. He would never snitch.

"When you came to my house looking for Clown, we left. He never kidnapped me, you fool. I told Cruz where to find us. And after Cruz pulled us over and arrested Clown, I took the Lincoln. I set fire to Cruz' place. I planted the suicide note. I went to your house. I did the drive-by. I tried to kill you and Christina. I called and threatened her. I know she was the one who reported Javier. I left the notes. At least I gave you guys a choice. Bullet, blade or flamingo vase.

"I did it all. And Javier knew everything. You fool. Javier wanted you dead as much as I did. You don't have a right to come into my life and take my daughter away from me. I don't care anymore. I'm facing life. I've lost my family, my daughter, my world. All because of you," says Bess.

"Why did you kill Deputy Cruz?" I ask.

"Because he saw everything. He came back to the room after he forgot his wallet. He grabbed the vase out of my hand. He stopped me from killing Laura. He didn't get it either. So he paid with his life. Just like you and Christina will," she says.

The entire courtroom grows quiet.

I sit down, exhale and hope justice will keep working its magic.

32

UNIVERSAL MAGIC

Dear Señor Luis Santiago-Borges,

Since I met you in the Walled City, I've come closer to forgiving myself and finding closure over my mother's death. Experiences we have, sometimes abroad, can bring the magic to give you a better focus in life. They can show you what is important and what is not. Like you said, allow my mother's spirit to dwell in my mind and in my heart. Hug those you love a little tighter. Love those that are right in front of you, ready, willing, and available to love you. For me, those people are Dylan and all women of all ages who come through The Mamacita Club.

There're times in your life when you're not sure about what's right or what's wrong, especially when it comes to love. Sometimes it's hard to know who the right person is for you or when to let go when they're not. Someone once told me that when you're in love, you can make magic happen. I've waited for a long time to see the magic when it comes to being in love. I see Dylan in a different light today than I ever have. I don't stand here thinking that he's the one or he's not. I stand here knowing that I want him in my life right now and that he makes me feel cherished in a way I haven't felt before. Sometimes it's just enough to have those around you that love you. It doesn't mean he has to put a ring on my finger, that I have to commit to him being my husband, or that we will marry in the Walled City.

If you live and let live, the Universe in time will answer all of your questions. The dots will connect someday. For all of these lessons about love, loss, hope, and forgiveness, you are one of the people I wanted to thank.

xo,
Gaby Ruiz

P.S. Please thank the Walled City Police for helping us achieve justice for Laura. Because of your help, the defendant was sentenced to life in state prison.

ACKNOWLEDGMENTS

Thank you Papi,

One of my many heroes like R.I.P. Nicole T., Molly Huckabee, John Ruiz;

And others like Kathy E., Nadia C., Jennie, Nana, Dada, Lu and Auntie Coochie, who taught me about love, loss and how to let go;

Suzi G., who has been there along the way;

Big D. and Oli, who reminded me how to play;

Sean B., who taught me to keep looking to build my treehouse in the right tree;

Sissy, Christian P. and Aaron B., who have taught me about recovery;

Michael L. & Candice B., who have always supported my choice;

Martha F. & Gayle B., who helped me find my voice;

Anna & Terrie, who edited my words perfectly;

Gerry, Ms. G and Room 203 in the L.B.C.,

W.W.W. and its original posee, Tara & Nikki, Karyssa, Daisy & Andrea G., Socorro, Jessica & the Y.O.C.,

And the new posse, Zulma & Kacey, Plan-It Life & Rancho D.,

G.I.F.T., Dave G. and Cregor D., Z, R.C.D.D.A.A. feat M.A.H. & J. Aki,

And the rest of the gang in Rivertucky, who have inspired me to serve;

But most of all, thank you Rosa y Mamí, who have taught me how to find the key.